Beast

ISBN-13: 978-1-8381273-1-2

Last orders called at the Whalebone
Staggering your way home
Hey lads don't take no short cuts
Stay out them ten-foots

Beware The Beast of Barmston Drain – Black Kes

CHAPTER ONE

Tony's father is dead. The nurse pulls the blanket up over his pale head and looks at Tony. She smiles with a face that says I'm sorry and, this is how it is, at the same time. Tony puts his plastic chair back into the stack of other chairs in the corridor. He doesn't feel real.

The nurse has put all his father's things into a clear bag, the wallet, the silver watch and a mobile phone. His wedding ring is in there too. Tony picks it up. He walks, vacant, out of the hospital cubicle and down the corridor. People bustle past him - nurses in blue scrubs, doctors in white coats. There are visiting patients in a mix of their own clothes and washed out hospital gowns, two soldiers in full uniform pass, one carrying a wooden box in his hands. Someone else must have died.

He gets into the big lift and stares at the steel wall as he rides all the way down to the ground floor, then walks out into the afternoon and waits at the bus stop on the main road. On the bus home, he does not catch anyone's eye, nor does he speak or look out of the window. He gets off the single-decker at Greenwood Ave after the Pilot pub and walks down 6th Avenue to the third terrace on the right. He fumbles with his key, opens the door, and goes inside. No one is home.

No one will ever be home again.

Tony thinks this is where he will cry. He thinks at this point, surrounded by the walls he has grown up in, the tears will flood down his face, but he finds they do not come. He sets the clear plastic bag on the kitchen table. Tony does not want to look at the things inside. The items that, only a day since, his father wore.

The house is clean, tidy and silent, just as he had left it and although Tony and his father have prepared for this moment for three months, now it is here, Tony is not quite sure what to do. He knows he must grieve; he and his father talked about this before he went, well before, but somehow, he doesn't feel ready. Tony does the one thing he is sure is good for him, like he always does.

He trains.

In his back bedroom, overlooking the little river that snakes through the city, Tony lifts dumbbells in front of the mirrors so he can be sure he is doing them right. He is fifteen and already has an athlete's body with a well-defined wiry torso and muscular legs. His hair is shaved, and he has a young face. In the garden, he skips till he is dizzy, then shadow boxes in the dying, summer evening light. He's good at this. He knows where he is when he trains.

The big kitchen clock says six when he has finished. He stands looking up at it and wonders if the tears will come. There will be no hospital visits to make, no treatments to attend, nothing to arrange for the death. All of it done, the funeral set already by his father's hand before he died.

Tony cooks beans on toast, eats it, and cleans up. He washes the plate and the pots, the knives and forks, dries them, and puts everything away. He has to do it right. There is no need to draw attention to himself and his situation. Details matter.

In his bedroom, Tony pulls out his laptop and sits down on his bed. He clicks open a file named 'Tony' and there, in a long list, are the videos. All fifty of them. Each one between three and five minutes long, more or less, and each one covering separate items. They range from how to change a plug, how to train, how to cook, how to operate the online banking website, how to shop online, what to do if you are sad, how to deal with a cold, how to stop bleeding, how to shave. Each one, filmed by his father as lasting advice for his son. Tony scrolls through the videos but does not click any of them. He thought the tears would come when he saw his father's face, frozen in time on the screen, in the little square of a video, and ready to play. They do not.

At nine, Tony showers and stretches his muscles in the tiny bathroom then sits down in the kitchen with his medical book. While his father was sick, he wanted to know as much about the body as he could, so he could understand. Now, he just likes the book. He sees the lines of nerves like tree roots around the body and the smooth sinews of muscles. He notices the clear plastic bag on the table again, with the wallet, mobile phone, and the watch inside. The phone begins to buzz. Tony picks it up and looks at the screen. It is a number without a name. He does not answer. The fewer people who know about what happened the better. It could be social services already or it could be the hospital or the police. At fifteen, with no guardian, Tony knows he should not be in the house alone and he should not be living without anyone to look after him, but, this is what they planned for, his father and he. Tony can do this. Like his father, he is independent, aware and capable. If he can last another year, till he is sixteen, then he will be free to do what he likes. He can keep the house and his father's money, and nobody can take it away from him.

Just like they had planned before his father died.

Tony lets the phone ring and then puts it back in the bag. He knows how to survive, he can wash his own clothes, pay the bills, operate an oven, take and give a beating, he can change a light bulb, pass his exams, he can survive.

When it is dark, Tony stands in the kitchen again, looking at the clock and listening to it tick. He has prepared for this moment, but he doesn't feel ready for it. He needs to be out of the house. Upstairs, he dresses in joggers and a sports top and slips on his trainers, then, he opens the front door, steps out and runs.

Tony runs up Greenwood Ave then takes a right through Orchard Park. North Hull Estate was built at the edge of the city between the wars and Orchard Park in the 1960s. They have bad reputations but like anywhere, the bad and the good sit side by side. At the top of Orchard Park, the city ends and fields stretch out in front of Tony in the light of the summer evening. He keeps to the road. He runs in a big horseshoe, right around Hall Road. He jogs past the Pint and Pot with the smokers standing outside, then past the medical centre, past the traffic lights and the gang of kids on street bikes, cuts down 8th Avenue and then he is nearly home. It's not enough. He doesn't feel tired.

He jogs onto the path down the side of Barmston Drain - it's not a drain but a river, about as wide as a road with a very steep green bank. Tony used to come here a lot with his father. Along the thin path beside the river, he runs for a long time until he feels sweat dripping down his face and all the while, his mind is blank. He has travelled north and to the edge of the city once more. Night creeps in over the top of the North Hull Estate.

Tony does not know where he has got to. It's dark away from the streetlights and into the forest. He has followed the drain a long way out without thinking where he was going. Light summer rain begins and Tony loses the track as he jogs into the trees. The forest is cramped, but this not quite the countryside, he stumbles on a carrier bag full of empty beer cans. The rain begins to get harder; it drums on the leaves around him and his nostrils fill with the fresh smell of summer. The river is dark and colourless at his side and the moon a pale white circle between the clouds. Tony does not want to stop. He doesn't want to go back to the house, or to school, to face all those people, to pretend somehow that he is okay. He doesn't want to deal with the house or the money. He doesn't want to look after himself. Inside, tight like a knot in his stomach, there is anger and fury, growing like his father's cancer. He knows he must control it, that the bitterness will eat him if he lets it, and so, he begins again, running harder through the trees. His feet catch on a slippery branch on the forest floor and he slips in the mud, falls forwards and bloodies his nose on a tree trunk as he goes down. He gets back up and carries on running. Tony thinks the tears might come as his body nears exhaustion, but they do not.

The rain starts heavier and he moves out of the forest to a wide field with wind turbines creaking against the light breeze. He stops. He sees something up ahead, a movement through the bars of rain. Tony narrows his eyes and sees the shape of a huge dog in front of him, a black dog, wolf-like but anemic looking with gangly legs and a long snout. It is bigger than any dog he has ever seen. He knows he should be afraid as he walks

5

towards it. He knows he should be running away, but, what has he to fear? If it should kill him, then... well, there's nothing left for him here. The black dog stalks towards Tony. In the thin moonlight, he can see its matted and filthy coat, the lips curled back in an ugly snarl as it approaches. Tony quickens his pace too. He thinks of his father, pale in the hospital bed, the man's eyes milky with fear and holding Tony's hand for the last time. He feels a knot in his stomach, a blaze of anger and fury and pain. The sweet man who brought him up, who read him stories at bedtime, ironed his shirts, walked him to school, helped him with his homework, cooked, listened to him, trained him – he's gone.

The dog-wolf does not slow.

Its head dips as it gets ready to jump. Tony does not slow down either; he feels his hands clench into fists as the beast approaches and his nostrils flare. The rain is heavy. The creature is as long as he is tall and jet black, like a blur in the darkness. Tony feels the burning in his stomach becoming more powerful and emotion swells in his chest as he gets closer to the dog-wolf.

He feels rage.

Close enough to smell the animal, Tony stops. His stomach heaves as he yells as loud as he can, feeling every muscle in his body tense up as the anger releases. This is blind fury as he is face to face with the beast.

How could he leave? How could he leave Tony to deal with all of this alone? Why didn't his father try harder not to just die?

Tony does not stop shouting for a long time and he collapses on his knees in the mud. He cannot see. His fists are so tight his nails have made cuts in his palms.

When he comes to his senses, Tony is exhausted, wet, and whatever he thought he saw has gone. He feels better that the rage is out of him, but he knows it will return and that he has to control it, use it, own it even. He knows too, as he jogs back the way he came, that his mind can play tricks on him, he has read so in his medial book. Tony runs back through the forest and down the drain side. 6th Avenue is quiet because it is so late. He opens the door to his terrace and goes inside, takes off his dripping clothes, puts them in the washing machine and sets the timer so the clothes will be washed for when he wakes up. He can hear the rain outside and the blaring telly from the neighbours. He goes up to bed and pulls the covers over him and lays awake. He cannot sleep, so he sits up and stares out of his window.

In the moonlight, along the bank of the little river behind his house, Tony thinks he can see a thin shape on four legs, slinking off into the trees.

CHAPTER TWO

Tony wakes and washes his face in the bathroom then examines the cut on his nose from the evening before in the mirror. He opens the medical cabinet, takes out two steri strips, and applies them to his face like any good boxing medic. No one will notice it, not on his nose. Three times a week or more, Tony visits the run-down boxing gym on 1st Avenue, behind the Pilot pub, so it's not unusual he might have picked up a cut. It's the six-week holiday, early-August, and Tony does not have to go to school, but that does not mean he can rest.

At ten, he leaves the house and walks down the street, so that people can see he is out and about. He nods hello to a neighbour and kids he knows from school on their bikes. They are dressed in hoodies, grey joggers and trainers that their mums paid way too much for. They know Tony, and they know somehow that his father is ill. They are aware also, he trains at the gym and is handy and that he keeps himself to himself. Now they see him along the street, they give him a wave and an 'alright mate,' only. There's something a bit unnerving about him, something they can't put their fingers on, a difference in his smile. Like the animals in the forest, they sense something is dangerous.

Tony goes into the budget supermarket, and inside, he gets potatoes, beans, noodles, frozen sausages, flour, and a frozen joint of ham. Tony's father taught him to cook healthy food that requires effort to make and will keep him strong. He smiles at the old women and exchanges pleasantries with the tall, effeminate cashier. He smiles too at a big Congolese woman who walks with a stick. She is wearing a long-patterned dress, which makes her look bigger. Her son trains at the gym with the younger kids, and that's how Tony knows her. Some people on the estate don't like the foreigners, the Poles, the Kurds, or the handful of Africans who make their lives there. Like his father, Tony has time for everyone until they do something to lose his respect. His father grew up here in North Hull and his granddad as well. A woman with a mean face stops

Tony. She has red hair and green eyes with heavy wrinkles running from across her forehead. When she smiles, her face changes. She's pretty.

"How's your dad?" she asks. She is Tony's neighbour to the right, Emma. She might once have been a fine-looking woman, but age has withered her face. She still has the curves in her figure-hugging dress beneath the denim jacket. She still looks good.

"He's fine," says Tony. He tries to smile and makes quite a good job of it. He doesn't want anyone to know his dad has gone. Not yet.

"That's a lie, right there," says Emma. She knows how people work and can read them, perhaps not as well as she thinks. "He's still in hospital, isn't he?" she guesses.

"Yeah, he might get out soon, though, and my Auntie Lynn from Doncaster is coming to look after me."

"Right, well, if you need anything, then you just have to let me know. If you want to come round for your tea and play on the Xbox with our Sam, you're welcome, you know." She has a twelve-year-old lad. He's quiet, good at football and has a sweet smile.

"That's a bit young for me," says Tony, "but thanks."

"And who's cooking for you?"

"I'm doing it myself until my Auntie Lynn gets here."

"Oh yeah?" says Emma casting her eye over his food basket and nodding with approval.

"You know we're always there if you need us, don't you?"

She said the same thing to his dad when he started to get sick. She says it every time Tony sees her. They both know he will not take her up on the offer. Emma has a little, stocky, grey-haired husband who used to work nights at the abattoir. He's angry and volatile, full of energy and noise. He likes to work nights because he can't get drunk when he's on the late shift. Tony has heard Emma screaming before and the little stocky man shouting and banging. Who knows what goes on behind those thin walls? Sometimes she wears dark glasses.

"We're a community," she says. "We look after each other."

Tony smiles. She's nice. Kind. She bakes sometimes, and he can smell the cakes and buns when her kitchen windows are open. Tony wonders if his mum was a bit like her. Emma smells nice. When she smiles, she has perfect teeth.

"Thanks, Mrs. Stevens," says Tony.

"You should call me Emma," she says, "you're older now."

The gym is run-down. It was not built to be a gym. Once upon a time in the eighties, it was a supermarket. It's long and wide with a raised boxing ring right at the far end. In front, there are blue mats on the floor and two rows of tatty bags hanging from the ceiling along both sides of the wall. Near the front door is the weight room with a bench and rows of bars and dumbbells. The door is open today, but Jacko usually keeps it locked. Kids will nick even heavy kettlebells round here. There's the not unpleasant stale smell of sweat and grease and a giant, faded poster of Mohammed Ali hanging on the far wall. Tony looks at the picture as he always does and says hello in his head. He likes the eyes of the big man on him. The gym is empty at this time in the morning. Kids will begin training at eleven as part of a programme the old trainer Jacko puts on in the summer holidays. That means Tony has about an hour before the gym will be full of noise and kids jumping and training and shouting, with Jacko growling at them in his gruff, low voice.

Tony warms up with stretches, then does shadow work in the cracked mirror, which covers the full side of one of the walls. He keeps moving, with jabs and roundhouses, bobs his head, blows out air as he punches, he gives it a good go, like he always does. Rage is in him, somewhere deep, stirring but silent, wrapped up in the moves he has performed a thousand times. He works the bags and repeats the same series of punches, jab, jab, jab, hook or jab, jab, jab, uppercut. He's good at this. He knows what he's doing, and it feels right, watching the bag swing as he belts it and feeling his fist take the shock of the blow. He likes the squeak of his trainers on the floor and the slapping of his gloves on the bag.

"You won't be able to train it out, kid." It's the voice of Jacko behind him. "No matter how hard you go at it. Training... won't get rid of it."

Tony does not stop, he keeps at the bag with the punches, one, one, two. Sweat runs down his face. He likes Jacko, so did his dad. He likes the way he speaks out the side of his mouth and the rough way he approaches life. Tony stops training and turns. The old man is small and stooped; he rests on a walking stick and has silver hair and bright eyes. Jacko had a stroke a few years back that left one side of his body at an angle. It doesn't stop him running the gym, and the bigger lads say because he can't train himself, he makes it harder for them.

"Get rid of what?"

"How angry you are."

"I'm not angry," says Tony with a smile.

"You see anyone else here hitting the bags like that? This time of the morning?"

"I like training."

"How's your dad?" asks Jacko, his speech is just a little slurred, but he's sharp.

"Still in hospital, getting better..."

In some ways, Tony believes this to be true. They will all find out what has happened at the funeral next week. It's when Tony will be under the most scrutiny.

"You're a good lad, Tony, and I don't say that sort of thing, you know me. You're a good lad, and anytime you need anything, you make sure you see me. I'm always here, and my door is always open. I won't say it again."

It feels good to have Jacko say this, and, for a second, this display of kindness has caught Tony off-guard. His stomach wobbles and his lip trembles, he feels like he might tell Jacko everything that has happened, how desperate it feels, and how worried he is for the future. In the same second, Tony buries his feelings back into his chest. He has to stay strong, like his father said, accept the help by saying a few words of thanks, that's all people are offering anyway. Tony gets the feeling Jacko means what he says more than Emma did but still knows

Jacko's door is not always open.

"Thanks, Jacko,"

"Now go back to hitting them bags. It'll make you tired, at least."

Tony turns and draws his gloves to his chin. Jacko stands next to him and watches the way he lands the punches, twisting his back leg as he delivers the rear hook.

"Lighter on the feet, let the twist put the power in. When's the fight?" asks Jacko.

"Two weeks on Friday," says Tony as he punches.

"You ready?"

"Yeah." Tony will face a kid from one of the big schools. It's a dinner event where two local amateurs fight and young lads are the warmup. The boy he's against is meant to be good, from the rich part of town, fast and up for it. Jacko knows Tony can beat him. Tony isn't sure, yet.

The younger kids filter in over the next twenty minutes, and they fill the gym with their fights, quarrels and laughter. Jacko lets them mess for a few minutes before striding out into the middle of the gym and banging his walking stick on the floor. The kids fall silent as he begins. He sets them running round the gym in a big circle. As Tony leaves, he can hear Jacko barking more orders at the children. There's sniggering, and Jacko demands twenty press-ups from everyone. Tony misses those days.

It's evening. Tony makes bread like his father showed him. He mixes and kneads the dough, leaves it to rise while he loads the washing machine, flips through the pages of his medical book, and then makes two perfect loaves which he transfers to the oven. He fries onions in some butter, boils the left-over vegetables from the bottom of the fridge and blends it into soup, then leaves it to simmer while the loaves bake. When Tony sits down to eat, he thinks about how he and his father would make the same meal together and take the same places. The food makes him feel better and stronger even though his hands are shaking from the training. Tony hears banging from next door, someone running down the stairs, probably, then dropping something, then a loud thump and shouting. He stops eating. It is the little grey-haired man who is married to Emma. Tony can hear his voice through the thin walls; there's an angry shout. He cannot make out the words. He hears Emma screaming and shouting back and a dull thud and then silence. Tony pauses for a minute until he is sure the sounds have ended then carries on with his meal. It's got a bit worse lately. Tony finishes up and washes the bowl, rinses out the saucepan, and cleans down the tops. Anything to make noise, anything to keep him busy.

As he finishes mopping the kitchen floor, there's a knock at the front door. Tony wipes his mouth. He is worried by who would call. It can't be social services because it is late, but it could be the police or kids messing about. Tony stops at the frosted glass and wonders if he should open the door when he hears a voice,

"You there, Tony?"

It is his friend, Will, from the next street up. They play Xbox together online, either football or shooting games. Will is one of the good kids at school. He has older brothers and a real family with a mum and a dad who still go out to the pub together. "Are you there, Tony?"

"I'm just about to go to bed," says Tony through the door, "I'm knackered."

"I haven't seen you online for ages mate. How's your dad? Is he back home?" Will has a high-pitched voice. Some of the other kids call him Granny.

"He's still in hospital. My Auntie Lynn is coming from Doncaster soon to look after me."

"You not online tonight, then, mate?"

"Nah mate, I'm off to bed."

Although he cannot see the boy on the other side of the door, Tony can sense his face is frowning in concentration. Another voice sounds from behind Will. It's a man, sincere and more serious.

"It's Will's dad here, Tony. We're worried about you, mate.

Someone at work told me that…" Tony can feel the strain on the man's voice. Will's dad doesn't want to be here doing this. He doesn't want to have to say what he's going to say. "Someone told me your dad died, Tony. They said he died this morning. Are you there, son?"

"Yes, I'm here, and I'm okay," Tony feels his blood run cold. If Will's father knows, then everyone will know. The whole street will know and the entire estate. "I'm just tired and I want to go to bed." Tony feels the urge to cry. He fights it.

"Is anyone there with you, Tony?"

"Yeah, my Auntie Lynn is coming from Doncaster tomorrow."

"She's not there now?"

"She'll be here in the morning."

"You can come and stay at ours tonight if you want, son. We'll get a takeaway, just us lads… Tony, are you there?"

Tony feels his hand on the key that has locked the door. He doesn't know if he should open it. He doesn't want to face this big man or go back to Will's family where they laugh and eat, where the house is warm and not entirely cleaned properly, where they are a real family.

"I'm alright, Mr. Black, I'm alright. I'll be fine in the morning when my Auntie Lynn gets round." Tony hears the big man draw in breath and consider what he has said. "The funeral's next Wednesday at the crematorium, at ten o'clock."

Tony can hear the man thinking, almost. Mr. Black looks at his son. It would be easier if he didn't have to take the lad home. He's only here because his wife sent him when she heard what happened, but he does worry for Tony, he knew his dad well, liked him too.

"Right, well. I think you should open the door, let us see you're alright."

Tony swallows and opens the door. Will Black and his dad are standing in the darkness of the summer evening.

"She's coming tomorrow, then, your Auntie, is she?" Asks Will's dad.

"Yeah, Auntie Lynn, from Doncaster."

"Right then," says the man. Will Black steps up, through the door and hugs Tony.

"I'm sorry, mate," he says. Tony tries not to hug him back. It might give too much away.

He watches the Blacks walking away down the street, bathed in the glow of the orange streetlight, closes the door and locks it. He is tired.

In his bedroom, Tony opens his laptop, clicks to the file of videos his father left him and reads through the list. There's too much to take in.

<u>VIDEOS</u>
1. Life
2. Hate
3. Home electrics
4. Loneliness
5. Fear
6. Auntie Lynn
7. Boxing 1: Losing
8. Boxing 2: Winning
9. Boxing 3: Moves
10. Boxing: Your first match
11. The story of the Lonsdale Belt
12. Buying clothes
13. Haircuts
14. The black dog
15. Making bread
16. Money
17. Accounting
18. Learning: You can teach yourself anything
19. How to lie
20. Shaving
21. Sexuality
22. Talking to girls
23. Having a girlfriend
24. Sex and contraception
25. Getting dumped and dumping
26. 10 places you should visit
27. Getting a job
28. How to behave at work
29. Dealing with the police
30. 10 essential books you should read
31. How to act when you feel shy
32. Training: Running
33. Training: Weights
34. Training: Yoga
35. Your grandma and granddad
36. Your mum
37. Our family history
38. Music
39. Drinking and hangovers

Tony hovers over some of the files with the mouse pointer, and the duration pops up. Each one is no more than five minutes. His father didn't like to waste words or time. Tony wonders which one he should watch first, but he's not sure he can take looking at his father's face when he was alive, right now. He can still see him there in the hospital bed, his skin yellowish and his fingernails growing too long from hands that had changed from strong to frail. The cancer killed him quickly. Tony hovers again over 'your mum' and then clicks it. The screen changes, and he sees his dad, standing in the kitchen downstairs. The man looks like he always did with a light beard, short hair and a big smile. He's athletic looking with his shirt sleeves rolled up over his elbows. He starts straight away in his soft voice.

"I met your mum in Beverley, in the Green Dragon on a Saturday night at the bar. It was how people met back in those days, I saw her standing there and I just said, 'Can I buy you a drink,' and she said yes. We bought this house together. It was meant to be a starter place. We thought we'd move out quickly." Tony's father rubs his chin with his big hands and he looks back into the past through his brown eyes.

"She was a lovely girl, your mum, full of fun and smiles, liked a drink, too much, and she had ups and downs. Sometimes she was happy, really happy, and it was infectious how much she felt alive. Everyone wanted to be with her and near her and then, there were other times when she was in a dark place, and you couldn't reach her or talk to her. She was good and bad; I didn't think there was anything wrong back then. When you came along, she kind of exploded with joy and was on top of everything. She wouldn't let me hold you too long or put you to bed, and then she started to get sick. You're a big lad, I can say, I guess, I have to say. She was depressed we'd call it now, manically. I used to come home from work, and she was cleaning the house for the third time, then washing your clothes three or four times even after they were clean. She scrubbed your bottles and cleaned everything over and over again, even the walls. She worried you might get sick and it might be her fault. Sometimes I'd find her crying, and sometimes I'd find her screaming. I couldn't leave her with you in the end. I took time off work, she got worse, she started taking pills from the doctor and they didn't help. She said she felt the world closing in on her. One night I found her outside, on the banks of the drain back here, screaming and crying, saying she was going to throw herself in ..."

Like an electric shock, Tony clicks the pause button on the video and sees his father, frozen there on the screen with his hand to his head as he tells the difficult story. Tony knows his mother lost her mind. He knows that she was locked away somewhere. She was ill and she's gone. It's still hard to hear. He clicks the button, and the video starts again.

"...so, she had to go away, and I used to visit her in hospital. We visited, you were a little lad, we went every week. She started to get distant and not like the woman I knew, like she was someone else." Tony's father stops talking and looks like he's trying to grab the words from a space somewhere inside his brain. Despair seeps out of him in a sigh, and then he stands up straight and remembers where he is, he's making a video for his son. He takes a deep breath through his nose and carries on.

"That's the past though Tony, what we have, or you have, is the future. She loved you and she loved us, and it didn't happen because we did anything wrong. It was just the way she was made up. Some people lose their kidneys, or their hearts don't work, but for your mum, it was her brain. We talked about this, I want you to know, she loves you, the woman I married and knew, she loves you and she always will." The man reaches forward, and his finger becomes as big as the screen. He stops, then pulls back. Looking down at the screen, this time, he cannot afford to brush it under the carpet, he has to tell Tony the truth. He has to, he will not get another chance.

"She died when you were two. We went to the funeral. We wore suits and sat in the front row of the church. It was a summer day." The man is overcome. It is all he can say. He clicks the button, and the video stops. Tony thinks perhaps now he should cry, but, like always, he feels numb.

In the darkness of his bedroom, he tries to snuggle up under his covers, but it is too hot. There is banging again from the house next door with sharp shouts and thumps which are over soon. He plugs in his headphones and tries to get to sleep.

CHAPTER THREE

After the funeral, Tony gets a taxi to take him home. He is dressed in the over-large suit his father made him buy for the occasion, and he wears black shoes that shine. He sits down in one of the armchairs in the front room, and the stiff but cheap jacket makes a crumpling sound as he does so.

He looks out of the window at the street and sees the North Hull estate drift by, kids on their bikes, a woman with tattoos, a pram, a man with a paper under his arm in a string vest, a woman with a Jack Russell, a man drinking out of Polish beer can. Everything is still normal, just like it was yesterday, and just like it would be tomorrow.

The service was unpleasant.

Tony's father's workmates from the abattoir carried the coffin from the black car, the vicar he had never met made a speech. It rained. Tony stood alone in one of the pews. They watched the coffin move slowly through the curtains of the crematorium and then, Tony stood at the doorway as people left, people he had never met before, shaking his hand and saying they were sorry. Some tucked money into his shirt pocket and tapped him on his shoulder saying, 'he was a good bloke, your old boy,' or something similar. Emma from next door wore dark glasses and gave him a kiss on both cheeks and a hug. Lads from the gym came too and Jacko passed him an envelope of money which they must have collected for him. There was no reception after. There was no Auntie Lynn.

Tony rubs his eyes and tries to take stock. It has been a good week so far as it could have been for him. Like his father said would happen, the world has begun to forget Tony almost immediately. Yes, there have been more concerned looks from those in the street, and a few kinder words from old men who knew his father, a card of condolence through the door, but quickly, things have got back to normal. They have forgotten Tony and forgotten his kind, big-hearted father ever existed. This is where Tony needs to live now, in the real world. It is also where he will hide.

He picks up his father's phone and powers it on, waits for it to start up, and then scrolls to a name called 'Auntie Lynn' in the contacts and presses call. He holds the phone to his ear, swallows, and wonders what the woman will say and why she was not at the funeral as she was meant to be. The ringing goes on for a minute and then there is no answer. Tony tries again, this time, after a few rings, someone picks up.

"I thought you were dead," says a woman's voice on the other end.

"It was the funeral today," says Tony. "My dad said you'd be there."

"Well, I was busy. Is that Tony?"

"Yeah."

"How are you?"

"Yeah, good, you?"

"Alright." The woman's voice is monotone and bleak. She already sounds angry. "Was the service okay?"

"Yeah. My dad said you'd be coming here for a few days or maybe a few weeks, just so we can get things sorted with social services."

"Well, I've been busy, it's not like I can drop everything here in Doncaster, Tony. I've got a family here too, you know. Who's going to look after the dog?"

"I thought my dad paid you."

There is silence on the other end.

"Yeah, but, well, you wouldn't understand, Tony. Why don't you tell me when social services are coming round and then let me know? I'll get there to you and I'll talk to them then. How does that sound?" Auntie Lynn's voice has taken on a kinder quality now she has an idea of a way out.

"Okay," says Tony. "You won't let me down, will you?

I can get you more if you don't let me down. Money, I mean."

Tony, like his father, realises this is a business proposal, with only a very thin family connection underlying it. You can't trust anyone.

"It's not about that, Tony. Who's going to look after my dog? I mean, if you pay the kennel fees then I'd be happy to stay for weeks, but she needs special care and that costs money."

Tony thinks about his Auntie Lynn, a woman he cannot remember, sitting somewhere in a city he has never visited, in a house he has never been to. He hears a dog bark somewhere on the other end of the line, and the woman says something to her animal.

"Your dog could come and stay here, Auntie Lynn," says Tony, the name Auntie seems strange on his lips.

"Oh Tony, you're going to have to call back, Shebaa's going mad at the postman. Let me know when social services are coming, and I'll be there. I owe your dad that, at least," and the phone cuts out.

It's noon and Tony knows he has to eat. He makes tinned mackerel on toast and has two oranges then ice cream to follow. He washes up and dries the dishes, loads the washing machine and sweeps the kitchen floor, wipes down the windows and then packs his gym bag. For a while, he sits at the kitchen table and looks through his medical book, losing himself in the coloured diagrams of the chest and lungs.

There's a knock at the door.

Like before, this makes Tony uneasy. He walks to the frosted glass and sees greying hair on the other side. A hand comes up and knocks again.

"Is anyone there?" says a voice that is at once calm and official. Tony forgets himself and answers.

"Yeah, I'm here, I'm fine," he replies, and instantly

wishes he hadn't said anything.

"My name's Ian, I'm from social services," says the voice through the glass. "I just wanted to have a word with you, Tony, to make sure everything is okay. We know about your dad."

The boy feels his feet cold, his fists clench, and his heart judders. He did not think this moment would have arrived so soon and has not had time to prepare himself for it. He had also expected letters and correspondence, phone calls perhaps, time, a lot more time. Either way, there is no getting away from this. Like a sparring session with one of the heavy blokes from the boxing gym, the only way out of this is through it.

Tony opens the door. Standing not much taller than he, is a grey-haired man with a peaked haircut and a wide smile. He looks like some sort of faded, sanitised rockabilly. The man has a clipboard in his hands and papers attached to it.

"Are you Tony?" he asks.

"Yes, that's me."

"Can I come in?"

Tony steps back to let the man from the social through. He walks back into the kitchen, and the grey-haired man follows.

"Would you like a cup of coffee?" asks Tony.

"No thanks, it's a quick visit while I'm in the area. I'm Ian."

Ian's eyes dart around the room checking what he sees, clean surfaces, the light smell of a bleached floor, everything in order, the tiny lawn out the back mowed and short, the bushes pruned.

"Your dad actually got in touch with us, before… we talked quite a bit. He organised things pretty well for you. He told us you'd be living with…" and at this point, Ian checks the documents on his clipboard, "Lynn Petersen, your father's sister, is that right?"

"Yeah," said Tony. He remembers what his father told

him about lying; the best way to do it is to believe it was true yourself. It doesn't come natural to Tony.

"Is she here?" Ian asks.

"Not right now, she's gone out to the shop."

Ian eyes the boy up and down. He looks well, with a smart short haircut and clean face. He smells good too. There's a cut on the boy's nose, but Ian already knows that he is a boxer, he has read the notes. Ian notices the windows have been recently cleaned; he likes this. It's what he does in his house. It's organized.

"Could you get her to give me a call when she gets back? There are a few things I want to ask her, a few details, nothing to worry about."

Tony takes the card with Ian's details.

"She'll be back later," Tony says.

Ian briefly looks around again. The house is clean and well-presented and the boy, okay, considering he has just lost his father. Ian knows he will begin to fall apart in the next few months if he is going to. Right now, life will be much the same. Somewhere in the social worker's mind a box has been ticked - this kid is okay. How okay he can't be sure and he will investigate. Ian holds out his hand and Tony shakes it. The boy has a good grip and wiry arms.

"I'm sorry to hear about your dad," Ian says. He is being truthful. "If there is anything we can help you with, then you can call me on that number there." Ian hands him his business card. "We have a group set up for young people dealing with this sort of thing, up at the hall behind the shopping centre, every Monday night. You're invited, you have been for months. It's going to take a lot out of you this, Tony, and we're here to help."

Tony considers the cool blue of Ian's eyes, his wrinkled late forties skin and his strong chest under a semi-smart checkered shirt. He understands straight away, this social worker does not care for him in a family way, more like a farmer looking after his animals. Tony remembers what his father told him, that he must feel thankful for any help offered and he must accept it gracefully, despite how he feels inside, whether it be rage or indifference, or in this case, fear. This man from social services could wave his hand and have Tony taken away from his home and school and friends and the gym down the road, so the young man smiles at Ian from his office somewhere far away from the North Hull Estate.

"Will she call me today then Tony, your Auntie Lynn, when she gets back?" Tony nods. "It is important, if there's nobody here to look after you, then we'll have to find you somewhere, but it's the last thing we want to do." There was no threat in the social worker's voice, just concern.

"She'll call," answers Tony. He watches Ian get back into his small car and drive off down the street. Already, Tony is lost.

In his tracksuit bottoms and a t-shirt, Tony steps out of his front door and turns to lock it. The door a few metres away opens just after, and his neighbour, Emma, steps out. She has a bruise on her cheek and is thinner than she was a few days ago. He has heard a lot of banging. She catches Tony's eye and smiles as she locks the door. Tony stares at her a little too long as he notices the mark on her cheekbone. Her face changes as she senses this.

"What are you looking at?" she asks, and Tony looks down. Emma can read what people think.

"Nothing," he says.

Tony glances back up at her.

"You don't know anything about me," she says. With only a glance, Tony has punctured her confidence. She guesses he can hear her fighting with her husband and her screaming, maybe he can even hear her crying too. "You stay out of my business, and I'll stay out of yours," she adds. "I know you're there on your own, all this talk about your Auntie, smells of shit to me. There's only you in that house."

"I do stay out of your business," says Tony, he keeps his head down as he locks the door.

"Just so you know, he's worse now your dad's gone."

"Who is?"

"Him... the one who's asleep upstairs. He used to worry your dad might come round and give him a hiding."

"I could do that," says Tony.

"You don't need to get involved. It's his way," she is apologetic. "It's the way he is. It doesn't mean he doesn't love us any less. He's a good man, and I can deal with it. Like I said though, you stay out of my business and I'll stay out of yours."

Tony nods.

It is Wednesday at the gym. Weights night. After the warmup jog around the block, Jacko orders the lads to grab two one-kilo dumbbells from the weight room. There are six of them, two kids from the estate, the big Lithuanian lad, a lanky new bloke in his late thirties and Tony's friend Apple. He's meant to be called Abdul, but the kids at the club call him what they like. He calls himself Apple now.

One kilo is not a lot to lift, but after Jacko has finished with them, their arms will burn. The lads are already sweating and Jacko has them do press-ups for a minute without stopping with a ten-second break. Then shadow box for a minute and a ten-second break, then pump the weights for a minute. It goes on. The new lanky kid is a trier, but he's in no shape at all. The Lithuanian is too muscly to be great at this. Apple knows all about pain. All the while, Jacko makes barbed comments about the boys and asks rhetorical questions, especially to Tony, who is working the hardest.

"Are you taking the piss?" he asks, or, "Did your mum show you how to do that?" It makes Tony feel at home and it keeps him from having to think about Auntie Lynn and the social worker. She will not call Ian today, that much is impossible, but, he will expect her to call soon enough.

When Jacko is done with his lads, he makes them stretch out their muscles and continues with the comments. At the sweat on Apple's chest, 'Have you wet yourself?'. 'When I was your age I used to train like this every day.' As they are leaving, he shouts to the lanky bloke, who has tried hard, 'I don't expect we'll see you again, Granddad.' If Jacko doesn't say mean things to you, he doesn't like you.

Tony does not like the thought of going home. After he has dropped his bag inside his front door, he goes for a jog. He tells himself it's a recovery run and will stretch out his muscles and calm him down.

It's turning dark on the North Hull Estate. The summer sun is orange in the sky, and the heat is disappearing out of the day. The pavement radiates heat back, and Tony starts at a jog, but the pace quickens. He overtakes another runner and dodges round dog walkers in the early evening sun. His legs start to heat up and loosen as he does so. Tony feels his anger bristling in him, just under the surface. He sees the wrinkled face of the social worker Ian and thinks about how he could get taken away. He thinks about his dad too and feels his muscles tighten and his back begin to gather with sweat. He runs along Barmston Drain and out of the city to the place where he ran the week before. He hopes it will make him feel tired but the more he runs, the better he feels. Tony's heart is pounding hard when he reaches the scrub field where he saw the dog-wolf.

The wind has picked up. His sports top sticks to his chest, and somewhere in the early evening darkness, he can hear the faraway creaking of a metal windmill. It *is* here somewhere; he can sense it. He feels the hairs standing up on the back of his neck and his stomach churning.

He crosses a ditch to the next field where there is an abandoned metal container, the huge kind that hook up to lorries. In the dim light, he picks his way through the overgrown weeds and rubbish around it. He does not know why he is here, what he is looking for, or what he hopes to do if he sees anything. Tony clambers up the side and then hauls himself onto the roof of the metal container. He stands up. From here, he can see the lights from the North Hull Estate and Orchard Park on one side and the main road out of the city on the other. Behind him are the still waters of the drain. The light is dying, setting orange across the fields ahead. Quite far away, he sees it, a shape that could be a big black wolf silhouetted against the sun. It does not move there in the distance, if it is there at all. He feels like it's watching him, but he can't be sure. Tony watches the sun go down and keeps his eyes on the shape, blinks and then it is gone.

When Tony gets home, he calls Auntie Lynn and there is no answer. He calls every half an hour until eleven and then, when he dials the number, the mobile phone is switched off. He hears shouting and banging from the house next door.

CHAPTER FOUR

Tony wakes early and stretches his muscles. He showers, cleans the bathroom and bleaches the toilet, makes his bed and folds his clothes. It has to be this way, like his father taught him. Everything has its place, and though it may take a little more time to do things the right way, it makes Tony feel good doing them. With every clean surface and hung up t-shirt, he senses his father's approval. He makes himself a breakfast of porridge with coffee.

On the way to the gym, the streets are quiet. Tony stops in the newsagents to buy chewing gum. It helps him train. Behind the counter is a ginger-haired lad with a round face who usually talks too much. The kids on the estate call him all sorts of names, Dean the Gob, Gobbo, Gobby or anything rude. It's early and he looks tired.

"I'm hungover," says Dean. Tony is thankful he doesn't talk as much as he usually does. "I heard your dad died."

"Yeah," says Tony.

"Sorry about that," says Dean.

"It's ok,"

"I wish my old man would kick the bucket," says Dean. He's about to follow up with a funny story but Tony has shot him a glance that cuts him short.

Inside the gym, Jacko sits on a fold-out chair with his eyes on the ring. There is a man holding pads and a boy of about seventeen, already covered in sweat, dancing around and throwing jabs. It's Apple. Every so often Jacko calls out with some advice, tuck lower, move or keep your chin down. Apple is a hopeful of the club and one of Jacko's boys, a hardworking lad, if a little dull.

"Good to see you, kid," says Jacko when he notices Tony. "You need to get warmed up."

Tony runs, skips, works the bags and shadow boxes in the big, cracked mirror before Jacko calls him over and tells him to get some gloves on. Tony pulls on his head guard and fits his black gum shield as he climbs into the ring and the man with pads climbs out. Both boys are panting lightly, with their arms warmed up and ready for it. There's no anger at all in Tony here, there can't be, any sense of fury and he will be too easy to hit. He has to control his emotions and his temper, let the pressure out slowly in bursts of power. Tony puts his gloves up and Apple steps forward, throwing a few searching punches which don't have anything in them.

"Now then, Apple," says Jacko. "We're gonna do this properly. Five three-minute rounds, like a real fight. Dave'll ref, and I'll score. Keep it clean but go hard. Tony, don't kill him."

Tony has fought in the ring many times before. He likes being used by Jacko like this. Sometimes the old man will ask him just to defend or just to move or to go easy or go hard. Apple is a solid fighter, brave, well trained, keen and, with a bit of luck, he might do something. For the first twenty seconds, the two lads circle the ring feeling each other out until Jacko tells them to stop messing about and fight. Apple steps forwards and tries a jab, but Tony is much too fast for him. Tony moves his head and counters with a hook that catches Apple on his chin. Tony steps on the punch but does not deliver another, Jacko has told him not to kill the boy.

They fight for the full five rounds, and in the ring, Tony is free. Although Apple is older, he's not a better boxer or stronger, he doesn't have the grace or the speed, but he can still hit. Tony takes body shots and a few good head blows shake him. Here, with the sweat spilling down his face and the gloves flying, Tony does not have any room in his brain for social workers or beasts or self-pity. There is just simmering rage, but he must not let too much of it out.

When it's done, and Jacko calls time, Tony takes off his gloves and spits out his gum shield. Apple is flustered and breathing heavy. His vest top is wet with sweat.

"You fight like your dad," Jacko says to Tony. "You're not aggressive enough on your back foot. It's like you're waiting to get smacked in the head. Keep forward Tony, knock 'em down."

"You told me not to kill him," says Tony. He does not want to explain to Jacko that he has to keep his anger inside, that if he takes the fight to Apple, he will explode.

It's half-past ten. Two big men walk into the gym. They are strangers, and Tony looks up at them. One is tall with silver hair and the beginnings of a stomach. He's dressed in a sharp suit with crisp, black trousers, and walks like he knows how to handle himself. He's past his prime certainly, but still strong. Next to him, the other man is shorter with a fat belly squeezed into a red Liverpool top, a flat cap and long greasy hair. He's ugly. Something is unsettling about these two men. As they walk down the centre of the gym, Jacko stops talking mid-sentence and walks to greet them. Tony puts his gloves in the cupboard and eyes Jacko as he talks to the two strangers.

"Those two want to buy this place," says Apple as he removes his gloves. "They've come all the way from Liverpool."

"Jacko won't sell though, will he?"

"Depends on what sort of offer they make him. He's getting on. He might not be able to refuse."

Tony wrinkles his nose. The bigger man in the smart suit leans down as if explaining something to Jacko and his gold watch catches the sunlight. Tony does not like him already.

"What would they want with a place like this?" asks Tony. "There are better gyms. There's a gym with an Olympic medalist in town. Why don't they buy that one?"

"Who knows?" says Apple. "This is the third time they've been down this week, with their big flash car." Tony watches Jacko shaking his head at the two men, shaking his head and then waving his hands as if to say no.

"The only good thing about this place is Jacko, without him, it's a dump," says Tony.

"This whole town's a dump, mate, the houses, the schools, the shops; it's all a dump."

"What are you doing here then?" Tony replies in a playful tone.

"It's where I belong," answers Apple.

"Me too."

The two Scousers continue to talk to Jacko as Tony gets changed into his tracksuit at the side of the ring. He watches them as he walks out, holding a stare on the taller one with silver hair. Tony makes his face unfriendly, but the Scouser sees him and smiles.

Outside, sat on the wall in front of the gym, Apple tells Tony about a girl he's been seeing, and they trade light insults. Tony feels normal for a few minutes as they chat there, in the sunshine with the streets coming to life in front of them. Summer brings out the kids and a little gang passes by kicking a football. Cars pull up in The Pilot car park. Losers wander in and out of the bookies opposite. Apple points at the big black car parked up in front of the gym, twice as big as anything else and gleaming, with silver wheels and blacked-out windows.

"You looking at my car?" The tall, silver-haired Scouser has walked out of the gym and stands behind the two lads. His hands are in his pockets, and he has a broad smile across his face.

"Yeah," says Apple, "no harm in looking."

The Scouser walks forward.

"No harm in looking," the man repeats. "It would be if it were my wife." He is suntanned and smells of aftershave as he gets closer. "Just kidding. I'm thinking about buying this place, you know. Have you lads been coming here long?" His accent is not sharp, coarse Scouse but something a little more gentle. Even so, it's alien to Tony and Apple.

"About three years," says Apple.

"What about you?" the man asks Tony.

"All my life," he answers.

"Did a bit of boxing myself. You might have heard of me. I'm Wallace. I did quite well back in the eighties and nineties. Too old for the game now, but I still train, got some good lads back in Liverpool, some of them are doing well. I could help you lads, get some cash into the gym, start changing things."

"It's a shithole," says Tony. "Why would you want to buy this place?"

"That's a good question," answers Wallace. He has charisma this man from Liverpool. He speaks well. "I wanna buy this place because I can make something of it, I can change it. I can make better boxers. I can get some real fights going, and I can make some real money. That's why I want this gym. I've got no reason to lie to you lads." It is a very reasonable answer to Tony. It's honest and to the point.

"Do you want to make something out of your life, like I did?" Wallace asks. Apple nods. Tony does not respond. The bit about making something out of your life is unreal to him. "I can see you're good lads… I hope I'll meet you again soon."

Jacko and the fat Scouser appear behind him, Jacko is not happy and even looks frail against these two. The fat man in the red Liverpool top has a gruesome smile.

"Thanks for your time then, Jacko," says Wallace. "Me and Whalebone here will be back on Saturday with a few more lads." He turns as he puts on silver dark glasses "It would be a shame if this club got any more run-down, you might lose it forever," he mutters.

The fat Scouser called Whalebone laughs. He has a bulbous nose and dirty face, but his arms are thick and powerful.

"A real loss for the community," says Whalebone. His

accent is grating. The two men walk back towards their big car, get in and drive away.

Jacko stands in the doorway of the gym staring down the street with a blank expression on his face.

"You ok?" asks Tony.

"I'm going to have to sell lads; they've got me."

"You don't have to," says Apple.

"Everything changes lads, everything comes to an end. Seems like yesterday I was as old as you, I was learning how to fight with my whole life stretched out in front of me, and I blinked, and it's gone. Wallace will bring money into the gym, like he said. He's an arsehole, a greedy arsehole, but he gets what he wants. He'll get my gym, in the end."

"You'll get a good price for it, though, won't you Jacko?" asks Apple.

"I won't get much, but it's better than anything else."

"What do you mean?" asks Tony.

"Well, like I said, Wallace gets what he wants. If he doesn't get what he wants, then…" Jacko gives one of his knowing smiles. "You lads will still have somewhere to train, that won't change," he added.

"He'll charge more," says Apple.

"Of course, he will. You pay five quid a week lads, for as many sessions as you like. There's no boxing gym in Yorkshire where you can train for that."

"What about you?" asks Tony.

"What about me?"

"Where will you go?"

"I come with the gym, Tony. I might not own the place, but I'm not going anywhere."

Tony has not thought about the social worker because the gym has taken up all of his brain. As he walks back down 6th Avenue to his house, the street is in full, summer action. A gang of little kids bounce on a giant trampoline that takes up the whole of a tiny front garden, a shirtless, skinny lad rides his pushbike on the pavement, there's the sound of a motorbike revving somewhere, a bus streams past. Tony does not notice any of it. As he approaches his house, he checks for any cars in the street he has not seen before. He keeps his head down. At his front door, he turns the key, goes inside and makes sure the latch drops. In the kitchen, Tony turns on his father's mobile phone and sees missed calls from a number and a message waiting for him. There's nothing from his Auntie Lynn. Tony listens to the social worker explain on the message, that he was expecting a call and that he'll have to visit again. His voice sounds disappointed.

Upstairs, Tony stares out of the window. He wonders how fast Ian will work, and how long he might have till he is sniffed out. If Auntie Lynn does not come through for him, then, he might have to face the possibility that social services will put him into care, but more than that, he would have lost the game he and his father have prepared hard to play. He would be beaten.

Tony cooks himself spaghetti bolognese with lots of spice like his father used to make it. There is no point cooking a small amount, so he makes enough for four. He'll freeze the rest and eat it another day. Tony keeps a nervous eye on the window and the door, expecting a knock to come sooner rather than later.

After he has cleaned up, he calls Auntie Lynn again and there is no answer. He does his laundry and takes the wet washing outside to put on the line. He has hung half of his clothes up when his next-door neighbour, Sam, appears playing keepy up with his football in the backyard. The fence between their little gardens is waist-high. Tony's dad used to spend time chatting over it. Sam is a good football player with a light, natural touch. He keeps the ball up easily on both feet and nods a hello to Tony.

"I wish my Sam could hang clothes out like you," Emma remarks as she comes out of her backdoor. She is wearing sunglasses, this time because it is sunny, possibly. She walks down the garden, and her flip flops slap against the soles of her feet. "Has you're Auntie Lynn got here yet?" She asks.

"Not yet, later on today, I hope."

Emma folds her arms.

"She's not coming, is she?"

What's the point in lying to Emma?

"I don't think so. She was meant to get in touch with the social worker. She won't even answer my calls." Tony does not sound defeated, just put out.

"What were you hoping to do, Tony? Were you going to live in that house all on your own, bring yourself up?"

"Yes," answers Tony. It was the plan.

"Where will you get your money from? Who'll look after you? What would your dad think?"

"It was my dad's idea," says Tony. "If I go into care then I'll miss the last year at this school, I'll miss my boxing training, I've got a fight coming up. You know me, Emma, I can look after myself. I've got enough money to last. I can cook, clean, train. I can pay the bills. I can do it on my own."

Emma glances down at her feet and her painted toenails, then at the young man standing on the other side of the little fence. He has hung his washing out in a neat line.

"It's not about all that, Tony," she sighs. "You need someone to care for you. I mean someone to tell you things are alright, emotionally." Emma worked for the council in the adoption agency a few years ago. She completed courses on emotional abuse and heard stories about neglected families, distant fathers and drug addict mothers. She knows people need other people more than they need anything else. "You have to go into care, Tony," she says. "Really, it's for the best."

"I thought we were going to stay out of each other's business, me and you?"

Emma cocks her head.

"It's a bit of advice, that's all. I saw a bloke come round

before, looked like a social."

"He was," says Tony.

"You know, if you want something to eat or just a friendly face, then my door is always open, Tony. I've got my problems as well, but that doesn't mean I don't want to help." Tony's tired of all this. It's all hot air.

"I can look after myself, and I don't need your advice." His anger is visible only for a flash.

Emma darkens. Tony has done the one thing his father told him not to do; he has thrown help back in someone's face. He should not let the mask slip, but he cannot help it, especially to people who are kind to him.

"You've been through a lot, Tony. You have to let someone help you. You're too young to be doing this on your own."

"I would like to get some sleep at night," he says, unable to stop himself. This isn't a soap opera. "So, the next time your husband starts swinging his fists, why don't you give me a call and I'll come put him in hospital for you. That way, we can all get some peace."

Emma shifts her weight onto her other hip. She's angry.

"You're just a little boy, Tony," she whispers. "What do you know about anything?" Her tone is bitter. "You've got a nerve, talking to me like that. I thought your dad brought you up better."

"I'm sorry, Emma," says Tony. He swallows the fury down into his stomach. "I know you mean well, and I'm sorry."

"Your dad was a good man, stay like him, if you can. Next time you hear any banging from my house, turn your TV up and don't worry about me. I've been with him for fifteen years. If anyone knows how to handle him, it's me."

They stare at each other for a minute, neither saying a word.

"I better hang this washing out," says Emma.

Tony tries to call Auntie Lynn again. The first time it is engaged, then she does not pick up. Tony now sends a text. 'Please call me as soon as you can,' and then sets the phone down. He is beginning to realise that she will not come through for him.

Upstairs on his laptop, he watches MMA fighting and boxing matches on YouTube. He forgets himself. Tony likes the art of the men as they swing and duck, trade punches and sweat. He can see errors in their foot movements, see where their head should be and how they should react. He's learning all the time. Tony's father did not like MMA where the men pound each other and grapple, not because he didn't like the fighting but because they were over too quick. He loved the game and the slow tactics.

As Tony brushes his teeth, he realises he hasn't heard any banging or shouting from next door. He wonders, as he looks in the bathroom mirror, if somehow, Emma has got the better of the ratty little man she has married. He hopes so.

Out of his bedroom window, Tony watches the river stretch off between the houses behind his house. The moonlight makes the trees glisten as they sway in the darkness. Could there really be something down there? He tries to unpick what he saw that night in the rain and then last night, stood on top of that container.

He knows he saw something.

CHAPTER FIVE

Tony does not sleep well. He tosses and turns and is at once too hot but still needs the comfort of his covers. He sees images of wolves and the face of the fat Scouser, Whalebone, with his bulbous nose and rotten teeth. He smells the drain. He wakes to someone knocking on his front door. The knock comes again, rat-ta-tat, swift and professional. He waits for a minute in bed, waits for the noise and whoever it is to go away, but the knock comes once more. The letterbox opens, and a voice comes through,

"Are you in there, Tony? You're going to have to open the door, son."

It is Ian, the thin social worker from the day before. He knocks again. Tony dresses. His heart is in his mouth as he walks down the stairs.

He does not see a way out of this.

"I know you're there, Tony, I can hear you banging about." Ian sounds calm.

He could run, but there would be no point, the whole idea was for him to stay where he was, finish school, sell the house and leave. It has been some minutes since Ian arrived at his door. The man taps on the glass again. Even his knock is patient and measured.

"Come on, Tony," Ian says from behind the frosted glass now he sees a figure inside. "We want to help."

Tony opens the door and Ian is concerned. Today he is dressed in jeans with roll-ups and a red checked shirt with the top button up.

"Are you alright, mate?" Ian asks. The young man shrugs his shoulders. "Your Auntie didn't call. Can I come in? We have a few things to talk about."

They are standing on the front step when Tony sees Emma coming up the street carrying a shopping bag. She considers the official-looking man, thinks the worst and then, she walks past her own front door and up to Ian and Tony. She doesn't know what she's going to do or why, then again she did always want to be an actress, and she is very good at it.

"Sorry, I'm a bit late, Tony love," she says, "I've been at the shops." Emma stops at the doorway and glances at Ian. "Who's this?"

Tony struggles with things that are not true. He doesn't understand what Emma is doing.

"The social worker I told you about," says Tony, not yet aware the game Emma is about to play.

"Wasn't I supposed to get in touch with you?" she asks. Ian is confused.

"Who are you?" Ian asks.

"I'm Tony's Auntie Lynn, from Doncaster. You better come in. Tony'll make you a brew."

They go inside. Emma puts her bags down on the kitchen counter like they belong there and takes the social worker into the front room.

"I did mean to call," she begins, "but yesterday I was just flat out. You know what it's like." Ian smiles. "Tony, love, fetch us in a cup of tea, would you?" Ian nods. She has a gift for untruth.

"I'm relieved to see you," he says. Ian's whole life is based on telling and finding out the truth. He is happy that this woman exists.

Tony makes them two mugs of tea and listens, with his stomach churning in fear as Emma tells him her story. She explains to Ian what she is cooking Tony for his tea and how the shops are much better here than they are in Doncaster. It's the beginning of an excellent performance. Tony takes the two drinks through, and they are both sitting down, Ian on the sofa and Emma on the edge of the armchair. In her new role as Auntie Lynn, she does a fine job on the man from the council offices. She talks about the funeral and how well Tony is coping, says she always wanted to move back to Hull anyway - that's where she's from and what she knows. She was hoping to get in at the meat factory behind the river, but now it's moved, she doesn't know what she'll do. Tony sits down as they talk it through. Emma is perfect, she's brave, warm and funny. Tony only wishes that she didn't have the slight bruise on her cheek. Ian shows he's interested, asks the right questions and smiles when he has to. Like Emma, Ian is playing a game too. He's here to find out if this woman really is okay and trustworthy to look after this boy. Tony gets the feeling Ian is not as wet as he looks, there's mettle here in the way he switches the conversation around to what he needs. You don't have to be a hard man to be hard.

Ian asks, in his roundabout way about the finances and the rent, and, though Emma does not have any idea at all about this, she does not miss a beat in her delivery. Tony's father has provided for them, well, she explains. It's partly the reason she's here. Emma, as Auntie Lynn, speaks with clarity and is honest. She struggled in Doncaster, financially, now she's here in a house that is paid for, she can start to build a new life, get a job, move away from a relationship back in Doncaster that was less than perfect.

After ten minutes, Ian sets down his mug of tea and makes his way to the front door. He's seen what he needed to see and ticked the boxes in his head again, for now. He invites Tony to the group that meets every Monday night and Emma, as Auntie Lynn, says he will definitely be there. He shakes their hands at the front door. Emma closes the door.

Relief spreads over Tony's chest. She turns to him, standing in the tiny hall of the two up two down terrace.

"Thank you," he says.

"You owe me," she answers. "I'll stay here for a few minutes. He might come back. If I get found out, I'll be in more trouble than you."

"I won't forget this," says Tony.

He feels defenceless. Even with his knowledge of boxing and all the training, he feels inadequate in the face of this woman. Here is real power and bravery. He wonders also, why anyone would be so kind to him.

"Why did you do that?" he asks her.

"You need a chance, Tony. I've seen the kinds of places they send kids like you. You've got a better life here. I'll keep an eye on you."

"That's not what you said the other day."

"I've changed my mind. I'm allowed to do that, aren't I?" She smiles, and they hug, like mother and son. "You'll be alright," she says.

Emma goes into the kitchen and picks up the shopping she set down on the counter earlier. At the back door, she turns back to Tony.

"Not a word to anyone about this," she says.

Tony agrees. He can't help himself.

"Why does that man want to hurt you?" Tony asks. "Why would anyone want to hurt you?"

Emma gives him a weak smile. She swallows. She might have asked herself that too.

"It's his way of showing he cares." She sighs.

"I'm sorry," adds Tony, "it's none of my business."

More relief comes to Tony when she has gone. He washes the mugs and hears the clock ticking as he dries them and puts them away. For now, he's safe. Like his father said, the longer he can pull it off, the less chance he has of getting discovered altogether. The first week was always going to be the hardest, but soon, people will forget about poor Tony who has lost his father, and he'll go back to being a normal lad who goes to school and trains at the gym.

Tony takes a bin liner and goes to the main bedroom. It is as his dad left it before he went into hospital. The picture of Tony and his father on a sunny day sits in a frame on the bedside table, the mahogany wardrobe is closed, and there is a large sailor's chest at the foot of his father's bed. This is all his father owned. Tony opens the wardrobe and begins to take out the shirts and trousers. He places them into the bin liner and watches the material crumple and fold as it falls. It is an unpleasant job. He takes out a green t-shirt and remembers his father wearing it at Christmas. He will take them down to the charity shop before he goes to the gym tomorrow. When he has filled one bag, he ties it up and sets it at the top of the stairs.

Back in the bedroom, Tony looks down at the sailor's chest at the foot of the bed. It contains things that must never be thrown or given away. He kneels and opens it, just like he has done since he was a child. He takes the objects he knows are there, a carved elephant his father brought back from India, a big shoebox of photographs of which there are many, his father's beret from when he was in the army, a pale chess set and, at the bottom, wrapped in soft cloth, the boxing belt Tony's father won in 1989. The Lonsdale belt is a stretchy strap covered in decorative faux gold metalwork and a picture in the metal plaque at the centre of two Victorian boxers. Tony has held it a thousand times, and he knows how it feels and every detail of the picture in the centre, yet, he likes to savour it, and slowly turn the belt over in his hands to inspect each element. Tony knows everything about the fight too, from his father's trip in the third round to the knockdown in the eleventh. He's heard the story a thousand times. His father, hammered by the Welshman in ten rounds, knocked him out in the eleventh. Tony never got bored by it. He puts the belt back into its soft cloth cover and then places it gently at the bottom of the chest. It's worth a lot of money, his father said. It is what Tony must use if he ever needs cash in a hurry. He leaves the removal of his father's things for another day though he knows he must complete it soon.

After his tea of pork chops, sweet potato mash and green

beans, Tony sits on his bed staring down at his feet. The training from the morning has left his chest and arm muscles sore, but it is not enough. He needs to run, but not yet, it must be dark.

On his laptop, Tony searches for black wolves, lone wolves and wolves in East Yorkshire. He reads about werewolf legends and the stories of a black dog that stalked the docks in the city in the eighteen hundreds, a beast named 'Old Stinker'. He considers the etchings from the old books which have been scanned and added to the Wikipedia page and tries to find the wolf he thinks he saw. Tony reads newspaper articles about the girls from Halsham, a few miles away, saying they saw a creature that walked on four legs and then two, running after their car in the twilight of a winter's evening. He looks at the Guardian article where a psychologist explains these sightings are our collective guilt that all the wolves in the UK have been wiped out. He wonders what the creature would eat and remembers there is a video on his list of life tutorials which his father left him, something about a beast. He brings up the files and sees it, *Number 14 The black dog*. He clicks the link and there is his father, wearing a beany hat because it might have been cold back then in March or April. He has short brown hair and brown eyes, a gaunt face and a twinkle in his smile. Tony clicks the play button. His father begins.

"My granddad, so your great-granddad, worked on the docks. He was a foreman, and it meant that when everyone else got laid off, he kept his job. During the great depression of the 1930s, there wasn't much work down there. People were desperate, and gangs of men would turn up at the docks hoping to get a day's work if they were lucky. One evening, he'd just got paid and, standing outside the dockyard was an angry mob of blokes, all poor, all hungry and none of them paid for months. All with families to feed as well. Hungry men do bad things, and granddad had a pocket full of his wages. He told me that, as he walked up to the gates with his wages in his pocket, a big black dog, like a wolf, appeared through the evening mist. It didn't bark or snarl and the crowd of poor men, stepped back to let it through. The black dog led him safely all the way home. That's why there's a wolf picture on the wall in the front room, from your great granddad." Tony's dad tells the story like he does not believe it.

"My dad said he saw the black dog as well. He used to live in Cottingham when he was a young lad after they got bombed out during the war. He told me that he'd seen it at the train station there waiting for him in the darkness." Tony's father looks back into the past. "You could never trust what my old man told you. The black dog." Tony father smiles. "It was a joke, of course. My dad said it had followed him here, right to North Hull, he said that the drain behind us leads to the dock and it was still out there. He used to see it on his way home from the pub. I never saw it. I've lived here all my life, and I've been up and down by the side of that drain for more than forty years, but never saw anything like that. Your mum said there was something there though; she said she'd seen something big on Beresford Park, past the fishing lake and the boating sheds. She said she saw it moving between the trees. That was a long time before she got sick. We used to talk about it like a joke." His father's finger appears to touch the button on the phone, and the video stops. It hasn't told him anything.

Tony clicks back along the timeline bar, so he can play it again and watch his father's face as he tells the story. When he says he hasn't seen it, the man looks out of the window and does a half wince. Tony knows his dad inside out. He knows his father is not a good liar, and when he does try to lie, you can always catch him out. Tony recognises the look as he freezes the video.

The man is not telling him something.

Tony runs down the path by the side of the drain in the

late evening sun. He is dressed in a black t-shirt and shorts. It's warm but not too hot. So his muscles get a chance to stretch, Tony goes slow to start with. He follows the same path that he did on the night it rained, down, through the little forest and past the creaking wind turbine. Why would his father lie to him? The whole point of everything they had talked about over the last few months was honesty, but then, his old man never did make everything easy. Tony learned to throw a proper punch before he could talk, he trains as hard as his dad did, spars with the same boxers, eats the same food and so his father expects him to cope the same, understand the same, reason the same.

He runs hard, out past the disused container and along the side of the field. The evening is fading around him. Dog walkers and joggers don't come this far out. He swings left through the overgrown weeds and up, onto the banks of the river, and then he is running down the path in the evening, his breath is heavy in his ears and his heart is pounding in his chest. He feels free as the sky begins to darken. Tony checks to his left and right, up ahead and sometimes behind, wondering where the creature is. He has run far along the banks of the river. Fields stretch out around him with bales of wheat that have been rolled up and covered in black plastic. He does not slow but carries on, feeling the stubble of the corn whip at his legs. Although he is only a mile or so away from the city, the landscape is flat and wild. Rabbits scuttle away from him as he runs. The muscles in his legs are beginning to tighten, and he feels the rush of endorphins release into his body, they flood his veins with calm.

Up ahead he sees a copse in the middle of a field, where five or six big trees are huddled together with bushes around the bottom and darkness inside.

Tony stops.

He feels fear running up his legs. There is something in this copse of trees, something frightened behind the leaves. It is motionless, and Tony can see a creature crouched low to the ground, he can smell it too. He approaches on unsure feet and is sweating in the late summer evening. As he gets nearer, there is a rustle from the bushes, and the animals burst free. There are two of them, two deer. They rush out on brown, fast legs and run from him across the field. Tony gives chase, watching their heads dip and their white tails bob in the half-light as they get further away. One of the deer springs over a gate and the other stops and turns to glance back at Tony, as if she is laughing at him.

A black shape looms out of the darkness over her, and she is gone, pulled into the corner of the field and the shadows. It's the black dog—Tony's beast.

Tony approaches at a jog and then slows to a walk. There is a low growl as he comes upon it. The large black shape is nuzzling at the belly of the deer and burrowing into the stomach as it feeds on the insides. It growls louder as Tony approaches. He squats down on the stubble of the cornfield and watches it eat from a distance, pinches himself to make sure what he is seeing is real. Low to the ground as it is, the dog-wolf dwarfs the deer it has killed, and it eats in aggressive snaps and shakes of its black head. Tony edges forward. The animal stops and pulls its snout from the carcass. Even in the darkness, the boy can see the wet blood on the beast's fur, and he can smell the hot reek of its body too. It growls, peeling back its lips to show white, sharp teeth, long canines and black gums. Tony does not retreat. Instead, he feels that anger in his stomach, tight and hot. He feels the fury in him, and it rises to the surface. Tony can about keep it wrapped up in the gym, in the street and his house, but out here, with his heart pumping hard, and sweat rolling down his temples, alone, he cannot hide it. The growl has brought the fury out.

Who are you to snarl at me?

He stands up, walks forward, and the beast turns its head to him again, low and aggressive. It is half as tall as he, with short black fur covered in nicks and cuts, eyes yellow in the darkness and thin, but powerful legs. Tony is not afraid; he does not know why. He will not step back. He will not give in. Not to this. He feels rage, and a shout rises from his chest. Sharp and loud. It shocks him. He walks forward, and another shout rises, then they all come at once, and he is yelling and roaring at the beast like he did all those nights ago in the rain.

So what if this dog, or whatever it is kills him, so what? What has he got to live for? Another year at school with thick, arrogant kids? Going to sleep every night and listening to a woman getting battered near to death? Going to the gym owned by arseholes? Eating the same, healthy food day after day? Not having anyone to talk to, the tick of that clock in the kitchen, cleaning up all the time, dealing with the social worker, pretending he's okay, holding it together, watching those stupid videos his father left him? Watching three minutes of absolute nonsense from a man who managed to get cancer, and die, at 48?

Why shouldn't he shout? The beast turns from its kill to face him.

Tony is still yelling in the near pitch-black night. He hates his father in this moment, a man so weak as to just die without putting up enough of a fight. He took months to do it as well. Wouldn't it have been easier if he'd just got killed in a car crash or fallen down the stairs or took a bad punch to the head and died, quick as a flash? Tony hates thinking these things. He's angry with himself as well.

He moves closer to this dog-wolf that cannot somehow be real, so close he can smell the fetid air and see the black nostrils covered in deer blood and gore. Tony does not stop, he cannot stop. He steps forward, still roaring and the beast, which is twice as powerful, bigger and more dangerous than him, steps back in retreat.

It is not angrier than this boy.

Like any animal in the forest, the beast knows there is always something more powerful.

Tony does not remember the run back home in the darkness. He feels exhausted, free, relaxed, himself. He is calm as he opens the front door of his house under the streetlight. In the kitchen, he pours himself a glass of milk and wipes the grease off his face with the back of his hand. His heart beats quiet in his chest. It is the stillness he needs.

The clock in the kitchen reads half-past twelve, and Tony switches off the light. He hears noises from the house next door, shouting and slamming of cupboards, banging and a woman screaming. Tony turns the light back on.

He feels calm enough to do something.

He opens the back door, goes out into the garden and climbs over the fence into next door. Through the window, he sees figures inside the kitchen. The short, grey-haired man has Emma pinned up against her tall, American style fridge with one of his hands around her throat. He is whispering into her ear, and his teeth are bared in anger. Tony can't hear what he is saying, but Emma's face is white with fear and pain. Tony taps at the back door lightly with his forefinger knuckle and hears the man inside swear and shout. He listens to the handle turn, and then, he is looking at the little grey-haired man in front of him who snaps:

"What do you want?"

"I wanted to see if everything was ok," says Tony. He can smell the booze on the man's breath. "I heard banging and screaming." His voice is calm.

"Everything's alright, mate, and even if it wasn't, it's none of your business" The grey-man is red-faced from effort.

Tony does not move.

"So?" says the man.

Tony can hear Emma getting to her feet somewhere inside the kitchen.

"Don't hurt him…" whispers Emma. Tony is not sure who she is talking to.

"So," says the little man, "are you gonna get off my

property or what?"

Tony blinks up at him.

"You know it's not right all this… don't you mate? It's happening most nights; I can hear it all." Tony's voice is level and unafraid. "It's got worse since my dad left. Did he have a word with you? Like I'm doing now? Just because he's not here, that doesn't change anything."

"Get off my property," yaps the man. "You think I don't know about you … I know you're on your own and one call to the social and you'll be packed off to wherever."

"Give them a call," whispers Tony. "The first thing I'll do is pay you a visit." Tony is solid. Though the little man has worked in manual jobs all his life and his arms are strong and he is fit, he cannot match Tony's measured tone and measured aggression. Perhaps Tony's father did have a word with the little man some years before.

"It's just a misunderstanding, Tony," says Emma. She has composed herself but, appearing at the door next to her husband, she looks washed out and exhausted. "Everything's fine here. You can go home."

"She's right," says the angry little man. "There's nothing happening, so clear off."

"Whatever my dad said to you still stands," says Tony. "Do you understand that?"

The little man stares at the boy, his eyes are serious, and Tony thinks he can see fear there, painted across his face and in his beady eyes.

"You're not your father," says the little man.

"Would you like to try me?" offers Tony.

The man hesitates. He frowns as he looks at this boy from next door, taller than him, faster and fitter. Tony lets him pause long enough before he says something to help and calm the situation.

"Anyway, it's probably nothing," and all of them know that is not really what he means. Emma pounces on the words:

"Yes, it was nothing really. We're just having a bit of a row, after a few drinks. Sorry it was a bit loud. I hope it didn't keep you awake."

"Well I'm next door if you need anything. I'm always there in the evening." Tony makes his voice sound steady. He thinks about Emma's face, white and fearful held up against the American style fridge freezer under the sharp kitchen light.

"Thank you, Tony," says Emma and closes the door.

Tony does not hear anything at all from the house next door until the morning when little Sam turns on his Xbox, and Tony's room fills with the sound of laser guns and explosions.

CHAPTER SIX

In the gym, Jacko sits on one of the fold-out chairs. His face is a grimace, and the wrinkles look deeper than usual. He takes off his beanie hat and scratches his head. Tony and a couple of other training lads have been cleaning up the damage from the night before.

There's been a break-in.

Someone wriggled into the gym through the little office window and trashed the place, chucked the gloves everywhere, slashed some of the bags, wrecked the kitchen and tuck shop and smashed the big front window. Tony has swept up the mess of broken coffee mugs and turned off the water, so the tap they kicked off doesn't leak any more. He's stacked up the ripped off cupboard doors and has finished boarding up the smashed front window with pieces of cardboard and duct tape. He stands in front of Jacko.

"Have you called the police?" Tony asks.

"There's no point," says Jacko. "You know that."

"Without a crime number, you won't be able to claim on your insurance." Tony knows this from when they got broken into a few years ago.

Jacko puts his hat back on his head.

"I haven't got any insurance," he says.

Tony agrees. There really is no point.

"Who do you think did it?"

"I dunno," says Jacko. "In the twenty-five years I've been running this place, no one's ever broken in. They've nicked from the tuck shop, robbed gloves and bags and stuff, even weights, but this is…like…"

Tony knows the kind of things kids and teenagers round here can do. They'll scratch posh cars, trash new playgrounds, set a car on fire and then chuck bottles at the firemen who come to put out the blaze, but why would they do this? There's no arrogance to Jacko or the gym, no air of fake aspiration, only the smell of sweat and hard work;

everyone understands that. Like Jacko, Tony realises this can't be the work of anyone from the estate.

"I called them blokes from Liverpool last night," says Jacko. "I told 'em I'd changed my mind and I'd sell. Played right into their hands I did… stupid old git."

"How?" asked Tony.

"Soon as I told him that I'd sell, he said he didn't want to buy this place anymore, said it was a run-down pit." Jacko rubs his prickly chin and Tony looks at the wrinkles coming from the side of his eyes. "He said he wouldn't be surprised if someone burned it to the ground, the bastard."

"If he doesn't want to buy then that's a good thing, isn't it? He can stop coming round here acting like he owns the place."

"I wish he would, lad. It doesn't work like that. It's not that simple. This has happened." He waves to the wreckage in the gym. "Something else will happen next, maybe one of the lads here will get his head smashed in. Next, those two Scousers will drop in and smile and say good things about the place, and they'll tell me they know someone who can stop all this happening and they'll ask me to start paying. Before you know it, they'll have cleaned me out, and they'll have the keys to this place. That's how it works. I should have sold the moment he made me an offer."

Jacko stares down at the floor of his gym, Tony has never seen him sound defeated before and never heard the gravel in his voice as bitter or hopeless. The old man stands himself up, dusts off his trousers and looks at Tony through his tired eyes.

"I won't let that happen," says Tony. At this, Jacko smiles and the twinkle returns to his eyes.

"It's just kids, Tony," says Jacko as he walks away. "Kids having a laugh, nothing to get upset about, we'll brush it off like we always do."

"What about the Scousers?"

"I was pulling your leg, kid." Tony hears Jacko clattering

around in the smashed-up kitchen, looking for a cup.

It's afternoon. Whalebone has been sat in the corner of the gym for about an hour. He is wearing a flat cap which does not go with his greasy hair, and his bulbous nose sticks out. It's red and puffy. He has the same Liverpool top that is stretched tight around his stomach. It must stink. Whalebone has the feel of someone nasty, beside the fat belly are powerful arms and the beady eyes are hollow. His teeth are beginning to turn rotten, but you can only see them when he smiles, which he does not do unless he has made an unpleasant comment.

Tony watches the Scouser from the corner of his eye while he trains on the bags and skips and then shadow boxes in front of the cracked mirror. The man does not move. He just sits at the back under the big, faded poster of Mohammed Ali. He doesn't appear to notice the boys who train in front of him and his eyes are fixed on some point in front of him, waiting, like a statue. Jacko tries to engage him in conversation, and the fat Scouser responds with clipped answers as he keeps his muscular arms folded across his stomach. Apple whispers what he has heard to Tony about 'Whalebone', who has a reputation far away on the other side of the country. He cuts people up. According to Apple, he has a machete in the boot of his car that he keeps sharp as a razor. He's done time for it back in Liverpool.

"Now then mate," says Tony as he walks past and Whalebone nods at him, a movement designed to indicate he doesn't want to talk. Tony doesn't like this man, and he doesn't like that he sits in the club where he trains and pays subs. This is the boxing club his father used and helped build. "You alright there mate?" adds Tony. The response tone is not friendly.

"Oh yeah," says Whalebone.

"It's just you've been sitting there for ages, watching… Makes me a bit nervous, mate, if you know what I mean."

Each time Tony says the word 'mate' it comes out cold and flat. Whalebone is not at all his mate. It's the way people talk round here.

"It's a free country," comes the response. Whalebone does not even move his head.

"If you wanna train, then you can, but you'll have to pay your subs and join the club. The first one's free."

Tony understands he should not be saying this. It's not his gym and not at all his place to question why this man is here. Whalebone is there to intimidate the members of the club. Tony does not like this.

"Are you saying I should clear off?" asks Whalebone as he turns to face Tony. His eyes are tiny, his breath stinks.

"Yeah," answers Tony.

The Scouser stands up straight away, and the fold-up chair scrapes the rough floor of the gym, echoing under the strip light above them. Whalebone does not stand like a fighter. He stands like a fat, ugly man who has done a great many unpleasant things.

"That's not very friendly," says the Scouser.

Whalebone's shoulders are strong and broad and he's much bigger than Tony. In the boxing ring, Tony fancies he would kill him, but in a street fight, the Scouser's experience and disposition might win through. Tony steps back.

"You know why they call me Whalebone?" he asks.

Tony wears a deadpan face.

The Scouser carries on, "because I'm hung like a whale," and he breaks into loud and false laughter which rattles round the gym and makes some of the lads training look round. No one is smiling and even Jacko who is standing by the side of the ring, has no expression on his face. Whalebone is still laughing as he walks to the front of the gym and through the door to the street outside.

"He's dangerous," says Apple when he's gone.

"I think it's all front," says Tony, but he can't be sure.

In the evening, Tony makes bread in the machine his father used. It's a slow process, but the bread is good and cheap, and it fills his house with the sweet and homely smell of yeast and goodness. He used to eat the same bread and soup with his father on Saturday lunchtimes, right here at the table where he sits. Tony looks through his father's mobile phone. He reads the text messages, ones from mobile phone companies trying to sell more data and one from Auntie Lynn which simply says,

"I'm sorry, Tony."

There are other messages, from work friends perhaps or men he played football with on Tuesday nights, maybe people from the pub, someone called Sharon, perhaps people he was in the army with many years ago. Tony does not read them. He sets his father's phone back in the front room, plugs it in to charge, and leaves it. He brings the laptop down from the bedroom upstairs and opens it on the white kitchen table. He does not want to watch the videos, he does not want to see the man who was once here, the man he watched die, but he feels he has to. Tony clicks on a file, and the list comes up again. It's hard to know where to start. He scans the files searching for something then clicks *Number 9. Boxing: Moves*. The screen expands, and there is his father. It's a more recent video than the last because he is gaunt and thin. He is wearing his training gear, shorts and a vest. He smiles like he always did.

"It's not the size of the dog that's important in a fight," he says, "it's the size of the fight in the dog," one of his favourite sayings. It was his way of explaining that you can do anything you want. Tony doesn't listen, this is too basic for him. The man moves and throws punches, snaps his hands back to his chin and bobs his whole body down as he dodges. It's actually nice to see his father move and smile, as he explains you should keep your legs bent and the weight on the back foot, shoulders down and for God's sake don't stick your chin out, unless you want someone to hit it. Tony watches his father go through what he knows about boxing. The man explains that if he's going too fast, then Tony can rewind the video and watch it again. Tony guesses that rewind means go back to the start. His father moves quickly onto jabs and hooks, explaining all the while what he's doing and why. Keep your chin in, again, twist your body as you land the heavy punch, uppercut. He explains how to hug and how to deal with the buzzing in your head when you've been punched too many times, how to keep moving in the ring, that you shouldn't be afraid and you shouldn't give in. He explains you should show no mercy until the bell sounds; it's only a game after all. Three minutes and it is done. Tony's father is smiling, his finger going for the off button on the mobile phone that is recording the whole thing. The screen returns to the thumbnail, Tony's dad is frozen in time, the kitchen quiet again. For a moment, Tony forgot himself, forgot he lives alone and he has no mother or father.

He chooses another video to watch, *Number 35: Your grandmother and grandfather*. He clicks the button. This time, his father is fresher faced and more healthy. It is late at night in the kitchen, and he has a bottle of beer next to him and his arms crossed. He is wearing a red Black Kes t-shirt. He tells of his mother and the East Hull street she grew up on, of her time at school and how she ended up a cleaner in an old folk's home. He tells too of his father, Tony's grandfather, a lorry driver who grew up round the corner from them, a heavy drinker and a womaniser who used to leave Tony's dad sat outside pubs while he got drunk on a Saturday night. He tells also of how the old man spent all the money on ale, and they lived the sixties and seventies on a shoestring. Tony can see his father is angry with the man. It's easy to spot, especially when Tony's dad has a good word to say about everyone. Tony's grandfather was a boxer too, a heavyweight, slow but graceful with an iron skull and an ugly flat nose. He could work a ring. Tony has heard the

Hull Fair story before, but he likes to listen to it again.

"Back in the day, a long way back before I was born, there used to be a boxing tent at Hull Fair. It wasn't like it is now. There weren't any video games or big rides. There were freak shows and halls full of funny mirrors, and, there was this big, boxing tent. You paid to get in and watch. If you thought you were hard enough, you could get up in the ring and fight. It would never happen these days; health and safety wouldn't let it. So, there was always a journeyman fighter, a handy lad who boxed anyone and every one day after day, he was as hard as nails. If you could knock him down, then you'd get a pound – a lot of money in those days. I mean it was big business, I only saw it a couple of times myself in my late teens, messy too, lads would come onto the fair after having a few pints in The George, and they'd fancy themselves, get up and try to knock the fighter down, and of course, he'd put them on their arses. You know how quickly a nose splits open when it's not used to it."

"Legend is, your granddad got up there one night. Anyone who knew him would tell you, given long enough, he'd beat anyone, but he didn't that night. He dragged it out for five rounds, gave as good as he got and finally, the prizefighter caught him a right hook that knocked him down. Of course, the crowd loved it, and your granddad made sure he passed his hat around for the folks to show their appreciation of his fighting skills. He got a lot more than the quid he would have got if he'd laid the prizefighter out. He came back the next night and did the same thing, and the next, and the crowds came to watch him get knocked over in the fifth round before he passed around the hat, every night for a week until the Saturday night, the last night of the fair. He'd made a packet, and he steps up into the ring, and as soon as the bell goes, he watches and pokes and looks for the opening and then, knocks the prizefighter down and out in less than a minute."

"They call him 'the beast' after that, and he says he's going to buy your grandmother a fur coat with the money he's made but he doesn't, he spends it on drink, and it's all gone in a month, and it was downhill from then on. I didn't know him when he was like that. Jacko knew him, he can tell you about him, he saw him train." Tony's father looks out the window of the kitchen into the dark sky, "Me old man used to say the booze kept him from the beast in himself. He reckoned he couldn't cope with the world if he didn't drink. He got the shakes, got scared. One Christmas he came home, plastered, pissed like I hadn't seen him and he..."

The video stops and jumps to another frame of his father stood in the same place, and then the footage begins again, back to his father talking, with the same red t-shirt. His father must have said something he didn't like and has been back through the film and cut it out. The man is apologetic, he tells of his grandfather's battle with throat cancer after all the cigs and his tracheostomy, (Tony remembers a man with a hole in his throat), he tells of his last days in hospital. As he pushes the button to turn off the video, Tony can see he is worried. Tony scans back through the video again to the jump. Something has been cut out of the video, crudely, a whole section. He tries to see the time on the microwave behind his father, but it is unclear. It makes Tony wonder. What would he hide?

Tony puts the laptop away. He cleans the kitchen and the bread-making machine and puts it back in the cupboard where it lives. He cleans the cooker and mops the kitchen floor though it is late. He does not want to look outside at the night that is out there.

In the shower, Tony scrubs the mildew off the glass screen, he works on the porcelain tray with a cloth and feels the hot water roll off his back and into his eyes. He washes the radiator, bleaches the sink and cleans the top of the bathroom cabinet to make sure there is no dust. Everything he does must be done right.

In his bedroom, with the light off, he approaches the window and stares down on the little square of garden. Who's a beast? His grandfather? That's what they called him. The darkness of the night outside bleeds into the bedroom, and there is a glimmer of light from the windows of next door's kitchen. Tony blinks. There, resting on its hind legs, is the creature. It looks up at the window, but Tony backs away. It's waiting.

Tony lays in bed, staring at the ceiling and feeling his chest rise and fall evenly in the darkness. He is calm. Knowing there is something outside which wants him is soothing. He can sleep easy. It is his beast. He's not going to drink it away like his grandfather or pretend it's not there like his father. He feels power.

The next morning, early, Tony hangs his washing out on the line in his tiny garden. He hangs his trousers in the way his father taught him, the legs first, a peg on the hole for your feet. He hangs socks too, two per peg. Putting it all in the dryer might be easier, but it costs more money in the long run. Tony, like his father, doesn't have money to lose just because he can't be bothered. Emma appears from her back door. She has washing in a hip basket and is wearing her running clothes that hug her smooth figure. She has a tight bum and a light step.

"You didn't have to come round the other night," she says.

Emma is straight to the point. She has heart.

"I couldn't sleep, the banging was that loud," Tony is joking with a half-serious tone.

"Listening to me own head banging the fridge, I had a worse headache than you," she mocks, but the words are deathly cold. "Don't do it again," she says as she begins to hang up her own clothes. "I know you mean well Tony, but it's me who has to live here, with him, I mean. You make it worse. Sometimes getting battered is better than anything else," her green eyes are deep-sea cold, lifeless, hanging in her wrinkled, mid-forties face.

"What did my dad say to him?"

"I dunno, he respected your old man, he was scared of him a bit too, but respected him. That's how he got through to him if he ever did say anything."

"Why don't you leave, take Sam and go? It's what I'd do."

"Got all the answers have you?" she asks with her head cocked. "It's not easy, and anyway, who says I want to?"

Tony has finished hanging out his washing.

"It's school in three weeks," she says. "Have you got your uniform?"

"Yeah, I bought it at the end of last term."

"Right," she says, "proper organised, aren't you?"

Tony likes being asked questions.

"I have to be," he says.

"Well let's get back to the way it was before. You stay out of my business, and I'll stay out of yours."

"It wasn't like that before," says Tony. "Why does he get to treat you like that? My dad would never have treated you like that. I'd never treat you like that."

"Just leave it," she says. "You don't know what you're talking about. You don't know my husband or me. You don't know who I am. Maybe I'm worse than he is. It might be me makes him do it, Tony. It might be me that makes him hit me." She says this with light humour. "What you training for?" she asks.

"A fight, Friday night."

"At the stadium?"

"Yeah."

Emma smiles.

"Knock the shit out of him," she says. "Pretend he's my husband if it makes you feel better."

CHAPTER SEVEN

It is Friday night. Tony has caught the bus to the stadium because Jacko isn't allowed to drive anymore after his stroke. He's alone. In his rucksack, he has his boxing equipment, his gumshield, shorts, wraps, gloves and his boots. Tony has been told to be there by six, and it's ten to as he walks through the big, wide car park with the oval stadium in front of him. His fight starts at half eight and guests arrive an hour before. The plan was that his father would be with him, as his trainer and coach and the one who would give him a drink between rounds and make sure his boxing gloves were tied on. Tony doesn't like being alone, but he knows this is the situation, and he must deal with it. He worries he will have to ask someone in the changing room to tie his gloves for him. He'll be nervous. Tony has already watched one of the videos his father left him on his first boxing match. His father explained the fear and panic of standing in front of a crowd and the noise they make. He told Tony of the shouts, the smell of stale beer and aftershave.

Tony goes to the reception at the arena, gives his name and explains why he's there. The grey-haired lady looks down her list and finds his name. She ticks it off and smiles, giving Tony a badge on a lanyard that he must wear. There's a man with a blue 'staff' t-shirt waiting for him at a door where spectators are not allowed to enter. He too smiles.

"You on your own?" asks the man, glancing past the boy to the electric double doors at the front of reception and expecting someone to come through. It was meant as a joke.

"Yes," says Tony. "My coach is sick."

"What about your mum or dad?" asks the man.

Tony doesn't want to go into detail.

"It's just me," he says.

"Where do you train?" he asks.

"North Hull Boys."

"Jacko?"

"Yeah. He had a stroke a few years back so he can't drive."

"I heard." The man sighs. "The other lad should be here in a minute."

Right on time, at six, the electric doors slide open opposite reception and through them, walks a young man of a similar age to Tony. He is dressed in a white tracksuit with a fancy design across the front and has blonde hair, a tanned face and a big smile. Tony notices his expensive trainers straight away and how he carries himself, confident but not cocky. Behind him are two men dressed in matching tracksuits, a well-heeled woman, and an old couple. There are more, teenagers and young people, maybe twenty of them, in a state of mild, steady excitement. The boy gives his name to the grey-haired lady, and she ticks it off and passes him his badge. The man with the blue 'staff' t-shirt greets the well-kept lad.

"You can't bring all these into the changing room with you," he jokes.

The two men behind the lad smile.

"We've brought a bit of support," he says. "Everyone's here, granddad, his mates, we're all behind our Bob. He's gonna do us proud."

This is the boy's father. He's a bit fat with a round well-meaning face, soft brown hands and a kind smile. The boy's mother is there too, well presented and tanned also. Perhaps they have just come back from a week away somewhere. Tony examines the words 'gonna do us proud', he's going to do something good for himself and his family. Uncles and grandparents, friends and brothers are here to lend their support.

"Only two of you are allowed through, I'm afraid."

Tony feels embarrassed. A lump rises in his throat as he stands there in his jogging pants which are old but clean, and his blue trainers that are a bit worn and were in fashion a few years ago. He wants to disappear.

"This is the lad you'll be fighting tonight." The staff man peers at Tony's badge on his lanyard.

"Tony" he reads. "This is Robert Hall."

It is the first time the boys have met. They shake hands on Robert's call, his grip is solid, and Tony looks in his eyes. This kid seems well trained, well-schooled, firm, but not arrogant. He's measured, disciplined and polite. He'll be a good fighter, Tony hopes.

"Come on then, let's go through,' says the staff member.

As they pass through the door, Tony hears a comment from Robert Hall's entourage, something like 'is that the boy he's fighting...' and, 'North Hull...?' He glances back over his shoulders as he is the last to go through and catches the eyes of an old man, Robert Hall's grandfather. The man holds his stare for a second and there, Tony can see what he saw in Emma's eyes in the kitchen as she was pinned up against the fridge by her throat. He sees fear.

Along the corridor they walk. The staff member and the other three are talking and Tony is following behind.

"My granddad was a boxer in the army," says the boy. "We're keeping it in the family."

Tony understands the old man's face now. Perhaps the boy hasn't trained hard enough or doesn't have the aggression he needs or can't take a punch, or maybe, like the kids on the estate, the old man knows an animal when he sees one. Somewhere perhaps, he walked mean streets and has seen things in places that these ordinary people don't see.

Tony gets changed in the space of the dressing room usually used by football players. Robert Hall does the same. His bag is big and full of kit, there are towels, bottles of energy drinks and sachets, armbands and three different gum shields in different colours, different shorts and boxing boots and various bottles of shampoo. His father helps him with his hand wraps, but they don't talk.

"I'll be back to call you out," says the staff member before he disappears.

Eventually, the father asks Tony something predictable.

"You here on your own?"

"My coach is sick. I'm with North Hull Boys." Tony has answered the man's next question before he can ask it.

"What about you?" Tony adds.

"Robert trains in Beverley, John Lloyd's club. Do you know it?"

"No," says Tony.

"It's a great club, there's a state-of-the-art gym, a sauna, a swimming pool and three full-size rings," the man describes the splendour of the place with his hands. There's nothing else for Tony to ask.

"Haven't you got anyone to wet your mouth between rounds?"

"I'll be alright," says Tony.

"Couldn't you find anyone? Not anyone from the club?"

Tony shakes his head.

"I thought we were going to have a proper fight," says the father to the coach like Tony is not there. "This kid hasn't even got anyone with him. We wanted to give Bobby a real go here. What sort of a fight is this going be?"

The man looks down at Bobby apologetically and then back to Tony and tuts. This is even before he has stepped into the ring. Tony's old trainers and his battered kit have already told his story for him.

They stand in front of the doors to the arena, Tony next to Robert Hall. Tony's gloves have been tied by Robert's dad. The blonde lad is jumping on the spot to warm up. Tony's heart is thumping. Through the doors, he can hear the murmur of the crowd. They are around big tables and have just had a meal. There are pints of lager and bottles of wine on the tables, men dressed in suits and ladies in posh frocks. Not too posh, but enough to show they're on a night out. Tony hears their names called over the loudspeaker and the doors in front of them swing open, and they walk out, into the arena. The noise is louder than Tony expected with the roar of chatting and then clapping as the audience sees them making their way into the ring. They are only the warmup, and kids at that, so there's no fanfare or showboating as they climb through the ropes. Tony is pointed to his corner, and he stands there, feeling terror run up and down his legs. In the centre of the ring, with a microphone, is a tall compère dressed in a sharp suit. He explains who is about to fight and their weights and ages. When he says Robert Hall's name, there is a cheer from the crowd. The compère introduces the referee, a white-haired man who then approaches Tony.

"Where's your coach, mate?" he says in a whisper.

"He's sick… I haven't got one."

The referee looks pained at this.

"Who's gonna throw your towel in if he starts beating the hell out of you?" Asks the referee. Tony doesn't reply. "We'll have to hope that doesn't happen."

Then, Tony is touching gloves with Robert Hall, and parts of the audience are chanting 'Bobby, Bobby', and he's listening to the ref tell him he wants a clean fight with no blows below the belt. Tony steps back and feels the board of the ring bounce a little under his weight. He looks up at the bright lights above him and listens to the 'ping' of the bell as the fight starts. It's the feeling you get before you go down a huge roller coaster.

Time slows. The two young fighters are surrounded by people and light. There is near silence as the crowd watches. Tony's body and back are tight with muscle, and he feels himself loosen up. Robert Hall approaches. Here, Tony knows what to do, he knows where to put his feet and what to do with his hands, knows how to move his head. He has done it a thousand times. As the boy steps towards him, Tony feels the knot in his stomach. He feels the same anger welling up. He knows to fight it down and that a boxer who is angry won't be able to do as well.

Tony blinks. He sees flashes of his past. His frail father linked up to a drip in a hospital bed, Emma's eyes wide as she is choking against the fridge, the fat Scouser, Whalebone, angry and sullen with his arms crossed over that red Liverpool top, the eyes of the beast he has seen in the woods. He has to narrow everything down into one point, let the anger out bit by little bit, keep the technique, move the right way but, when the time comes, focus. Robert Hall is buoyed by his supporters and confident of a win. He is loose, his face is greased in his head guard, and he jabs as Tony moves closer. Tony pats three searching shots away. Now, Tony can see Robert Hall has not trained as much as he has, his arms are not as strong, his chest not nearly as broad and he has not been in the ring as much. His feet are at the wrong angle, and the expensive gloves are held too far away from his chin.

Tony lunges forward and swings for the stomach, everything around him emptying into space, the lights, the crowd, the line of sweat running down his temple, everything dulls and fades out, and, on the end of his right glove – there is pure and bright fury. He feels his fist connect and crunch against Robert Hall's stomach and lower ribs. Robert has never been hit there, or like this and the pain is instant. But Tony is not finished. He follows with a left hook to the unguarded jaw, sending Robert stumbling back. He continues with his left hand ready to land another punch on the boy as he falls backwards. Tony stops himself going on anymore. This is a boxing ring and a game, and he must remember the rules. He stems the flow of anger and steps backwards. Robert Hall staggers in pain. Tony glances towards the rich boy's corner and catches the father's eye. He sees the same face that the grandfather had. Robert's father now knows his son is not in the ring with another, well-meaning young man who will make others proud. He's in with a fully-grown beast that is measured and dangerous. Robert Hall comes at Tony again with jabs he has learned in the gym, his face is worried. It will be a long three minutes.

Once the bell for the first round has been rung there are murmurings between the judges and some of the more boxing savvy members of the audience - it's not a fair fight. The kid from the well-off part of town has been outclassed already. With his smart, new boxing boots, tight pants and bright green gumshield, he looks out of place, more like a child. The referee squirts some water into Tony's mouth from the bottle.

"Don't kill him, will you?" he adds as he gently slaps the lad's face.

Robert, over the other side of the ring in his corner, has his father talking in his ear, he is telling him what to do, where to strike, and how to dance. He is a man who does not know he is blind, telling another blind man how to see. The boy does not want to get back up for another two rounds. He's scared. Robert Hall's grandfather strides down from his seat somewhere deep in the big arena and muscles past the judges and up to the side of the ring to say something into Robert's ear. It's a message from the old man's days in the army.

"Now listen to me, Robert," he whispers. "There's no way out of this. You stand up and make yourself proud."

The bell pings, again, and they are standing up and moving into the centre of the ring. Tony is loose and Robert Hall is frightened. They go to it, a mix of jabs and hooks. Tony lets Robert Hall tire himself out and then manoeuvres him onto the ropes and works the lad's body and stomach with thudding, solid blows. Robert Hall begins to defend and goes to grab Tony in a boxer's hug, he misjudges, and Tony steps backwards and thumps him in his cheek with a cross. The lad goes down onto his side. The blow has caught his nose and there's blood, so the referee steps in to make sure he is okay. Robert Hall gets to his feet, and the referee asks him to count to ten as he does so, all the time looking into his face to see if he is still with it. The referee glances up to Robert Hall's corner to see if the lad's coach is going to throw in the towel. He does not. From the audience, Robert Hall's grandfather stands up and shouts.

"Get up, Bobby," and there is applause as the blonde lad gets to his feet for the last minute of the round. Robert is shaky, white, with blood running out of his nose and onto his vest. When the referee waves them to start, Tony steps forward and works Robert's body again. He can feel that the lad is wearing out. In the last 30 seconds, Robert attempts a few punches that Tony absorbs. The bell rings.

As Tony sits down at his corner, he hears whispers from the audience and the judges – 'he's doing well, that lad, all he has to do is keep his head down for the last round' and, 'he's got heart, that lad'.

The bell rings for the last time, Tony steps to the centre, knowing that if he keeps at it, he will win. Robert comes at him renewed, centred and ready to give this everything he has. Tony ducks and absorbs the blows with his arms and hands and then snaps out, feeling the fury in him, white-hot and desperate. He catches the boy on the chest and follows up with jabs to the face. Robert retreats around the ring. In the last minute, Tony is on him, pounding him with those solid thudding strikes across his head and face. It is too much. The referee steps in between the two lads, and it's done. Robert Hall cannot be allowed to stand this for even a few more seconds.

There is applause, and the judges make their decision swiftly. The compère with his smart suit steps back into the ring on the microphone and the two boxing lads stand next to him as he recounts their fight. He announces Tony as the winner and holds up his glove. There is applause. He has done well. The compère announces Robert Hall and also holds his glove to the roof, to applause and hoots from his family and supporters, much more than there was for Tony.

As the two boys leave the ring, the clapping is louder, and there are shouts from the audience of 'well done Bobby,' 'great work Bobby' and whispers of how well the lad did against that brute from North Hull Boys.

In the dressing room, Tony listens to Robert Hall's father telling his son how well he did and how he carried on against all the odds and battled through against an opponent who was twice as good a boxer as he was. Tony pulls on his old grey joggers. The sound of the real fight begins through the walls as the compère's muffled voice echoes over the speakers and the roar of the slightly drunk crowd starts. Robert Hall's face is a mess and already puffing up from the battering Tony gave him. He will wear the bruises with pride, for even here in absolute defeat, Robert Hall has won. Perhaps even before they stepped through the door of the arena, he had won, maybe even as he put on his new boxer shorts that morning or opened his eyes in his soft bed.

Tony does not feel anger. He feels sadness. He wonders how different it might have been if his father had been there. How he would have spoken to Robert Hall's dad and shared a joke and swapped stories, the fight would have been the same, but the result would have been different. Tony would have been a winner rather than a lonely, shy boy from the poor and ugly side of town with his cheap clothes and sad face. He would be legitimate rather than something dangerous, and he would not be an animal from the wild that they let in to show how brave they all are.

It begins to rain as Tony waits at the bus stop in the darkness and pulls up his hood. He does not know if his father would have been proud or disappointed with his performance. Did he hold back because he didn't want to hurt the boy, or did he finish him in a gentlemanly manner? Tony is never sure of himself. He does not know how to please a man who is not there and will never be there again.

He gets off the bus and walks home, past the Pilot with the smokers standing outside then the silent stone of the

Methodist Church. When he arrives home, he is soaked through. Just before the turnoff to 6th Avenue, behind the metal rails of a fence after the little bridge, Tony sees a flash of movement from the overgrown bushes behind. He approaches. The rain is heavy on him, and he pulls down his hood so he can see better without the rain in his eyes. Behind the railings, in the darkness of trees and bushes that make up the bank of the river, he sees wolf eyes looking out at him. The great beast is hidden in the blackness. He can smell its breath. It makes Tony feel good to see it.

Tony sits in the bath and feels the warm water around his muscles. He is tired. After a fight like this, his father would make him something good, maybe a fry up, and he'd let him have a bottle of cider or beer. There'd be music playing and the smell of cooking. Tony's father would drink whiskey, and there'd be comfort in the house.

It's not the same now. Laid in the bath, Tony feels the bubbles around his toes. It is relaxing, and though he's safe, something is missing. There's a dull thud from next door that sends shockwaves through his bathwater. Three or four more thuds follow. He hears shouting and Emma screaming. Tony sits up in the bath. The screams are a higher pitch than usual, but perhaps this is because he is sitting in a different room. He is suddenly conscious of the time; it is a little early for the man to begin hitting her. There's more banging on the stairs next door and another scream and then silence. He waits for a moment and slides back down into the bath; glad it is over. Why would Emma stay with someone like that?

In the kitchen, Tony prepares a treat of cheese on toast. He finds a can of lager in the back of the cupboard and then goes in the front room, barefoot and dressed in his dressing gown. Here, sitting in his father's room, he relives the fight again, sees Robert Hall crumple under his fists and the look in the grandfather's eyes. Tony does his father's job of examining the ins and outs of the punches and blocks. He knows he did well, but he should have finished Robert Hall much more quickly. Tony is halfway through his second piece of toast when there is a tapping sound at the front door. It's half-past ten. He sets down his plate and creeps to the hall. In the dim glow of the streetlight, he can make out a figure waiting at the door. The light tap comes again. Tony pauses in the hall and a light voice cuts in through the glass.

"Are you there?" The accent is foreign. It's a boy. Tony opens the door. It is the little Congolese lad who comes to training on Saturday morning. His name is Lionel. Standing behind him at the end of the path to Tony's front door, is the big woman he saw at the supermarket, Lionel's mother, Mwamba. She speaks Kirwanda and Lingala and some Swahili, but her English is not great. She takes Lionel with her when she goes anywhere important so he can translate for her. He is ten but looks more like seven with his wide eyes, Arsenal shirt and closely cropped hair. They live in the tower block two streets away.

"My mother wants to give you something," Lionel says.

Although Lionel has been here for four years, his accent still has the twang of the Congo to it. He is pensive, even a bit afraid. Tony has held the punch bag for the little boy many times. He wonders why they are here. Mwamba is carrying a silver biscuit tin. She struggles up to the door with her metal crutch clinking on the stone floor as she hands it to Tony. She begins in Lingala, a long string of vowels with u and o and a throaty nod. Lionel translates.

"She is sorry you lost your father," says Lionel. "I am too."

Mwamba stands back, she looks worried. She says something else. Lionel continues, "We brought you foofoo, my mother cooked them for you. She wants you to…" Lionel looks back at his mother, and she repeats the same sentence in Lingala. "She wants you to know you are not alone, you are not alone in this world, and there is always someone who will help you."

Tony feels touched but senses there is more, there is tension. Mwamba's voice becomes low and throaty as she speaks, Lionel translates what she says.

"She says you do not need to seek out new friends. She says she will cook for you every night, clean your sheets and wash your clothes and look after you like her own son. You do not need to find anyone new."

Tony does not understand. It's creepy.

"My Auntie Lynn is here," Tony says. Lionel does not translate. Mwamba has not yet said what she wants to say.

"She saw you. She saw you talk to it. Here, in the street through the fence. She saw you talk to the animal." Mwamba's voice has become jerky and fearful. "She says your loneliness has brought him here, your anger too. He feeds from you."

Tony cannot believe quite what he is hearing, but he feels a chill run down his spine. He sees Mwamba's arm is quivering while it is holding her walking stick and Lionel is wide-eyed.

"I don't know what you mean," says Tony, shaking his head. Mwamba babbles back, Lionel responds.

"She is very afraid; she says you must not look for it or think about it. Try to be with friends, your family - you have your people. If you do not have any people then you can be our people, we will be your family, the animal will not help you."

Lionel is scared by his mother's words; perhaps he has not heard her speak like this before. Mwamba is also frightened in the late summer darkness. She is worried for herself and her boy.

"My mother is afraid," says Lionel. "She is a Kakamamdu in our country, and she can see the spirits.'

"Tell her not to be worried," Tony replies. "Everything will be okay. There's nothing. It was a cat I saw, a cat in the bushes. There isn't anything like that here."

Lionel translates back and Mwamba shakes her head.

"She says you're lying." Mwamba suddenly steps forward, and her large frame moves close. Her face draws near to Tony. He can smell her perfume and see the white in her brown eyes below his face. She says something in Lingala, it's impossible for him to understand, but the feeling is there and her sense of worry. Tony blinks back at her. "She says we are here if you need us," translates little Lionel.

As Mwamba and Lionel hurry away from his door, the little boy looks back over his shoulder as his mother pulls him by the arm.

"Do not let it in," Lionel shouts.

Tony closes the door and the silence of his house envelops him. He can only just hear the ticking of the clock from where he is standing in his dressing gown. He does not know what to think. The idea frightens him and electrifies him at the same time, but he knows what he has seen, and it is real, not some demon or figment of his imagination.

He is still holding the biscuit tin in his hands as he walks through to the kitchen and he pulls off the lid. Inside are two rows of perfect, round dough balls. Tony sniffs at the contents and then sets it down on the work surface. He does not want to be rude. He will say he ate them all as he empties the contents into the black recycling bin. It's good people care about him, even if it is misguided.

In the darkness of his bedroom, Tony watches a video on the laptop, *Number 4: Loneliness*. It's not a video he particularly wants to see because sometimes, his father could go on a bit. This must have been a very early one because his father is fresh-faced and healthy, wearing a suit and tie like he sometimes did if there was a meeting at work or a business night out. He is sober and honest with a cup of tea in front of him. The man adjusts the camera for a minute, and there is wasted time, the video is not edited as well as the others, perhaps he had not learned how to do it yet. The man begins.

"Just a few thoughts about being on your own…" The introduction is apologetic like he can't quite get to what he wants to say even though he's started. "It's not so bad. Everyone says you need to work as a team and support people, that you need to look after your mates and your family, and… that's true. You have to. It's what we're all about… but then, when you're standing in a boxing ring, with your fists up and thousands of people shouting at you, even though you've got a trainer and a coach and a wife and friends - you're on your own. I think that's what I'm trying to say. Everywhere you go there are people being together, couples, gangs of kids on their bikes, boxing gyms, pubs, people being with each other, maybe sometimes, so they aren't lonely. You know, son, you're on your own. It's as simple as that. There isn't anyone looking out for you, not when I'm gone. I mean, people will say they're looking out for you, neighbours, mates, maybe even Jacko at the gym, but you have to know that they're too busy looking after themselves to care about you, whatever they say. So, you're on your own. That's not something you should be afraid of, it's only American films and soap operas tell you being on your own is bad, and I'm not even saying this in defeat. I'm alone too." Tony sees the wide and honest smile of his father crack as he says this, like he's telling a lie even though he believes it is true. "I was alone for so many years till I met your mother and then we had you. I didn't feel alone when I had you and I don't feel alone now, but I did. I took it all the way to the heavyweight championships alone."

What had started out as a message that it was okay to be lonely had simply become like every other little film designed for Tony. Another reminder of how much his father loved him, of how much he cared. Tony's father smiles at the screen and shakes his head. "We all feel lonely sometimes, Tony, and that's okay. Go and find a friend, but lonely is okay. I love you."

Tony does not feel tired as he lies in the darkness of his room. He can hear the rain outside hammering on the roof, running down the drainpipes outside and dripping off the window ledges. He would like to run, but he knows it would be bad for his body and he needs to rest. He looks out of the window and down towards the drain in the moonlight. What did Mwamba mean? Do not let it in.

He knows it is out there.

CHAPTER EIGHT

It's the next day. In the gym, Jacko is sweeping up. The folding chairs have all been moved to the sides, and he is pushing a long broom as he walks. Tony can only see him from behind, his gait is a shuffle after the stroke, but the limp is even more pronounced today. He is slower than usual.

"Why don't you get one of the lads to do that?" Tony calls as he approaches. It is half-past eight in the morning, and there is the smell of cut grass from outside as the summer air begins to heat up.

"Twenty-five years I've done this," Jacko calls back to him, "every morning."

"About time you gave it up then," says Tony.

There is something different about Jacko, something in his voice this morning that sounds slower. Tony does not like it and wants to look Jacko in the face. He strides past him and then turns. The old man has been attacked. Jacko's right eye is swollen to a red and angry slit, and his cheek is purple with an enormous bruise. The old man brings his head down in shame as Tony moves closer to him.

"What happened?" demands Tony.

"It's nothing…looks worse than it is."

"Well, what happened?"

"On my way home last night, got mugged, some bastard got me as I was coming out the ten-foot behind my house."

This is a shock for Tony. He has always thought Jacko was unbreakable. He notices the man's hands and long fingers, his lopsided shoulders, his face, unshaven under the damage someone has done to his head. Tony sees an old man.

"What did they take?" asks Tony

"Nothing… I got a few good ones in before they cleared off."

Tony does not know what to do. Jacko should not be

sweeping the floor, not after this has happened to him.

"Let me do this," says Tony and he reaches for the sweeping brush. The old man shakes his head.

"You're a good lad, Tony, but this is what I do. I sweep the floor, and then the kids come in. I teach them how to box. It's what I've always done."

"Who would hit you? Everyone knows you round here. Who'd be stupid enough to attack the coach of North Hull Boys? There must be two hundred lads who train here, some of them pretty hard. Did you get a look at their faces?"

Jacko shakes his head. His eyes are defeated and far away and, at once, Tony understands. He realises who would do this, someone who does not fear the two hundred boxers, the kind of person who would not think twice about attacking an old man as he walks home late at night, the sort who wouldn't need to rob him either. Tony glances up. Someone has come into the gym. It is the big, sliver haired Scouser, Wallace, dressed in a grey suit with a smart shirt and open collar. His well-polished shoes click on the floor, and the expensive show-off watch clinks on his wrist. He is smiling.

"I was just passing," Wallace says, his accent rasping over the vowels and consonants, rough-sounding and unfriendly. "Thought I'd drop in and see how you've been keeping Jacko. Looks like you've been scrapping there, grandad."

The words are coarse and harsh, even though the man grins.

"Nothing I can't handle there, Wallace," Jacko replies.

"Seems to me, mate, like you can't handle it very well at all. Are you sweeping this floor?"

Jacko does not respond.

"Not doing a very good job, are you?" Wallace adds.

"You aren't welcome here, mate," says Tony, straight to the point, like any street lad.

The Scouser smiles. He's a street lad too, but from a

bigger street and he's been at it longer than Tony.

"I don't like people speaking to me like that, son. It upsets me."

"I'm not bothered if you're upset, mate, just as long as you clear off."

Tony feels his anger bubbling to the surface, quick and hot. His hands clench into fists.

"Leave it, Tony," says Jacko, his hand coming to rest on Tony's chest.

"You haven't told him yet, have you?" says Wallace.

"No, I haven't told him yet," answers Jacko.

The eyes of the Scouser twinkle in cruelty.

"I bought the club last night, made a bank transfer over the internet. Jacko here works for me now. So, you see, mate," he addresses Tony, "this is my club now, and if you don't like it, then it's you that can clear off." His voice is half-serious, half-mocking.

Tony takes a breath. He could go for Wallace and break his jaw right now, but Jacko's hand keeps him still. It would be stupid. Wallace is much bigger than him anyway. The silver-haired Scousers smiles like he has all the answers.

"I like you lot actually, Tony," says Wallace, "I like you a real lot, I respect your spirit. I like this town too. It's got heart. I can work with that; it's like being at home."

"This was my dad's club as well, Jacko," says Tony.

"It was a good deal," Jacko replies. "He offered me more than I could turn down and your dad isn't around anymore in case you hadn't noticed."

"They beat you up Jacko. Maybe not him, but people who work for him. Why didn't you ask us lads to help? There are loads of us here would stand up to someone like this."

Tony is talking as if Wallace is not there.

"I don't like the way you're talking," says Wallace. "I'm the new owner of this club and I'm prepared to give you a chance, but you can only push me so far." Tony isn't going to back down. Why should he?

"If you two ladies want to fight," says Jacko, "then put on a pair of gloves and get into the ring. This is a boxing club, not a pub."

The Scouser smiles.

"I might not own this club anymore, but it's still my rules, I still work here," Jacko adds.

"The old man's right," Wallace says. "I'm here to make this place better. I've heard there're some good young boxers in this club, real grafters. Whalebone tells me Henry Petersen's lad trains here, a gifted little bastard who just lost his dad."

"That's me," says Tony.

The Scouser beams. He knew that already.

"Think of what I could do with a fighter like you, Tony," he says. "I didn't buy this place for the building. I bought it to get to train lads like you. I spoke to one of the judges who was at the stadium the other night, where you fought that kid who was tipped for something good. He told me you split him in half. Now… that is exactly the kind of fighter I am looking for, and if you let me, you and I can make a lot of money together, I mean, a lot of money."

Tony blinks at Wallace and then back to Jacko. The old man frowns.

"I'm gonna do my run," says Tony as he backs away.

"Just so you know, Tony," says Wallace, "you ever talk to me like that again, and you'll pay for it."

Tony holds the Scouser's gaze. Jacko breaks the silence.

"Three times round the block before you come back." Tony nods.

When Tony gets back, the summer school children are leaving the gym, tumbling out of the doors and onto the little patch of grass outside. It is lunchtime. Tony steps around them as he makes his way into the gym. He is wet with sweat but feels calmer than he did before. He passes

Whalebone, who sits on one of the fold-up chairs with his back against the wall and his eyes hidden by his flat cap.

"Weirdo," whispers Tony as he walks past, loud enough so the fat man can hear. Whalebone does not move at all and stares into the open gym as if he is a statue. Jacko is in his office. Tony walks the length of the gym and taps on the wood of the open door as he peers in. Jacko has a black carrier bag in his hand and is stuffing papers inside.

"I'm having a clear-out," Jacko says.

"I didn't know there was anything in here."

Jacko's face is worse as the bruise is coming out. It looks like he can hardly see. Inside the office, there's a mucky brown desk and black leather chair behind it. There are two rickety stools against the wall and a fading calendar that reads 2001. The place smells of mouldy paper with an old filing cabinet sat in one corner. Jacko has opened the drawers of the desk and is stuffing whatever is inside into the black bin liner.

"Do you need any help?" asks Tony.

The old man shakes his head. Tony does not remember Jacko ever coming into the office. Jacko is shorter today, older too, his head held down.

"They beat the hell out of you, didn't they?" asks Tony.

"Drop it, Tony. It's for the best."

"Their best or your best?"

Jacko drops the black bin liner on the floor. He swallows.

"Sometimes you've got to know when you've lost, Tony, that's what I mean. You can't go on winning forever."

"So you've let them take the club, your club, where you swept the floor every day for the last twenty-five years?"

"I had to Tony. It's easy for kids like you to dream of winning and fighting, but as you get older, you'll see it's just a matter of time before you have to give in and settle for what you've got."

"It's not giving in Jacko. It's standing up for yourself.

That's what you always taught me to do."

"What if they weren't trying to rip me off, Tony? What if they could do something for you, for all the lads in this club and on this estate? Have you thought about that?"

There is fear in Jacko's voice, almost invisible, but his tone is higher than it would normally be. At the door behind them is Wallace.

"Hadn't you better be training, lad," he says to the boy.

Tony blinks at Jacko and watches the man who trained him to fight carry on filling a bin bag full of papers like a cleaner. Tony has seen people who've taken a kicking before and the way they act afterwards. He's seen it on the lads in the gym when he's knocked them around in the ring and seen it in his neighbour Emma as well.

"I'm your coach now, Tony," says Wallace. "Get back in that gym."

Tony leaves. In a few seconds, they can hear him working the bags outside with heavy punches. Wallace steps forward into the office, which is now his, and closes the door so it's just him and the old man.

"Don't push them too far," says Jacko. "You push them too much, treat them too mean, and they'll give you it back twice as hard."

Now Tony is not around to hear, Wallace can pull away his mask of innocence and the well-meaning pretence.

"I didn't ask you anything," he snarls. "The only reason you're here is because Whalebone took pity on you; otherwise you'd be staring up at a hospital ceiling. I don't give a toss about the people round here. I don't care about this club or you, and... Jacko, I don't wanna have to remind you again, never speak to me, or look at me again, or I'll have Whalebone do something you won't like. You do know why they call him Whalebone, don't you?"

Jacko continues to put papers into the bin liner. He has lived around hard nuts and men of violence all his life, if he shows fear, they will sense it and come in harder.

Wallace whispers to himself, "I thought this was meant to be the hardest boxing club in the city?"

Jacko continues, opening another drawer and pulling out manila folders of receipts and bills from ten years ago or more. Wallace clicks his tongue.

"Hull…" he scoffs. "What a shithole."

Tony lays in the bath in the early evening after he has eaten a dinner of potatoes and beans. On his front step he found a thin, Chinese takeaway tray full of what smelled like curry. He guessed this must be from Mwamba and emptied it into the food recycling. He does not want charity.

In the warm water of the bath, Tony examines his knuckles, stretches out his fingers and then gathers them together in a fist. He imagines what they would have done to Robert Hall's face if they had not been in gloves. He thinks about the times he used to lay in the bath, the same, and he would hear his father singing in his bedroom, or on the phone to one of his friends. The house is dead without him. Music from the speaker connected to his phone gets sucked up into the sadness if Tony plays his old tunes. The TV sounds like doors slamming, and video games with Tony's friend's voices over the internet, seem garbled and far away. The only sound that remains in the hot afternoon or the dead of night, is the sharp tick of the clock above the kitchen door.

It's dark and Tony stares out of the front window at the street and sees the gang of pushbike kids roll past, ten or more of them, off into the more delicate parts of the city where they can cause a bit of trouble. Some have North Face jackets with their hoods up; maybe they say *innit* at the end of every sentence. They ride expensive mountain bikes bought by well-meaning grandparents or parents, or nicked, or found. If they make trouble around here, they will meet with honest fury. Who knows who is behind the doors of these streets, drug dealers or angry dads? Either way, here on the North Hull Estate trouble will be dealt with swiftly or by someone who knows their dad. In the nicer parts of the city, the residents will call the police before they throw punches. Tony shies away from the window as they drift by.

In his father's bedroom, Tony opens the chest, like he always does when he is lonely. He goes through the cuttings in a folder and looks at the yellowing news stories with pictures of his father after a fight. He is young in the tiny photos. Tony handles the belt his father won, the Lonsdale Belt and wonders, as he turns it over in his fingers, if he will ever win anything so special. From the bottom of the box, Tony takes out an old-fashioned packet of photos. He opens the flap. He's seen them before, these pictures from his mother and father's honeymoon. They are on the south coast where there are long beaches and where his mother is thin and pretty. She looks fragile as she stands in a see-through shawl with the wind catching her hair. His father is standing beside her, shirtless and strong. They are at odds somehow, a brute next to a flower, but they are both smiling. Tony's father said they were in love with conviction. Tony knows they were.

He hears a tapping. It is late, perhaps eleven. At once the hairs on the back of Tony's neck stand on end. The tapping comes again, a faint, light rat-a-tat coming from the kitchen downstairs. He remembers the Congolese woman, Mwamba, speaking to him through her son. 'Do not let it in,' she said.

He steps down into the hall. The lights are off, and the house is silent. Tony sees a pale face in his back garden against his kitchen window. It is Emma; her eyes are wide and makeup has run down her cheeks. She looks like a ghost. Tony opens the back door, but she does not come inside. She is shivering though the night is warm. Tony does not know what to say as she stands there in her long t-shirt nightie with nothing on her feet. Something has happened.

"We've killed him, Tony," she says. "We've killed him,

Sam and me. I hit him with a pan. We've killed the bastard."

Tony blinks as he hears the words. His feet go cold.

Inside the house next door, in the kitchen, twelve-year-old Sam is curled up in the corner, on the floor, with his knees up to his chest and his head buried in his arms. Tony stands above him with Emma behind him. On the floor, face down is the ratty little grey-haired man, dressed in his pyjamas. He is motionless. Tony reaches out to his neck to feel if there is a pulse. He knows from his medical book there should be a soft drumming from inside, but there is not. He looks back at Emma who is standing, horrified, in her long, shapeless nightie.

"It was me who hit him," she says. "I couldn't stand it anymore. He's done it to me for fifteen years." Her eyes are wide. "Fifteen years."

Tony swallows. His mouth is dry and his palms are tacky. He does not know what to do. From the corner, Sam brings his face up from his arms. His eyes are raw from the tears.

"I killed him, Tony," he says through a weak throat. "I killed him. I hit him with that pan, and then I hit when he was on the floor too. She's lying so I don't get in trouble."

Tony sees a heavy silver saucepan on the laminate, and it looks out of place.

He examines the man laid face down again. There is no blood, but he has no pulse. Tony rolls him over, and his eyes are wide open, hollow and cold. He stinks of booze.

"I could take his body somewhere," says Tony. He has an idea.

"What do you mean?" asks Emma. Her voice is shaking.

"We could get rid of his body."

"How?" she whispers.

"I know a thing…" says Tony. His lips are dry.

Emma blinks at him under the strip light.

"What thing?"

"Something I know," answers Tony. "Something that will get rid of his body."

Emma is confused.

"We should call the police," then thinks better of it when she looks at Sam.

"Maybe," says Tony, "but how will it look, when your lad has killed his dad? What do you think it's like in prison for a lad? What would happen to me? They'd find out I'm on my own and that you aren't my Auntie Lynn. Then I'd be shafted as well."

Emma blinks at him.

"Where are you going to take him?"

"Out into the woods."

"Tony, this is stupid," she says in a moment of clarity, fearing for the future and her son. "We have to call the police, get this sorted, or they'll find out, and then we'll all be for it, you, me and Sam. He's dead, laid out there dead. For Christ's sake."

"What you want me to do?" asks Tony quietly. "Why did you even knock on my window? Now you've got me mixed up in this as well. You have to let me help."

Emma swallows. She does not know what to do. The outward show of confidence and bravado she presents to the world every day has been ripped from her. Tony considers the body of the ratty little man. He has seen a dead body before and he's not afraid of this. Tony bends down, picks up one of the man's arms and pulls so the lifeless body sits. Then, he hoists the grey-haired man over his shoulder in a smooth movement. He turns to Sam as the boy sniffles in the corner.

"I'd have done it too, kid," Tony says to him. "Anyone would, anyone. You've got nothing to be ashamed of."

With the floppy and lifeless body over his shoulder, Tony turns to Emma as he walks to the door. "Don't say anything to anyone, about anything. They'll find his body, somehow. Say he was out walking, drunk, late at night. Say he was a good man. If you can, pretend like none of this ever happened. You have to believe it for it to be true."

"Where are you taking him?" asks Sam from the corner.

"There's something in the woods along the drain, something… I've seen it lots of times," answers Tony.

Emma puts her face in her hands. She does not want to think about it. By the microwave clock, Tony reads the time, ten past twelve. He lumbers out of Emma's back door and climbs over the fence at the bottom of her little garden and into the woods. On sure feet, he walks down the bank with the twigs and branches snapping under him. In the darkness, he can feel something watching as he goes, so he does not travel far. It is here already he can sense it. Tony eases the body off his shoulders and sets it down, on its back, on the wet, muddy bank. He stares down at the face of the ratty, grey-haired man, silent in the darkness. His eyes are still wide. Tony watches gravity pull the body into the water of the river, and it drifts away on the weak current.

As he walks back up the bank, Tony hears something in the forest move out of the shadows behind him.

CHAPTER NINE

A police car pulls up in front of Tony's house and the officer inside the passenger seat looks out of the window. He is young, in his mid-twenties, with concerned blue eyes. He gets out of the car and approaches Emma's front door. Tony hides behind the curtain when the older officer who has been driving scans up and down the street. He hears the copper rap on the door, then it opens, and Emma invites them in.

She is a very good actress. She lied to his social worker. She has lied to the world for so long about how happy she was with a man who hurt her. He sits down on the side of his father's bed and runs his hands through his hair. He has not slept. He does not want to think about the body he put in the river the night before or what happened to it afterwards, but he cannot help himself.

Outside, Tony locks his door and glances in Emma's window as he walks past. He sees the two policemen sat upright on the sofa, and her with her head in her hands on the armchair opposite. There is nothing Tony can do.

He passes bike kids on the corner, three of them with a heavy one smoking a vape pipe. They nod with the tiniest movement of their heads. Tony does the same back. In the newsagent's Tony buys a small plastic bottle of milk. The ginger cashier, Dean, is pale from never leaving the shop. He's not hungover this morning.

"Coppers pulled your next-door neighbour out of the drain this morning," he says with a morbid but gleeful expression. "Some dog walker found him, or what was left of him."

"What happened?" Tony asks.

"Something ate his face and his insides," says Dean as he hands Tony his change, "horrible business."

"Really?" answers Tony. He should say as little as possible.

"That's what everyone's saying."

Tony grimaces at him and Dean the Gob beams back.

"There is a beast you see, mate."

The gym is full. As Tony walks in, he sees Whalebone stuffing paper into a black plastic bag. It is the poster of Muhammed Ali that was on the back wall of the gym for so many years. Tony looks up at the space on the wall, and there is a clean, white rectangle where it hung.

"We don't like his sort," says Whalebone to one of the kids as he rips another piece of it up. Wallace is next to the ring. He is dressed in tracksuit bottoms and a vest and shouting at Apple inside. He does not sound angry; his voice is a mixture of enthusiasm and sarcasm as he explains what the lad is doing wrong. Tony can see the lines of definition on Wallace's arms and the way he holds his fingers when he shows how to throw a punch. He has been a boxer, this man, and a good one too. Apple is fighting a non-descript lad who Tony has not seen before. The lad is big and bulky but not light on his feet, and it is clear the new fighter has not done this before. Apple works hard. The bigger lad is beginning to tire. There is a line of big, doughy kids standing in a queue alongside the ring.

"Alright," says Wallace, "next," as the big lad steps out of the ring, another one steps in and approaches Apple who does not get a break. It is rugby training. The team from the local school turn up to train at the club once a week and Jacko shows them how to fight. Only now it's Wallace. Apple is being made to take them on one after another.

"You're late," says Wallace as Tony sets his bag down, "and you look like shit. Get yourself warmed up and on them bags, you're in here after this lad."

Tony sets to, and he runs around the gym, skips and shadow boxes before he hits the bags. He has a light sweat all over his body when he pulls on his head guard and gloves. The rugby team have given Apple the once over, and the young lad is tired when he comes out of the ring for Tony to take over, he spits out his gum shield and smiles.

"They're pansies," Apple whispers.

The rugby lads are on their second round of fighting and getting a bit more used to it, but they are in no way trained. Their footwork is all wrong. They are cumbersome and artless. Tony opens them up with jabs and keeps them moving with shots to the head. Wallace shouts tips from the side, more to the rugby lads than Tony. 'Get your chin in – move – put your arms up, or he's gonna belt you.' He whispers as Tony moves closer, 'give them some space, Tony, let them make the mistakes,' they change places with each other and grumble at Wallace because Tony is a better boxer. He sees they are flagging and changes the rules.

"Let's have two of you lads in the ring," he says, waving his arm at the rugby lads, "show him how you do it in your game." The rugby players do not need much encouragement to step through the ropes. Two lads crowd him into the corner and Tony jabs to keep them away. There is no malice in this. It must be nearly the end of the session. More lads are getting into the ring, and they circle Tony until one of them jumps on him from behind and pulls him down. Soon the whole of the rugby team is on him or each other in some way, wrestling and pummeling him with the soft parts of the heavy boxing gloves. It feels good to fight like this, friendly and heavy. He can smell the sweat on their bodies and the heat on their breath as they beat him up. They hurt him in the same way he hurt them, with good nature. Tony is smiling when Jacko climbs up into the ring and fishes him out by his arm, swearing under his breath. Tony sits down at the corner and regains his breath while undoing his gloves. Jacko seems to have some of his dignity back and the swelling over his eye has gone down.

"Right!" says Jacko, loud over the gym. "I need to talk to all of you about a couple of things, gather round." It is the old Jacko that is speaking now, his voice loud and sure.

"So that means stop whatever you're doing and come over here round the ring."

At the far end of the gym, the lanky lad from the weight session is tapping the bags and Jacko points over at him. "Will someone go and tell that deaf bastard he has to come over here?" and one of the smaller kids dispatches himself. Jacko steps around the ring as the small crowd gathers. Tony sits on the floor with Apple behind him.

"There are two things I want to say... first, you've probably heard, they pulled Mike Clarkson out of Barmston Drain this morning, poor bloke was in a terrible state, and you've all probably heard he was got at by something. Before you start believing all the shite, foxes have done that before, did it to a lad they found dead when I was a lad, ate his face. What it does mean, far from there being a beast, there is, or are, some right horrible bastards out there. We don't know what happened to him yet, but please take care of yourself and each other. There're some sick people around, and we stick together in this club, so watch out for each other."

Tony feels his ears begin to burn red when he hears about the beast. He does not look around; he does not want to give anything away.

Jacko continues, "but, there are some true things... I have sold the club. I've sold it to this fella here who's been helping us out with training this morning. His name is Terry Wallace, Kirky Boxing Club, Toxteth, Liverpool. Terry won thirty-four fights in his career and he's here to help you lot." From the skinny seven-year-olds to the bigger juniors and to Tony's rough grey eyes, they will do anything Jacko asks of them. "I can't think what he expects to find with you lot," he whispers then carries on in his usual, rasping voice, "I'll still be here, sweeping the floor and making sure you put your gloves back right and do proper press-ups. You can tell your mams and dads things are changing after this summer holiday. Subs will change, some of the rules will change, this place will start to change as well." There's a sadness as he says these things, but you would have to know him well to notice, "the only thing that isn't normal," says Jacko, "is things stay the same, so I'm sure you'll listen to Wallace here just as well as you listened to me."

Wallace nods at the old man as he stands up from where he is leaning on the ropes.

"Like Jacko said, my name is Terry Wallace," he says. He has a gift for speaking that perhaps Jacko does not have. His Scouse accent makes him sound strange but oddly powerful. "My office will be over there, and, if any of you lads have any problems, my door will always be open." Wallace stands at his full height in the boxing ring. "Jacko is right. There'll be a lot of changes here. We'll be updating the equipment, the bags, the weights, this ring, everything. It'll be a different club and there'll be new rules as well. Over there is a friend of mine, Whalebone."

Wallace points to the fat Scouser who sits in one of the fold-out chairs near the back. "He's a hard bastard. He's not a boxer like you lot, and he doesn't wear gloves, but when he hits you, it hurts. He sees everything, does Whalebone, everything, and he's everywhere all the time, even when I'm not. You lads leave him alone, and he'll leave you alone. Disrespect this club, me or the other lads here, and he'll come down on you like you would not believe." Wallace stresses the last few words. His message crystal clear.

Tony blinks up at Wallace above him. There is no need to frighten these boys. They are on his side.

"So, things are going to change, but one thing is not. We are still here to train and fight and whatever the world does out there has nothing to do with what happens in here. We still try and we still win, and I believe that this club can deliver. "As Wallace, the new owner of North Hull Boys, says his last line, he looks directly at Tony. "I think we can make a winner," he says.

The police car is still outside Emma's house. He tries not

to glance in her window as he walks past. He does not want to invite any trouble. It's coming anyway, like it always is. He turns the key in the lock of his front door and steps inside. The silence greets him, and this time, he is thankful for it. In the kitchen, he sets his gym bag on the table and he peels off his hoodie. He can hear his father telling him to put his gym clothes into the washing machine and to make sure he has cooled down. Tony takes the clothes out of his bag and feeds them into the round cylinder of the machine, sets the timer and adds powder. Over the last few months, Tony learned how to use all the appliances, how to cook and read the gas meter, how to bleed the radiators, how to defrost the freezer, even how to reset the router.

There is a tap on the door and Tony, again, feels his blood run cold as he closes the washing machine door. Tony expects to see the bright yellow jacket of a policeman at the other side of his front door, but there is someone else. He opens the door. It is Lionel, the little Congolese boy holding a Tupperware box. Behind him and some metres away is Mwamba. She rests on her walking cane at an angle. Her hair is braided and catches the orange of the streetlight. Lionel speaks.

"My mother made you this mikate, it's food from Congo," and he holds the Tupperware container out for Tony to take. He can see that inside there are the same round balls of dough she gave him a few nights before and some rice.

"I haven't finished the last ones," says Tony.

"My mother says you threw them away."

Tony takes the Tupperware container from the boy and he smiles at Mwamba. She says something. Lionel translates.

"She says the animal is near and is getting closer." The woman natters more in her language that flows and warbles like rich birdsong and Lionel interprets.

"She asks that you do not let it in."

"What if I want to let it in?" asks Tony.

Lionel translates for his mother. She shakes her head with vigour and replies.

"She says it will eat you," Lionel replies. "It is dangerous. It will eat your spirit." This is almost a game to Tony. He does not believe in ghosts and so he is not afraid of them.

"The only dangerous things on these streets and in those woods are people. What does she think is out there?" He can't believe he is having this conversation on his doorstep.

"She says there is a wolf. In our country, it was a monkey, a chimpanzee from out of the forest. A bili ape, tall and strong. It would come to the lonely ones of the village who did not think they had any friends."

"I have friends," says Tony. Now that his father has gone, he does not have anyone to talk to, except, perhaps, Emma from next door. "I have friends," Tony repeats as if to make it sound more real.

Little Lionel continues, relaying the story his mother told him.

"The bili ape takes them out into the jungle, far from their people and eats their spirit, their inside, their heart and their sadness."

"What for?" asks Tony.

"To make a new bili ape," says Lionel. The little boy is sweating. He is a conduit for the fear and anger, resentment and worry of the woman behind him as well as her translator. "My mother says she saw one when she was a child, she followed it out into the jungle, and one of her uncles stopped her and chased it away. She says she has brought it here. It must have followed her."

Tony frowns at the boy in his Arsenal shirt and shorts.

"She's tapped mate," Tony says.

"I know," says Lionel, like a spell has been broken, "I don't like it. I'm afraid."

"She scares me more than any spirit," says Tony, "but tell your mum there's been a beast down the side of this drain for as long as I can remember. Me granddad says he saw it. You ask all the people up and down this street, and this town and they'll all tell you they've seen something or other. Tell your mum she hasn't brought anything here and she doesn't have to worry about me."

Lionel cocks his head and looks back at his mother, standing a few metres away, leaning on her walking stick with her full, long dress over her legs.

"She will kill me if I tell her that," he says, "just eat some of her mikate, please? It will make her feel better."

"Tell her I will."

Tony watches the boy walk back towards his mother. Mwamba stands there, regarding Tony with a mixture of fear and anguish. Tony closes the door and looks out at the street through the frosted glass. He shakes his head.

In the comfort of his bedroom, he sits cross-legged on his bed with the laptop in front of him. He opens the list of videos his father made and scans down. He stops at *number 29: Dealing with the police*. It might be of some use, he reasons. He clicks the mousepad and the screen changes and expands. The face of his father appears, thin, with a baseball cap on to cover the hair loss from the chemotherapy. The man adjusts the mobile phone he is filming himself on. His father begins, and this time, in his hand is his favourite glass, a pint with a handle. He smiles.

"Quick one on dealing with the police," he says as he takes a sip of the black liquid. It could be the bitter, cold black tea he drank a lot of, or it could be Guinness. "They're not all bad, despite what the lads will say. Think of coppers as a big, organised gang, they run the city, the country and the roads and they pay themselves pretty well and like any gang. The most important thing for coppers is to look after their own. They have duties, don't get me wrong, they want to catch baddies and lock up child molesters, but to be honest, you probably know this, they don't give a toss about break-ins, fights, criminal damage and that sort of thing. If you have to deal with them, don't be cocky and don't be an arsehole. Help them as much as you can and make it look that way. A lot of these young coppers are a few streets removed from you and me kid. They could be the same as us, so, you treat them normally and with a bit of respect and, hopefully, they'll treat you in the same way. You won't beat them either, you can run from them, but if they've seen you, then you won't get away. Like I said, they're the biggest gang in town and they look after their own."

Tony pauses the video and wonders where he was while this video was being made. Maybe he was out in the street talking to Apple or one of the lads, maybe at the gym, maybe upstairs, thinking like he always did that his father would not die and all this would not happen to him.

There is a tap on the front door. It must be half-past nine. Tony does not turn on the hall lights as he makes his way down the stairs. He sees a figure outside, the dayglow of a police uniform jacket. The tap comes again, a little more forceful. Tony jogs down the stairs, and his heart begins to beat in his chest.

"It's the police," comes the voice from the other side.

Tony feels like he talks to everyone through the glass of this door. He undoes the latch. Like his father said, it's best not to mess about with them. He opens the door and in front of him is the same young police officer from earlier, the one he saw knocking on Emma's door.

"Is your mum or dad in?" says the officer. He has smooth skin, but his grey eyes are older. He wears his police cap a bit too far back.

"My Auntie Lynn's gone out," says Tony. The copper looks at him with total belief and even an air of apology.

"When do you think she'll be back?" he asks. Tony swallows. The copper's young face is not accusatory.

"Late on tonight," he answers.

"It's about the body we found in the drain," he says. "We just...well, my name is special constable Moore. We're doing a door to door, to let everyone know what's happened and about the body." Though the young policeman means well, he's a threat, more of a risk than the social worker. Tony tries his best to look scared.

"There's nothing for you to worry about… or your Auntie, it's a community call, to reassure. So, can I call back tomorrow?"

"I'm not sure what shifts she's working," says Tony, "so I don't know when she'll be in." The copper nods in agreement. Tony follows with a question, genuine, even though he has heard and can guess the answer.

"What happened to him?"

The young policeman is sincere and his remorse is real.

"Animals, foxes or, we think there might be a wild dog. It's nothing to worry about, nothing suspicious either. We're pretty sure he fell into the river first." The officer steps back. "I'll leave you our card with our details on if you need to get back to us."

Tony takes the card and closes the door. He listens as the policeman walks a few more paces to the next house and taps again. Tony swallows and feels his insides bubble.

He locks himself in the bathroom upstairs and sits on the toilet without taking down his trousers. His heart is beating shallow. He feels like crying, but there's no one to hear, and no one to care. Tony remembers the other voice of his father, the one that spoke sense and then looks at himself in the bathroom mirror. There is nobody at all now who is going to care if he cries or gets beaten in a fight or loses his father or his mother, or the coppers take him away.

So what?

Tony will look after himself, like he's been trained to, like he's designed to. He feels his chest harden and his fists clench.

CHAPTER TEN

It is late August. The summer holidays are drawing to an end. Kids who were bored for six weeks find something to do, finally, and kids who have had a lot to do are now, at last getting bored. Tony already has his school uniform. His father ordered it last term. He has a new bag and shoes. It's all set. In the early morning, Tony sits in the kitchen, listening to the clock tick above him as he spoons cereal into his mouth. He gets flashbacks of carrying the little grey-haired man over the back gate and through the woods. He was floppy and limp, still warm, hot even and reeking of booze. Tony wipes his lips as he remembers the feeling. What if someone saw him? He thinks about Mwamba. He reasons that, from her tower block, only two streets away, she would not have been able to see him, but there is something about the old African woman, she has an uncanny way. She notices too much, a bit like that Ian. He washes the bowl, dries it and sets it back in the cupboard where it belongs. He thinks, standing in the kitchen, that he is in the exact spot where his father made the videos. The washing machine beeps to signal it has finished its cycle, Tony unloads it into a basket and takes the clothes outside to hang up. He pins up a bed sheet as the back door of Emma's house opens and she wanders down the garden with her own basket of washing. Her face is drawn and thin, with deep wrinkles and weary eyes. She still has a swing in her step, but she's cold. There is something different about her.

"You alright?" asks Tony.

"Yeah, it's not been easy." She does not make eye contact as she hangs out a shirt on the yellow washing line. Tony looks at her face. She has not smiled once since she came through the door. Emma always smiles.

"How's Sam?"

"Upset. We're grieving. We're seeing a counsellor, the

both of us." She shoots Tony a glance, as if she wants to say something.

"I told you I'd help," says Tony.

"The police say he drowned. I told them about his depression and his drinking. I said he didn't sleep and that he lost his job at the factory. I told them about what he did to me and Sam, about how jealous he was. It wasn't right, was it, Tony? It wasn't right. I mean, he wasn't right." Her voice wavers with emotion as she speaks.

Tony hangs up the socks from his wash load.

"We look after people round here," says Tony, repeating her words from days before. She smiles. It's genuine and her teeth are white and perfect.

"It's like a new day every day," she says. "When I wake up and remember he's not here, I feel… I feel free, like I did before I got married, like I'm a young lass again. Sam and me have got plans now. We're gonna move away as soon as all this dies down and get away from round here, we'll go somewhere nobody knows us and start again." Her eyes have excitement in them. "I feel like I can breathe again," she whispers. "Do you think about what happened?" she asks.

"Sometimes," says Tony, "but it doesn't bother me if that's what you mean." He's lying.

Emma wants to smile again, but it drains away from her face.

"What is it? I mean… what is it out in the woods by the drain? Have you seen it?"

Tingles run down his legs when he hears the fear in her voice.

"It's a wolf, a dog, or something… a beast, bigger than you'd think… and it hides, so quiet and calm, like it's watching the silence. It heard me take the body down there. It watched me, too." Tony has stopped hanging up his washing and is staring into the distance.

"How come nobody else has seen it?" she asks.

98

"Oh, you won't see it unless it wants you to," replies Tony. "It's like it's not even there. I wondered if it was in my head for a while. I wondered if I'd made it up."

Tony realises he has said too much, Emma is scared by what he has said but he doesn't care. She has to be on his side now, after what's happened, so it doesn't matter if she thinks he's a nutter.

"You be careful, Tony," she says.

"I think it might have had me already, if it wanted to," he answers.

Emma's face is a grimace, and her green eyes are wide.

"How many times have you seen it?"

"Plenty," says Tony. "I think it lived out back of the meat factory. There's nothing for it to eat now that place has closed, except the deer." It feels strange to hear himself talking about what he has thought, as though his ideas weren't quite real until he told them.

"You should tell someone, Tony... before it does something else, maybe to someone who doesn't..." she does not want to say more.

"You mean someone who doesn't deserve it?" Tony adds.

"Yes, that's what I meant."

"It isn't doing anything other than what we all do. It's trying to survive."

"And how in the hell did you find it?"

"It found me," says Tony, "it's alone."

The beast might be more like him than he imagined.

"You be careful," says Emma. She fingers the little cross on a necklace at her chest.

"I will," says Tony. He picks up his washing basket and goes inside.

Wallace is a good trainer. He is younger and fitter than Jacko, he has a knowledge of the modern game that the old man does not. It was not so very long-ago Wallace himself did the training as hard as a professional, ate the four thousand calories and pounded the bags, skipped and sparred daily. He still has some of the body to prove this including toned arms that are fast and strong, flat knuckles and a broad chest, but his stomach has grown full from the beer and red wine, the meals in restaurants and the cheese. Wallace and Whalebone have moved over from Liverpool and are staying in digs in the centre of town. Whalebone has found the local haunts already and visits the sleazy nightclubs and the back streets where girls do things they don't want to do for money. He and Wallace have spread their feelers round the town and found the people who can do this and that, who are rotten and wrong.

Tony spars with Wallace. The Scouser is not wearing a head guard, but Tony is. The older man uses the space in the ring, he is agile for his size, and his shoulders are relaxed as he throws a jab. He steps in and hooks, Tony dodges and moves closer for a series of body shots. Neither is trying to hurt the other, but they must have weight in the punches and aggression, or there is no benefit to either of them.

"Elbows lower," says Wallace. His advice on boxing is spot on, "less dancing or you'll tire yourself out." This is true. Wallace sits in between the good and the bad, next to the law and the prison. He is honest and at the same time, rotten. He has a wife and children back in Liverpool, two boxing clubs including this one and all the trappings of success in his expensive watch and large car. He trains and drinks pints with the lads, likes football and has pictures of his kids up in the little office he cleaned out and yet, Tony thinks, he associates with a man like Whalebone. The two are friends, they share a joke and talk in whispers around the gym. Tony knew from the first moment that he saw the silver-haired Scouser, that he was wrong, despite everything which might not make him seem so. This does not make him a bad boxer, and Tony will use all this training, get faster and quicker, learn the mean tricks and the ways to win. He'll suck it up and listen. He'll take it with a smile.

Tony and Wallace drink water from the new fountain which has been installed. The walls are freshly painted and the punch bags are new, the floor is brightly polished wood laminate. It is like a different club, except Jacko is still here, training the younger ones, like he does.

"I've got a fight for you," says Wallace, "next week."

Tony wants to look surprised, but he doesn't let it show.

"Next week, that's a bit early?"

"I know, but you're ready. For this kid, anyways. It's out of town, Doncaster, a step-up fight. A lad called Paul Fogal has gone and got himself arrested for GBH and been banged up so he can't fight. They need someone to take on Mario Lacey, a kid from London, tough as hell and on the path to somewhere big. He's taller than you with a bigger reach, a better punch and he's got more fights under his belt than you. He's been tipped for the top."

"So why do you want me to fight him?"

"Because you'll kill him."

Wallace takes a sip from his paper water cup. His face is dripping, and he sounds like he is stating a fact.

"I want this club to succeed," he says, "and I want to make money and I can do that by training my fighters and letting them fight. I'm your manager too. I'll get paid. This club will make money."

"I'll get paid as well then?"

"You get trained for free. You use this gym for free."

"I pay you."

"You pay me nothing, five quid a week… it's nothing. You fight because you need this place, so, you're going to fight for me." Wallace is not being cruel. "It's your career, Tony, let's start it in style, eh? Take this London kid down, and everyone will know who you are, everyone, and you'll be in with a chance to be someone."

"What if I say no?" he asks.

"Well, then this isn't the club for you, is it? You do want

to be a fighter, don't you? The kid I see training in here every day, he wants to be a winner, that's why he trains as hard as he does and fights as hard as he does. I can see it in you, Tony, I can see the anger in your eyes, you're an animal, like me."

Wallace has got this wrong and he does not know Tony at all. The training is not to win. It is so he can stay normal and stay focused. The dreams of being a fighter have never been in Tony. He knows what a boxer's life is, he's seen it in his father and heard his father's words many times in his head, 'you don't want to be a boxer'. Tony does not. Wallace's expression changes as he sees Tony is hesitant.

"You do want to be a fighter, don't you?" he asks with a frown, "otherwise, what's the point? How else are you gonna make anything out of yourself, especially round here?" Wallace has him.

"I'll do the fight," says Tony. He sets his paper cup down on top of the new water fountain. Wallace smiles.

"I knew you'd say that, so I already told them you'd be there. It's next Wednesday night. I'll take you." Wallace claps his hand on Tony's back. "You're gonna do great kid," he says. "You're one of us now. I know we had a few differences when we first came here and it's natural for you not to trust people you don't know straight away. When I first took over this gym, blokes were falling over themselves to be my friend, an ex-boxer like me who's got a few quid. Everyone wanted to be my mate. Not you. You don't care who you're meant to like, if you don't like them, then you don't pretend. I respect that, Tony. I heard about your dad too. I wish I'd met him. Everyone has a good word to say about him." Tony stares at Wallace without saying anything. He doesn't like this man talking about his father. "I've worked out a plan as well, a way we can beat this Lacey kid, it should be easy."

People are coming into the gym. They are older than the day crowd, men fresh from work or their tea and young lads who want to train so they can look after themselves in the pub or get a six-pack to impress. They are easier to manage than the kids, much easier and Wallace leaves him to share a few words with a Lithuanian lad with muscles much too big to be anything like a decent boxer. Wallace has a way with these men. They respect him because of his reputation and his smooth manner, his success and the aggression that lies just under his skin.

Something is not right. Tony can sense it.

On the way home and walking with his hood up in the late summer evening, Tony sees the figure of Mwamba ahead of him. She is carrying a plastic bag full of shopping in one hand and using her walking stick with the other. At her side is Lionel, keeping her slow pace and even from behind, Tony can see he is bored. He too has a shopping bag. Every step looks like it hurts her. Tony catches up with them and pulls out his earphones when he gets level with Mwamba's full, short frame.

"I'll carry your bag for you," he says. Lionel translates, and she stops, then hands him her heavy plastic bag in silence. Tony walks next to them with Mwamba in the middle. The going is very slow.

"Has your mum got arthritis or something?" asks Tony.

"She got shot in the hip," replies Lionel in a matter of fact way. "Back in the Congo, she got shot in the hip by soldiers."

"Why?"

"People get shot in the Congo, sometimes."

Tony nods like he understands, but he doesn't. Lionel is a bridge between the two worlds. In the same sentence, he sounds like he could be born and bred on the North Hull Estate and Kinshasa. His mother says something.

"She asks, did you eat the food she gave you?"

"Could you tell her I did? Really, I threw it away; it didn't look great."

"She knows when I lie," says Lionel, "it's a mother thing. So, I will have to tell her the truth."

"Why does she want me to eat the stuff anyway?"

"She put a spell on it. A protection spell. You have to eat the food for the spell to work." Tony wrinkles his nose. He's never heard anything like this before. "I know…" says Lionel with a huff. "I deal with it every day. Would you eat some of it next time?"

"What will the spell do to me?"

"It will protect you from whatever my mother saw." Tony smiles.

"Does she have to kill a chicken or something?" asks Tony.

"No, I don't know what she does. It's embarrassing." Lionel sounds tired. "I hate the holidays," he says, "all I do is stay with my mum. I wish she could speak English a bit better."

"You'll be free one day, mate," says Tony.

Mwamba asks something and stops for a rest on her walking stick. "She wants to know what we're talking about."

"Tell her the truth," says Tony. He listens as Lionel's Hull accent changes into Lingala with its tones and rich vowel sounds.

"She says she likes you because you are brave and you'll help an old woman in the street. She will give you more foofoo, you know, and you will have to eat it in front of her." Lionel sounds tired.

"It's good to be thought of," says Tony and then he adds: "Can you tell her that? Say thanks," and little Lionel translates. She smiles and answers but addresses herself to Tony.

"She says she knows what it is like to lose your father. It happened to her when she was ten years old."

They have reached Mwamba's flat block. At the double doors, Lionel reaches up and keys in the number that will open the door. The mechanism clicks and the red light turns green. Mwamba says something to Lionel. He protests. She says it with more force.

"She says you have to remember you are not alone. We will be your family if you need one. She says she will help you if you let her." Tony looks at this old Congolese woman, standing at an odd angle on a hip that was blown out of her body thousands of miles away.

"Why don't you go to the shop for your mum, save her the walk?" Tony asks.

"She doesn't like me to go out on my own. I'm only ten." Tony thought he was eleven at least.

"Next time she needs something, write it down and pass it to me and I'll get it. She can pay me when I deliver." Lionel translates, and Mwamba smiles a wide beam Tony has not seen before. She has perfect white teeth with a large gap in between the two front ones.

"That's good, she says," translates Lionel.

CHAPTER ELEVEN

It's the evening. Jacko sits in Tony's little kitchen. It's late. The old man smells faintly of alcohol.

"I would have preferred to see your old man. What have you got to drink?" Jacko asks. He's wearing an old tracksuit and his trainers. He looks out of place. As far as Tony knows, Jacko has never set foot in this house.

"My dad has some beer left over in one of the cupboards, I'll have a look," answers Tony.

"Nah," says Jacko, "he's got some whiskey somewhere," and Jacko casts his eyes around the kitchen, at the clean cooker and bleached floor. He nods to the cupboard, "look on top of there," he points.

Tony pulls a chair up, stands on it and feels around on top. There is a bottle, on its side. He pulls it out and blows off the dust. It's a half bottle of expensive whiskey, Irish. Tony thought his dad drank the cheap stuff. Maybe he didn't know his father as well as he thought he did.

"There you go," says Jacko. "That's his emergency whiskey." Tony hands him the bottle, Jacko gives it back. "Put it in a glass," he says. Tony finds one from the cupboard and pours him three fingers.

"How did you know he had the whiskey?" asks Tony as he sets the glass on the table.

"I trained him," says Jacko. "I knew him. You'll have a drink yourself. You're old enough now."

Tony shakes his head.

"It's no good for me, Jacko. So, what can I do you for?"

Jacko takes the glass in his thick fingers and drains the tea-coloured whiskey, sets it down and reaches for the bottle to pour himself another. His eye is still bruised.

"It's those Scousers," he says with a grimace, his chin is covered in tiny white hairs that have grown since the morning. His hands are strong from a lifetime of work. Jacko was a forklift driver down at the docks until he retired and took over the boxing club. That's the way Tony has always remembered it and the way it has always been.

"What about the Scousers?" asks Tony.

Jacko takes another drink, just a sip this time. Tony thinks about what his father might say in this situation, and he doesn't know. Tony isn't a talker, so he states the obvious.

"They've changed the club," he says.

"Aye, they've changed a lot, new bags, new paint job, new ring coming in a few weeks, new gloves and all that, he's pinched my old office." Tony knows all this, but Jacko does not sound very angry, just weary and pragmatic; he has something he has to tell. "I wasn't sure at first. I knew Wallace wasn't okay, I mean, who in their right mind would come down to our run-down club, to North Hull Boys and offer to buy it? What is there round here?"

"You bought it, didn't you?" says Tony.

"I got it cheap. The lease was up. That was twenty-five years ago. It was a different world and I'm from here. I was an old man, even back then."

"Maybe Wallace thinks it's cheap." Jacko wafts Tony's ideas with his hand.

"I came here to ask you, Tony, what do you think of him?" Tony examines the old man sitting in his kitchen with the stubble on his chin and his tired eyes.

"I don't trust him… or Whalebone."

"So, what are we going to do about it?" Tony reaches forward and picks up the bottle. He pours Jacko another measure.

"Why am I included?"

"Because of your dad. You're his lad. I couldn't have started the club without him… he brought the fame to the place and helped me set up, we fitted the laminate floor together and built the ring. He's part of the walls. It's his club as well." Tony knows this, but he has never heard Jacko speak to him like he was important, like someone who could have an opinion, he was always just his father's son. Now he feels like his father. Jacko takes another sip.

"You're all I've got left now your dad's gone." Tony never thought Jacko might be grieving too and the old man's voice is just a whisper. Tony does not know if there was ever a Mrs Jacko or kids or relatives. He does not even know his first name. "So, what are we going to do about it? About the Scousers?" Jacko repeats.

"I don't know Jacko, what do you want me to do?"

The old man leans forward with his eyes glinting in the bright strip light of the kitchen. He is heady with the drink already.

"I want you to stand by me when I need you... There'll be a time when Wallace will come unstuck, he'll upset someone or make a deal he can't keep, and he'll look to the club to stand behind him. He'll look to the lads. I want you to promise me you won't be his lad. He'll burn you. I don't know what he's promised."

Jacko is concerned. His thick hand reaches out across the table, and he grabs at Tony's arm in friendship, the grip is tight and true. It is uncomfortable for both men, but the times are serious, and connections need to be secured. "I promised your dad I'd watch out for you and he promised me you'd do the same for me. Whatever Wallace has told you; it isn't true, he'll sell you out, he'll use you to get what he wants." Tony's hand goes out to grip Jacko's arm in the same fashion, and it's strong and firm.

"I've always been on your side, Jacko," he says, and the old man releases his hand. Jacko sits back, picks up the whiskey and drains the glass then sets it on the table and stands up.

"I'm glad we've got that sorted," he says. Tony stands also. "Your dad would have been proud of you, Tony. I'm proud of you." The words make the boy blink.

The old man zips up his tracksuit top to his neck and makes his way down the corridor with Tony behind him.

He pauses as he opens the door, as if he had more to say, then thinks better of it. In these situations, where he must deal with emotions, Jacko is hopelessly weak, like a child. He walks down the step into the warm, dark street outside. Tony closes the door and finds himself looking through the frosted glass. It is a new thought, to realise someone else might need him.

Tony is at the gym early. He changes out of his tracksuit into his shorts. There's no one around and the smells of the late summer morning fill the air and the dust particles dance in the sunlight streaming through the now clean windows.

It really is a different club.

Tony slips on his running trainers and walks to the door. He'll do the run all the boys do before they start training, around the block three times. Tony sets off at a good rate, down Greenwood Ave and past the new houses, then towards the fishing tackle shop, turning left at the off-license and its glass walls to stop shoplifters. He passes the cheap supermarket that sells frozen items and round in a big circle to the Pilot with patches of spew right outside the locked front door. Tony does not want to run through the park or onto the banks of the drain or through the forest. He does not want to see the creature or even know that it is there. Seeing Jacko the night before makes Tony strong, knowing someone is on his side makes him brave.

In the empty gym, Whalebone has drawn up a chair at the back and sits with, his face impassive as he stares into silence. Wallace is leaning against the far wall in front of the ring. He is dressed in his tracksuit with a lean and severe face. Tony enters and nods at Wallace. Tony checks out Whalebone but does not say anything. There is an air of menace here, now that these two men are present. It's clear they have been waiting for him.

"Where's Jacko today?" asks Tony.

"Dunno," says Wallace. His jokey demeanour is lost this

morning and replaced by a serious but blank expression. "We need to talk about the fight," he says.

Tony stands in front of the new mirror with Wallace behind him and stretches his arms after his run. He is sweating still.

"Go on then," answers Tony as if he is not bothered. He is intrigued by what these two have to say.

"Are you warmed up?" asks Wallace.

"Yeah."

"Come here." Tony walks to Wallace. "Stand there," Wallace points to the floor. There is silence as Tony stands in the spot. "You're gonna learn something Tony, right now, something you don't know a lot about, and before we start, I don't take any pleasure doing this. I want you to know that. All my fighters need to know how it feels."

There is no training Tony is afraid of, no weight he cannot try to lift and no physical exercise he will not be happy to do. He feels this is something more unpleasant.

"Whalebone," says Wallace and the stony-faced man from the back of the gym, stands up on command like a robot. He swaggers to stand in front of Tony, about a metre away and his hair is lank to his shoulders with his face cold, he reeks of dirty clothes mixed with aftershave. Tony senses danger like when he sees the beast. He feels fear. Wallace speaks low:

"You should be feeling scared, Tony. I've told you about Whalebone before, but you haven't seen him in action. I want you to let that feeling wash over you. It's fear, and it's that fear you need to keep you safe in the ring and on the street, it's fear that watches out of the corner of your eyes when there's something coming…"

Without warning, Whalebone springs forward, his right fist snaps out and connects with the centre of Tony's chest. The speed and the pain are intense and Tony recoils backwards. He crashes to the floor, clutching at his ribs. Almost as soon as he falls, he scrambles back to his feet, ready for more of the same, but Whalebone has not moved. He is still in the same position with his fist out.

"Thank you, Whalebone," says Wallace and the ugly man goes back to his normal standing position. "That's called karate. It's a bit out of fashion these days, no one does it anymore, they all do taekwondo or kickboxing or MMA or whatever, but growing up in Toxteth in the eighties, Whalebone used to get bullied, so he took up Wado karate and thirty years later... I don't think I've ever met anyone as strong or as cruel as him. You can try and outbox him, but he knows how you move, he knows how everyone moves. We used to work nightclub doors, and I saw him take out big men, small men, groups of men, women, anything. The thing is, he loves it too, does Whalebone. He loves to fight, not box or play games but fight and hurt people. That's why me and him have such a good relationship. Did you hit him hard, Whalebone?"

"I just tapped him." Whalebone's voice is nasty.

"So, you see Tony, you might think you're a hard case, and you are, but there's always someone harder, in your case, two people, me and Whalebone here. You should be afraid of him. You should remember that Whalebone could be behind you at any time, from out of nowhere."

Tony regards Whalebone as he touches his ribs where the blow landed. His heart is beating, and as Wallace wants, he feels fear. Like a child, Tony feels himself slipping into understanding, the understanding of being under, being controlled and being fearful. The three men stand for a minute or more, in silence. Whalebone is impassive and cold, Wallace wears an air of arrogance and Tony is slightly bent over, nothing at all like the proud young man who walked in. Wallace breaks the silence with his jovial, back to normal voice which as always, has a hint of malice.

"Back to your seat then Whalebone, we've got work to do here."

The friendly Wallace claps his hands together in a 'let's

begin' way and walks into the centre of the gym.

"This morning, we're gonna work on your breathing Tony..." and he sets off describing the training routine for the morning. Tony goes along with it, quietly, he is shocked by the violence, even though he fights almost every day, it is always in the ring and never unprovoked. He'll have to unpick his feelings later. As Tony is skipping at the side of the ring, he understands what Jacko must have felt when these two did whatever they did to him. As he is hitting the heavy bag with Wallace shouting orders behind him, Tony stares out at Whalebone, who sits at the back of the gym. He feels cold dread in his veins.

CHAPTER TWELVE

Tony does his shopping at the cheap supermarket. He buys flour and suet, and a joint of frozen lamb that he will leave for a day in the slow cooker to tender up. As he packs his bags and listens to the idle chat from the check-out boy, he sees four of the lads from his year at school. This close to the end of the summer holidays, they are bored and skint. Tony watches them sauntering down the street, three walking, one on a bike. They are dressed in tracksuits with tight legs and droopy groins, mostly, they have almost the same haircuts. Tony stares at them through the window of the supermarket and wonders what they will do for the rest of the day. One of the lads with his hood up pulls out his mobile phone and grins as he takes a selfie with his middle finger up. They may go for a walk in the park where Tony runs and smoke e-cigs, or real cigs or catch the bus to town and sit in the bus station talking to girls. Maybe they'll play on their consoles at someone's house and have their tea cooked by their mum or get a takeaway with the family all around. They have nothing to do but live their lives. It's a world that Tony doesn't understand.

As he moves away from the till, Tony feels suddenly conscious they will see him shopping for himself, and they might laugh at his trainers that are last year's or his tracksuit that has seen better days and his hair that is not covered in gel. He walks out of the shop. Wallace has knocked his confidence, or rather, the punch from Whalebone has. He can still feel his chest is bruised and his ribs are sore. The boy with his hood up has stopped to talk on his phone and they all pause to wait for him, meaning Tony will catch them up.

He has no choice but to keep walking.

Now he gets closer, he sees one of them used to train at the boxing club with him a few years ago. The one on his phone is mouthy and shouting at someone on the other side, loud and kind of cruel. Tony has seen him before. He's a joker who's not particularly funny but more annoying. Tony keeps his pace up walking and catches up to them. He feels nervous for some reason but tries not to let it show. The one with the expensive bike sees him.

"You got a fight this Friday, Tony?" he asks.

"Yeah," he answers in a quiet voice.

"Who you fighting?" asks the mouthy kid who has put his phone away now.

Tony shrugs his shoulders as he walks past.

"No one you'd know," he says. Tony's voice is not confrontational, but there is a weary quality to it. The mouthy kid asks again.

"You don't look like a boxer…"

Maybe he's not from round here. Maybe he's come from one of the wealthier suburbs that join onto the estate. Maybe he's from the village further up, and he wants to pretend he's tough. If the kids had said anything else, made fun of Tony's shoes or his clothes or the fact that he's shopping, then Tony might have withered and carried on, but this; to question his ability in the ring and who he is. This is the best thing he could have said. The other kids become instantly uneasy. They know Tony, they know what they hear from the lads and men who train at the gym, they know about the new Scouse manager. They have heard Tony is something else, and they know about his fight at the arena and his speed and his aggression. Like the animals in the forest, they stay away from the bigger beasts, not out of deference, but out of a sense of their own well-being. Tony here, with his shopping bag and his well-worn trainers and the darkness in his eyes, is much more like a man than they are.

"You'd don't look much like a boxer," repeats the mouthy kid. His friends do not give him any encouragement.

"Come down to the gym sometime," says Tony. The kid

is about to mouth off again, but none of the lads are listening, so it's not worth it.

Tony walks the half-mile down Endike Lane, past the rows of council houses and the Lord Nelson pub. At this time in the afternoon, there are men who stand at the entrance with pints in their hands and cigs in their mouths, overweight lads that are ill and unkempt. They stare at Tony as he stares at them.

At Tony's front door, little Lionel sits on the step with his hands under his chin and a football under his legs. He's bored and dressed in the pastel green jumper of the local primary school. Tony stops and puts his bag down. Lionel smiles up at him.

"What are you wearing your school uniform for? It's the holidays."

"My mum says I should try it on to see if it fits okay."

Tony grimaces. He doesn't like the idea that the other kids will make fun of Lionel, which they will if he wears his school uniform when it's not school.

"At least take the jumper off," says Tony, "and what's wrong, how come you're sitting here on my step?"

"My mum sent me round," Lionel holds his hand above his eyes to stop the sun shining in as he looks up at Tony.

"Why?"

"She wants a favour."

"What kind of favour?"

"You have to come with me."

Tony recalls telling Mwamba he'd help her if she needed anything and he meant it. After a heavy morning at the gym and lots of sparring, Wallace has given him the afternoon off. Tony unlocks his front door and sets his shopping on the counter. He rummages around for the ice-cream and puts this in the freezer while Lionel waits outside.

As the two walk across the road towards Lionel's flat, they fall into easy conversation. The young boy explains he will be in year six after summer and will be one of the oldest in his primary school. Tony asks about video games and football; he asks about his mother too. Lionel goes quiet at this.

"She's a bit off her head," he says.

"Oh yeah…," this is the way Tony encourages someone to say more.

"She sees stuff. She has nightmares. Wakes me and my sister up. I tell her to go to the doctor. She can hardly walk, as well. She's off her head."

"What do you mean by off her head?" asks Tony.

"Like, she's lost it."

"You mean she's sick."

"I guess."

"My mum was the same," says Tony.

"Did she cast spells on people?"

"No, I mean, she was off her head. She was sick."

"How did you get her better?"

"We didn't. She had to go into a special place for mad people." At this, Lionel looks horrified, and water gathers at the bottom of his big brown eyes. He looks up at Tony.

"She won't get taken away, will she?" Tony wishes he had kept his mouth shut.

"No. But don't go round telling people she's off her head, even if she is. She's your mum."

Inside the block of flats, they take the steps because the lifts are broken. It's a six-storey building and the last of the tower blocks left on the North Hull Estate. There were three more, once upon a time, but they've been pulled down to make way for better, more suitable housing. Lionel lives on the second floor. It's colder in the stairwell than in the afternoon sun outside, and there's the smell of bleach and rubbish. From far above them in the building, they can hear a woman screaming and a man shouting. The sound of the voices and cries echoes downwards.

"There are lots of bad people in here," says Lionel.

He leads Tony up and along a dark, wide corridor where a strip light flickers at the other end. They stop at the first door, Lionel unlocks it and they step through.

It is like walking into a different world. The smell of cooking hits them both as they walk into the tiny hall, and there is strange music coming from the kitchen. On the walls are colourful pictures of birds and a large wooden cross. Tony follows Lionel into the kitchen and next to her cooker, sat down on a high stool, is Mwamba. She has that big smile that shows the gap between her white teeth and is dressed in a long African style floral dress. She struggles to stand up when she sees Tony. On the cooker is a tall, bubbling pan of stew and one of sticky rice. The smells are alien to Tony's nose, like the music, sweet and pleasant but odd to him. The kitchen is connected to a little dining room with a long table that is set for dinner. At the far end, a young woman sits in front of an empty plate. Tony can't see her face because the sun is shining in from outside. He glances round the cosy flat, so different from the bleak corridor and the rubbish outside. He has been invited to eat. There is no way out this time.

"This is my sister, Susa," says Lionel as he shows Tony to his seat at the table. Mwamba struggles forward as she carries one of the pots of stew from the cooker. She sets it down on a tea towel in the middle of the table, and there is a ladle sticking out of the top. She moves to collect the other pan of rice, but the young woman from the end of the table has beat her to it and lifts the big pot on thin but steady arms to a metal grate. It is now Tony sees her face. She is elegant, perhaps seventeen, with delicate, smooth brown skin that shows off the whites of her eyes. When she has set the pan down, she sits back at her place at the other end of the rectangle table. Mwamba sits down. It's a struggle for her, but she has a grin on her face. Lionel stands up and scoops out the rice and the stew with a big spoon. He makes a good job of it. Tony is last. Mwamba says something in Lingala. Lionel translates.

"My mother asks you to say grace."

"I've never said grace," he answers. Lionel translates.

"She says you should just say whatever you say at your house before you eat."

Tony thinks back to the times he and his father sat down in the kitchen to eat. He sees, suddenly, his father's smile as he sits in front of him and Tony feels warmth from the memory. He repeats what his father said.

"Dig in," says Tony. Lionel translates, and this pleases Mwamba.

As they eat, Tony allows his eyes to search around this room in this tower block so close to his house. He sees a blue flag with a red stripe on it across one of the walls, and pictures of family members on the old-fashioned gas fire. There are frames with babies and children inside and one with a bride and groom in loose-fitting suits in a foreign place. It is strange to Tony, but he feels welcome. The food is thin and a little watery, the chicken boiled rather than fried or baked, but it is good. As he eats, Tony can see Mwamba is watching him. She says something to Lionel in Lingala, and he finishes his mouthful before he translates.

"She asks if the food is good."

"Tell her it's great."

"Really?" asks Lionel.

Susa speaks up. "She's put too much salt in it," she says. Her accent is clean and smooth, with a touch of French in it but good, clear and almost perfect.

"I like it," says Tony.

"My mother talks about you a lot," says the young woman. "She worries about you; she says she's seen you with a wolf."

Tony smiles but swallows.

"There aren't any wolves around here," answers Tony.

"She may be a bit old and she doesn't speak English, but

118

you can trust my mother," says Susa. She's intelligent, Tony can sense it already.

"Maybe she thought she saw me with something," says Tony.

"Maybe," answers the girl. "She's got us all this far, she got out of Kinshasa alive and survived a gunshot to her hip. She watched our father die and lived through things we can only imagine. So, I don't expect she'd make up a story about something like that."

Tony blinks at this girl next to him. He likes the way she speaks in a level, frank tone. He likes her cheekbones and her brown eyes that blink at him, calm and clear across the tablecloth with the Congolese music in his ears.

"How long have you been here?" asks Tony, "I mean, in this country?"

"Three years. In this flat for about two," she answers.

Like Lionel, Susa has a way of creating drama then drawing it back down to reality and making it all sound so normal. "We like it here," says Susa.

Tony spoons some more of the thin stew into his mouth. It's refreshing.

"You're a boxer, then?" asks Susa.

"Not really," says Tony. He's careful not to sound arrogant or full of himself. "I'm just starting out, got a fight tomorrow in Doncaster."

"Who are you fighting?"

"Some kid from Brixton."

"Will you win?" asks Susa.

Tony blinks back at her with his blue eyes. There's no front to him, no trace of his own importance or how strong he is.

"If he hasn't trained enough, I'll win," he says, and though Susa has never seen him box before, she believes him.

From the other end of the table, Mwamba begins chattering away in Lingala and laughing. Her voice is loud and clear and her laugh honest. Tony watches her explaining something to Lionel, perhaps a joke or a memory and she touches his arm as she does so. Here is a different woman to the shuffling figure Tony has seen walking up and down Greenwood Ave. Perhaps she was beautiful many years ago. Tony finds himself smiling too.

Pudding is a sort of flat cake that is meant to be a sponge. Tony has had a lot better, but he eats it happily enough. Like his father said, if someone invites you to their table, you're going to eat whatever they give you and say thank you. After his mother has ordered him, Lionel explains the story of how Mwamba got lost when they first got to the UK, how she got on the wrong train and ended up in Leeds and was so scared she cried. Mwamba watches Tony's face as her son relates the tale. She searches his face for the moment when the punchline comes, when she cried, and Tony realises the story has reached the point where he has to laugh, Mwamba claps her hands with happiness.

She serves tea without milk from a big teapot. Susa tells Tony she is in the last year of her A levels and has already been accepted to a university somewhere, far away that sounds grand and distant. She will train as an optician and maybe one day, when she has a job and money, they will all go back to the Congo. She speaks clearly, without any swear words or slang, like a woman in an office or an English teacher, each word is pronounced and smooth. Tony finds himself hooked. Though he knows it's rude, he does not want to stop looking at her, especially when she is talking. As he sips his black tea, Tony realises from the clock on the wall in the kitchen that it is just before six and he is late.

"I'm supposed to be at training," he says to Mwamba. She's unhappy as Lionel translates and then, as he sets his chipped tea mug on the table and gets ready to leave, he sees the old woman's face turn dark. The music has stopped, and the summer sun has lost some of its power outside the windows. Her forehead lowers as she speaks to him in a language he cannot know. She orders her son to translate and he answers back that he does not see why he has to, she snaps at him, and he begins.

"My mother says she knows the animal is still out there." Lionel's face is twisted with worry. The boy does not want to do this. Tony is becoming someone he likes, and he does not want to reveal his mother's fear and expose her eccentricities. Susa's smooth voice cuts in. She takes up the translation in a tone that relays only the facts without the emotion.

"She says she saw it behind your house, in the bushes near the river. From her bedroom window, she can see over the roof of your house. She says it is waiting for you."

Tony glances at Susa, and where there was a smile before, her mouth is straight and her eyes glass cold. "You must not let him in. She says she can feel the beast drawing nearer to you, winning you over, making you afraid. You are young and brave and strong too, you think you can go near to the fire without getting burnt, but I am here to warn you that, if you get too close to it, you will never get away."

Tony does not know what to say. He looks from Mwamba's earnest face to the girl he has just met, Susa and her smooth skin and brown eyes.

"Do you know what you are doing?" asks Susa.

Tony does not answer right away. The further away his father's death gets, the less sure he is what to do. He does not know if he should fight tomorrow or if he should search for the dog-wolf behind his house, or if he should visit Jacko to comfort the old man, or if he should be here.

"No, I don't know what I'm doing," answers Tony.

"My mother says you do not need to choose, be safe, trust yourself, and if you need to come here, then the door is always open." Tony stands up. It's time.

"Thank you for having me," he says.

Susa shows him down the little corridor to the front of the flat. At the door, he turns to her. She is a little shorter than he and she smells of perfume. They can hear Mwamba in the kitchen where she is washing the used plates in the sink.

"Why does she care about what happens to me?" he whispers.

"There have been people who have helped us along the way. There are people who help us now. My mother says it is a circle, a circle of good deeds and actions, and we are part of it too. This is why she wants to help you. It's repayment. She wants to help those who are lost."

"Do I seem lost to you? Do I look like I need help?" Tony asks. He has let his guard down for a fraction of a second, like in a fight, sometimes you have to run the risk of getting hit.

"Not especially," says Susa, "until I look in your eyes."

"What's wrong with them?"

"They're sad eyes," she answers.

From the corridor and in the stairwell outside the flat, there is the sound of a woman screaming and shouting and the banging of doors. Tony's face is quizzical.

"There are criminals here. I think they're running girls out of one of the flats upstairs. It's much worse at night."

"They don't bother you, though, do they?"

"We keep the doors closed."

"I hope I see you again," says Tony. "Maybe you'd like to come to the boxing club sometime?"

She smiles and shakes her head.

"It's not my thing," she answers. She opens the door, and Tony steps out into the flickering strip light of the corridor. He says goodbye.

As Tony walks down the stairs, he can hear a woman screaming and shouting below. It is the same high-pitched yell he listened to a minute earlier. He goes down one set of stairs and turns. A woman is leaning over the railings and shouting down at someone walking away. She has boney arms and blonde, spiked hair, a short skirt that does not fit and a leopard skin print top. Obscenities ring out as she shouts at the top of her voice and her whole body shakes as she yells. She turns and walks back up the stairs. Her nose is bloodied and her eye freshly swollen.

"What are you looking at?" she spits as Tony passes.

He does not answer but carries on down.

Outside the flat block, across the street and sitting on a bench is Whalebone. He is wearing a tight, cream, England football top and the same flat cap. He smiles as Tony walks past him. On his chest, there is a splatter of blood.

The house is cold when Tony gets back to pick up his training gear. Not cold because of the heat, it's still late summer, it's just that there is nobody there. There was always a radio on or the TV, always one of his father's friends here, or one of Tony's mates from school. It doesn't seem like anyone visits, not for fun anyway. He hears the slam of a car door outside and goes to the front window. It's Ian, walking down his street with a checked shirt done up to his neck.

Tony thought he'd gone through all this. He opens the door and Ian beams back at him.

"Hello Tony, just wanted to find out how you've been getting on."

Tony doesn't know what to say. He hasn't prepared for this, mentally. He's not like Emma next door. Ian carries on, "I've got a few details to go through," he holds up a file he's carrying. "Can I come in?"

In the front room, Ian takes a seat.

"Would you like a drink?" asks Tony. Ian nods. He opens the file and puts some of the papers on the coffee table.

"A few formalities Tony, something for you and your Auntie Lynn to read."

In the kitchen, Tony boils the kettle and pulls down a

mug from the cupboard. He adds dried coffee from a glass jar and swallows. He does not quite know how to play this one and is unsure how to act around Ian. He had put all thoughts of seeing him again to the back of his mind. Tony needs Emma from next door. She owes him, at least, he hopes she thinks she owes him. He takes a deep breath as the kettle boils and tries to get into some sort of character.

"How have you been keeping?" asks Ian, as Tony sets his coffee down on the coffee table.

"I'm fine," answers Tony. He takes one of the coasters from on top of the gas fire and slips it under the coffee cup he has just set down adding, "Auntie Lynn doesn't like it if we don't use coasters." He is, at once, pleased with his lie that will make it look like he is being looked after. Ian smiles.

"You never made it to the club on a Monday night. It's still running, you know, and you'd be welcome to join."

"Thanks, and everything," says Tony, "but, it isn't... something I'd be interested in. I have all my friends here and my family too. I have the boxing club down the road. They're helping me through."

Ian sips at his coffee. Tony does not like the way that Ian listens or the way his calm blue eyes examine him, as if he knows something Tony does not want him to know.

"And how is it going with your Auntie Lynn being here? Are you both getting on well? Is she around?"

Ian's questions are not designed to trick or hurt; he has a desire only to make sure Tony is okay. That's what makes it so difficult.

"She's at work and... it's all okay."

Tony wishes he could make up a lie to chase away the awkward silence, he wishes he could say more to allay Ian's concerns, but the empty, noiseless house eats up his imagination and the clock in the kitchen ticks. This man is not afraid of silence like most people are. Ian knows how it sounds and can also listen to what someone says when they don't say anything at all.

"How is the boxing?"

"Good," answers Tony. "I've got a fight tomorrow."

"Really?" smiles Ian.

"In Doncaster, some lad from Brixton. Should be good."

"Who's taking you?"

"My coach, from the club."

Ian picks up one of the forms and begins to write some notes with his left hand. Tony looks at his thin neck and arms. He smells clean and is well-presented. Ian does not have any of the gruffness Tony is used to on men, none of the coarseness of body or language. There follow questions, about his friends, where's he's been going, who's been cooking and cleaning, who does the shopping and who washes his clothes. Ian asks to use the bathroom and Tony explains it's at the top of the stairs. He can hear the man creeping into the bedrooms for a peek, and Tony feels powerless to stop him. In the bathroom the bowls and toilet are scrubbed clean, the glass shower screen is without a streak of dirt or mildew. He nods in approval.

Downstairs, Ian zips up his coat.

"She's a bit of a clean freak, then, your Auntie Lynn."

"Yeah," answers Tony.

"A bit like me," says Ian. "Everything has its place."

Ian says he will fill in the rest of the papers at the office. He thanks Tony for the coffee and makes his way to the front door. Tony watches him get into his family car and drive down to the end of the street and out of view. He breathes a sigh of relief.

CHAPTER THIRTEEN

With the laptop on the kitchen table, Tony scrolls down the list of videos his father has left him. He goes to number five; he knows it is there because it caught his eye, *Number 5: Fear.* Previously, he wondered why his father would leave him a video about this, but now, when he thinks about Whalebone, and the blood down his shirt, he knows why. The video begins, with his father's earnest face in the very same kitchen Tony watches it in.

"I've tried to start this one loads of times," says the man, squinting down at the smartphone camera that is leant up against a coffee mug. "Jacko will tell you it's good to be afraid in the ring. He'll tell you it's good to be wary of getting hurt, that it helps you to keep your head down and keeps you on your toes but... well..." here Tony's father scratches the back of his head in thought, "that's kind of for dickheads. He only tells that to the hard cases and the nutters, the kids who don't know how to be scared because they're too stupid to imagine what can happen. You're not like that. You've always been scared. You used to be scared when I left you to sleep alone as a little kid. I used to lay on the floor and hold your foot while you drifted off. You slept with the light on for many years. You worried about everything, about where your mum was, if there were spiders under your bed, monsters, everything. I tried to tell you then that it was all in your head."

Tony's father has a far-away look, like he doesn't want the words to come out, but he has to force them because there will never be another chance to tell this to his boy.

"I've been afraid before. I was afraid with your mother. I was afraid she would leave me. I was afraid of my dad, your grandfather. I've been afraid of men in the ring, but, none of it has done me any good at all, none of it. It made me question what I was doing. Like your granddad. When I was a young lad about seven, I drew on the walls of my

126

bedroom. I was with Auntie Lynn. We drew stickmen in pencil. It was easy to clean off. My mum told your granddad when he got home from lorry driving. I remember waiting for him to come into the front room and feeling my legs shake. He sent Lynn out and then when we were alone, he slapped me round the face, full force. My ears rang and my cheek burned, and then he hit me again on the same side, he gave me a black eye he hit me so hard. I saw the anger in his eyes. He was bitter and I looked right at him. He could see that he hadn't broken me and so he hit me again, and I didn't look back at him after that. I was terrified, petrified, all through my teens. Every so often, whether I broke the rules or not, we'd have a set to, and he'd find a reason to hit me. Slaps became punches. He broke my cheekbone once after I came home late on a Saturday night."

"Then, one Sunday afternoon, near Christmas, he'd been in the pub for the afternoon and came home, it was dark, and he was pissed. There was no reason for him to pick a fight with me, but he did. He told me to get into the front room, and I stood there, fourteen years old, my legs knocking together like I was seven again, as my own father pulled up his fists to hit me, again. Right there, staring up at his angry eyes, I thought, I've had enough of this. This man is going to keep doing this to me and I have to stop him. It doesn't matter if I get hurt - I'm going to get hurt anyway - he's going to batter me if I fight back or not. It was a kind of revelation, and it was that moment I stopped being afraid of him. I realised, the very thing I was frightened off, getting hit, was going to happen anyway. So, what was the point of being afraid?" The man's eyes glaze over into his past as he describes the scene, "I went for him before he could go for me, I caught him on his jaw and knocked him on his arse over the sofa. I think it was a shock for him. He got back up, and we went at it, smashed the front room mirror and the sideboard as we fought... he was a hard bastard your granddad, as hard a man as I ever stood against, even then when he was in his fifties. It was my mother who stopped it. She got in between us. He listened to her."

"After that, he never bothered me again and never picked a fight. He never tried to make me mad, and he told me, years later, he was glad I'd hit him, glad I'd stood up to him and told me too, he wished he'd stood up to his father. I realised that fear would stop me doing all sorts of things, fear and worry. I can't say I'm never afraid, but I know that fear won't help, and like every fight, you go in knowing you're going to get hit, it's going to hurt, and that doesn't matter, keep your eyes open, keep breathing. Don't be afraid Tony, and don't let them tell you to be afraid because whatever you're frightened of is going to happen to you anyway."

Tony presses pause, and there is his father's face frozen in time, creased in age with a light stubble across his chin. He is a terminally ill man. His biggest fear, that he cannot look after his son, has come true. His nightmare is real.

Tony closes the laptop and goes to the bathroom where he washes his face and stares in the mirror. He wonders what he is frightened of. He is afraid he will not be the boy his father wanted him to be, that he is not strong enough to stand alone and not brave enough to fight down the pity and sadness he feels.

By his father's logic, this is what will happen. So what's the point of being scared?

Tony runs through the darkness by the side of the drain, bare-chested in shorts and trainers. He is not even out of breath for the first mile or so through the summer evening wind is warm on his face. Above him is a clear, starry sky with a thin moon. He pushes on, past the disused container until he is out into the fields and running across the stubble of recently cut hay again with the weak moon to light his way. He feels sweat on his forehead and down his back. It's good. Tony doesn't look back at all, not even for a glance, but he knows it has been following him since the edge of the city. At the bottom of the field, he slows as he comes to a gate, slows and turns. It appears out of the darkness, head low, tail down. It is smaller than Tony remembers but more sinister, with its ears up and the eyes catching the moon above. Fear begins in Tony's stomach and the beast pads nearer. He cannot outrun it, cannot fight it, like the first time they met, he is at its mercy. His heart quickens. There is something different about the way it moves with eyes that are wide in the starlight. Tony's palms feel clammy, his mouth is dry, he's nervous. What is different about the dog-wolf tonight? Tony coughs and realises where he is, miles from the city, alone in the darkness. He feels the bruise on his chest from where Whalebone punched him.

It can smell his fear.

Tony steps back, his chest rising and falling as he draws in breath. He must turn his fear off somehow. He must stand as he did that first night and roar back at the beast, find his strength. He tries to think about his father in the hospital bed, hooked up to drips and tubes and his eyes milky with terror and sadness as he holds his son's hand.

Tony steps back again.

He sees the face of Whalebone smiling, with bloodstains down his shirt and Wallace next to him, laughing his false, loud laugh. He feels the world closing in around him. His legs are wobbling, and his feet are cold.

He steps back again and is unsure for the first time. The beast moves forward, with each step growing in confidence, bringing its long, canine face closer to the young man. Tony feels the fence at his back. There is nowhere left to go. The beast moves in. They have never been so close, and Tony can feel its breath on him, hot, and the eyes yellow and pale. He knows it will kill him and suddenly, on the realisation he is trapped, there comes a sense of calm. Tony's fists clench. He swallows and feels panic leaving him. Here, under the stars, a few miles away from North Hull Estate, with the summer breeze in his hair, Tony stands face to face with the beast, its jagged teeth bared and its muscles tense and ready to jump. Tony's muscles tighten.

From his stomach, white-hot and bitter, the venom of anger washes away his fear. Tony roars out like he did that first night he met the beast, but it is not quite the same. This time it is controlled. He does not care if he lives or dies, he knows he will lose in the end, like his father did, and so what matters now is the show, the doing of things in the right way and the fight. He will not bow down to anyone, nor step back, he is not the boy his father raised; he is the boy he wants to be, a fighter. He screams as loud as his lungs will let him and steps forwards as the beast cringes back. He senses the fear in it. In the darkness, this animal must be as scared as he is, as hungry as he is, lonelier, perhaps as unsure.

The two of them run through the forest at a light jog. The creature stays behind a few metres, keeping a noiseless pace as they move through the trees. They skirt around the side of the city, far from the lights so nobody will see them and scramble up a bank and then down onto the side of the drain itself. They run all the way back to behind Tony's house on 6th Avenue, walk up through the little forest and Tony climbs over his fence. He turns to the beast behind him and waves his hand for it to keep back.

"Stay there," he whispers.

He unlocks the back door with the key from under a stone but does not turn the light on for fear it might dazzle the beast. Inside, he opens the fridge door, removes the pork joint from one of the shelves and tears open the package with his teeth. Outside again, Tony sees the beast standing on the pathway, like a shadow in the darkness. He tosses the pork joint onto the path in front of him, and it lands with a slap. The beast steps forward and picks up the meat in its jaws, turns back to the safety of the forest, and in a few steps, it has leapt the fence and is gone, without a sound. Tony stands for a moment, contemplating what happened and letting the sweat run down his bareback. He feels drained.

A light goes on in the kitchen next door and Tony hears a key rattling at the back door. It opens, and Emma pops her head out. Her face is without makeup and wrinkled in worry.

"How long have you been standing there…like that?'" she whispers.

Tony breaks from his trance.

"I dunno," he mutters back, "a couple of minutes…"

Emma steps outside in the warm night, she is wearing a dressing gown, but her feet are bare. The light from the kitchen drowns the darkness in the garden and makes Tony blink.

"Are you ok? It's two o'clock in the morning."

Tony holds his hand up to shield his eyes from the light. "How long have you been standing there?" she repeats.

Tony shakes his head.

"I dunno."

"Haven't you got a fight tomorrow?" she asks. Tony nods. "You should be in bed."

Tony lays awake in bed, unwashed and still in his shorts. He looks up at the light from the moon on his bedroom ceiling. He does not have to look out of the window to know it is there.

CHAPTER FOURTEEN

Wallace drives, Tony sits in the passenger seat and Whalebone takes up the middle part of the back seat. The car is unlike anything Tony has ever been in before, with seats of plush leather, a mahogany dashboard and digital, space-age controls. Wallace is an aggressive driver and the car surges forward. He overtakes into the fast lane of the motorway and the other cars stream behind them. Tony watches the speedometer creep over the one hundred mark. There is no emotion on Wallace's face as he holds the wheel and they tear along the road. Every so often, Whalebone snorts and rubs his purple nose.

"Did you do your homework?" asks Wallace.

"Yeah," answers Tony. "I read everything there is on him and his trainers. I read everything on his club, on where he lives in Brixton and I read his social media pages."

"What's your approach?"

"Go in strong, show him who I am, keep on the back foot if I can and outbox him. He'll be as fit as me and at least as skilled, so there's no game playing and no tactics. From what I've seen of him, he's a straight-up kid."

"How do you reckon?" asks Wallace.

"He trains hard in his local gym and teaches the juniors like I do. He has a girlfriend and works in a garage as a mechanic, DJs sometimes but says he isn't any good at it. He looks like he's committed. Has a strong family, everyone's behind him, he's a handsome lad, too."

"So, you know all about him…" says Wallace. "I've done my research too. I watched him fight on YouTube. I've seen you fight - you're gonna wipe the floor with him."

They pull off the motorway and through streets that look run-down but unfamiliar. Tony wonders if he will see his Auntie Lynn somewhere, walking her dog or standing at the traffic lights. He wouldn't recognise her if he did.

They pull up in front of a stadium and the heavy tyres of Wallace's big car crunch on the stones. He presses the handbrake button.

It is early evening and the three of them walk through the spinning doors of a sports club, Tony first, flanked by Wallace and Whalebone. They walk into a busy hall full of those waiting for the fight. There are boxers and trainers, men in full-length tracksuits that match and squeaky trainers which have not been worn in. Although he only catches people staring from the corner of his eye, Tony feels them watching the three of them as they walk down the corridor. He keeps his chin up. Wallace has told him about this already, about how to be someone when you walk in a room, and to project the fear of what you can do and of who you are. It is almost the opposite of what Tony's father would say. Tony plays along and, somehow, he likes that people might be afraid of him. A bald man shakes hands with Wallace and they break off to talk, leaving Whalebone standing behind Tony. He's shown to the changing room, where Wallace and Whalebone join him. It is different from the last fight he had. At least now there is someone with him. Wallace returns and pulls Tony to one side:

"That was Mario Lacey's manager, an old mate from back when I was in the game. He's done very well for himself these days." Wallace moves closer and speaks in a whisper. "I put the fear up him, told him I'd never seen anything like my fighter. You see, Tony, you're an unknown to someone like Lacey and his crew, there's nothing to look at, nothing to read and no one to talk to about you. You know everything about Lacey already." Tony can smell the expensive aftershave. "Make them frightened Tony, like we talked about." Tony flinches as Wallace grasps his shoulders so he can add drama to his words, "and then beat the hell out of him."

Wallace turns to Whalebone and the ugly Scouser smiles back at him. It doesn't quite look genuine to Tony.

They leave the dressing room and follow a corridor, go down some steps then onto the stadium floor. There is no dinner party this time. It is a small arena with a boxing ring set up in the centre and hundreds of people sat around it. The lighting is low like a nightclub apart from the ring, which is bright with white neon. Wallace and Whalebone wait in front of Tony. They are both much bigger and cover him like a curtain as they wait for the compère to call out Tony's name over the clamour of the crowd in front. Tony's fight is still not the headline, but he's off the bottom of the bill, and the crowd has already seen two lads go at each other. It's got them going. The compère, with his high-pitched voice introduces Tony briefly, and a spotlight focuses on him as Wallace and Whalebone move out of the way.

There's no music as Tony walks through the chairs and clapping people with his hoodie up. He climbs through the ropes and looks at the crowd around him. There are too many faces to notice. There is no showboating from Tony, no dancing or fists in the air. He removes his hoodie and stands with his arms at his side with his nerves twitching. The compère gives Lacey a much longer introduction.

"Ladies and gentlemen, fighting in blue and white shorts, from Brixton, London, undefeated in twelve fights, the young dazzler, Mario Lacey."

The spotlight goes on for his opponent, and the kid from London makes his way down through the crowd flanked by others wearing the same white silk hoodies. Hip hop music blasts through the speakers as he climbs up through the ropes and takes off his robe. He holds his hands high and claps his gloves together as he smiles at the crowd. He is taller than Tony, with dark skin and well-defined muscles, his hair is in dreadlocks and tied up in a tight topknot. His thin beard makes him look older, and he's mouthing the words 'thank you' to the crowd. Tony instantly likes him.

There is no arrogance here.

He approaches Lacey, and they touch gloves. Tony stares into his black eyes and sees the nature of the young man. He is level, bright, calm and measured, committed too. It will be a good fight, Tony senses. Here is someone who might be better than he is, might be faster and stronger, with more heart.

When the bell rings for the first round, Tony comes out hard, he prods a few times, searching the air around Lacey for how he moves and then, he steps in, drops low for a body shot combo and up to the kid's face which is covered by his gloves. The blows do not hurt Lacey, but they let Tony know how he reacts and how solid he is. Tony works more shots that do not worry Lacey and he counters. Heavy punches to Tony's body shake him as they connect with his ribs. He staggers back and Lacey goes for his face in a wide swing as Tony ducks. Tony wants to smile as the kid from London advances on him. Already he knows Lacey is a better fighter than he is, much better, and it is a relief to fight someone like this.

Tony steps back to the ropes and covers his face as Lacey hammers him with pounding shots to the head and body. Tony does not want the fight to go this way. He does not want to be on the ropes as he is. He can hear Wallace from the corner of the ring roaring at him to step forward and the shouting from people around him. The bright lights above make him sweat, and the dull, pounding blows of Mario Lacey work Tony's body. He feels himself beginning to freeze up, a choking sensation as Lacey dances forward with a fresh combination of hammering shots. One of the punches gets past Tony's gloves and glances off the side of his head, shaking his skull and rattling his brain. His hearing slips in and out. Wallace is red and screaming obscenities. Tony sees the face of his father, withered in the hospital bed and feels the power building up in his stomach, the white-hot anger, the blaze of pure fury and, in a break between the hammering shots, he snaps forward and unleashes.

For a few seconds, he is beast.

Lacey drops back as Tony moves forward, dips his head and weaves. Tony jabs forward and catches the kid from London on his chin with a left hook. It was a lucky clip perhaps, but Tony follows it up with an enormous right cross with all his body weight behind it. The blow staggers Lacey, and he recoils. Tony is on him, anger on his breath, controlled but blazing. He rains down with punches and the tide of the fight turns. Just as Tony dances him into the corner, the bell rings three times. Tony does not move back to his corner right away but stands there staring at this kid from London. Lacey winks back at him. In another five seconds, Tony would have finished him.

In his corner, Wallace is red-faced and excited. His breath is hot in Tony's ear as he towels off the boy's brow.

"Keep it going, mate, he knows who you are now, they all do." Tony takes a sip of water.

"I wish me dad was here to see this," says Tony.

"Maybe he's looking at you from somewhere, mate," answers Wallace. He rubs Tony's shoulders. "You can't get caught on the ropes again; he'll knock you out, stay away from him, keep moving."

For the next round, Lacey does not get in close, and so Tony cannot catch him. He pats away the punches and stays clear. Tony chases, but Lacey is fast, sneaking in for the odd jab or headshot, outboxing Tony by keeping it technical. This is a sport after all and not a street fight. Like a game of chess, you can win if you stick to the rules and you know how to play well enough. Tony keeps his head down and works the ring, looking for space like Wallace has shown him. Lacey is too experienced to be tired out. He lands a right hook on Tony that gets past his glove and stings. Tony counters with a one-two punch, a left jab that sets up a right cross. It hurts this lad from London, and he buries his face in his gloves while Tony lands more punches on him.

After the bell has rung, Tony sits down on the stool in his corner, and this time, Whalebone passes him his water bottle with a straw. Wallace is at the other corner talking to Lacey's manager. The man is shaking his head. Wallace is telling him something and is angry. The Scouser turns and points at Tony and says something else to the manager. It's not natural. As the seconds between rounds tick down, Wallace is becoming angrier and angrier.

Tony heads into the next round, and Lacey has changed again. If he was trying to fight before he is hardly trying to at all now, he glances back at his manager and stays well away from his opponent. There is something wrong. Tony presses but Lacey moves, side steps, dodges and where Tony felt he had an opponent before, it feels like this kid from London is not attempting to fight at all. At the bell, Wallace whispers in his ear, hot and angry.

"You go down in the next round," he explains.

Tony frowns as he spits out his gum shield.

"What?"

"You go down in the fourth, that's what we've agreed."

"I can take him," says Tony incredulous "You want me to lose?"

"You heard me," says Wallace. "Unless you want Whalebone here to do something very unnatural, you are going to lose this fight in the next round. Get in close to him, let him hit you but don't make it too obvious."

Tony senses this is the true face of Wallace looking at him now, angry, mean and selfish. "I've told his manager that it's five thousand quid for us to lose in the fourth round. That's what we're here for, Tony. We're here to lose. How would it be if he lost to you, some run-down kid from Hull, an animal, some nutcase? They've invested too much money and time in Mario Lacey to let him lose here. They say he's been earmarked for the Olympics when he's eighteen. He didn't want to cough up, that bastard, but you showed him, Tony, you showed him you could finish his lad off. You've done well, but now it's time to make some money, to do the real work. You go out there and let Lacey finish you. That's the mission." Tony blinks up at him in horror.

Here it is.

Wallace sees his shock. "Oh, I'm sorry mate, did you think you were a real boxer like your father? Did you think you could make it? You've got the fists, but you haven't got the money. It takes years and years of training to make it to the big time, years and money and dedication, and you haven't got any of that. You're just some sad kid from the worst estate in the UK. You're a no one already. All you've got to do is go out there and do what people like you always do - lose." Tony's eyes darken.

"You go down in the next round," Wallace repeats.

"I'm not going down," says Tony, "I'm not one of your boys, and I'm not a boxer. I'm here for the fight, and I'm here to finish him."

Whalebone closes his hand around the back of Tony's neck. The grip is vice-like, his fingers dig into the muscles. The pain is sudden and Tony winces. Wallace leans his face down, "Tony, you are going down in this last round whether you like it or not. You're going down like your dead old man and your mad mum. They took her away to a mental asylum, didn't they? After she'd had enough of you and your dimwit dad. I heard she bit her wrists out and bled to death, looney. Is that what happened? Is that what you did to her?"

This is suddenly new to Tony that his mother killed herself. He knows she is dead, but he did not know. He thought it was cancer that had her, like his dad. Wallace can see his words have hit home, and he smiles.

"It doesn't matter to me mate, bad things happen, as long as you go down in this round."

The bell pings and Tony stands up. He's confused. If a minute in the corner can allow a fighter to gather themselves, it can also unravel them. Tony steps forward and manages to get his hands up as Lacey unleashes a flurry of blows. Tony weaves back with his face in his gloves. He tries to unpick the information he has heard from Wallace. How does anyone bite their wrists, and is that what he even said? Lacey steps to the right and hits Tony in his side with two jabs that sting and wind him. Why had Tony's father never told him about his mother if even someone like Wallace knew about it, and why did she kill herself? Tony has too many questions to ask. Or maybe, Wallace is trying to get inside Tony's head and screw him up. Lacey steps under and comes in with an uppercut, it connects with Tony's chin and sends him reeling back. Lacey presses home his advantage with blows to the head and body. Tony weaves backwards, but it is not enough, the kid from London has him. Lacey has everything, his own professional Facebook page with pictures of his girlfriend and family. He has trainers and managers dressed in matching white tracksuits. His hair is in a well-groomed topknot. His body is toned and smooth. He is supported and cared for, trusted by those around him. This is the kid that begins to win. He was always going to.

Tony feels his knees weaken and his chest heave. He takes a blow to the face, followed by another. His senses dim, the sound of the crowd is far away, the lights are bright above him, there is the taste of blood at the back of his throat, and then, almost without realizing, his face is flat against the canvas. The referee stands over Tony waving his hands to finish the fight, and as Tony comes round, he senses footsteps all around him and hears whoops of joy from the Mario Lacey camp. Wallace helps him back to the corner and puts a towel over his head. His hands are soft on Tony's shoulders.

"You did the right thing," he whispers. "We'll see you do right out of this."

In the car on the way home, Tony sits in the back and watches the streetlights from the motorway flash by the window. He has a swollen eye he can only just see out of. Wallace is driving and Whalebone is in the passenger seat. No one has said anything yet. They stop at a drive-through and Wallace buys a milkshake that he passes to Tony in the back. The boy holds the cold drink on his bruised face and eye and takes sips through the straw.

"So, you're not a boxer then?" says Wallace.

"No," says Tony.

"I'm glad. I don't train boxers. I train fighters," says Wallace. "Where to now? Do you wanna keep fighting for me? You're good, and you're tough, and we always need people with spirit, mate. We could do a lot together."

Tony looks out of the window at the darkness of the motorway again. He feels broken.

"I dunno," he says. He sips the sweet milkshake again and his lips feel swollen too. He's been hit that hard before, lots of times, but this is different.

They get back to North Hull Estate late, and the streets are silent as they park outside the boxing gym. It's Friday night; everyone is somewhere else. The three get out of Wallace's posh, black car and Tony begins to walk home. He does not want to spend any more time with these men.

"Where are you going?" asks Wallace.

"Home," answers Tony.

"You forgot something."

"Yeah?" Wallace signals to Whalebone.

"Pay the man."

Whalebone pulls out a wallet and opens it. He takes out a thick wad of notes and holds it up to Tony.

"You earned that," says Wallace.

Tony steps up and takes the money from Whalebone.

"I didn't see you getting hit," says Tony. "Looks like I did everything."

"Be grateful you got something, you did well."

Tony sticks the notes into his hoodie jacket and walks home up Greenwood Ave.

"We'll get a cup of tea tomorrow," Wallace calls after him.

Tony is too tired to think, but he has so much to work out. The feeling his father may not have told him the truth unnerves him. He turns the key in his front door, goes in, takes off his shoes and trudges up the stairs to the bathroom. He washes the blood off his face. In the shower, he examines the bruises on his ribs and chest. His muscles are sore. He checks his swollen eye in the steamed-up bathroom mirror. There would be a reason his father did not tell him about his mother. Tony unpicks the events of the fight, he sees how Wallace has played him, bigged him up, tore him down, made him feel special then brought him crashing into despair and all the while, Tony knew he was being tricked and, like a child, thought he could rise above it. Losing is the easy part for Tony, he's used to that. He's used to the sting of disappointment. He's already lost his family. He does not mind being injured either, it's part of the job but being part of something rotten, like the deal Wallace cut with Mario Lacey's manager, leaves a bitter taste in his mouth.

When he is clean, Tony goes down to the kitchen dressed in his boxer shorts. He opens the fridge door and sifts through the vegetables and the jars. He goes for a joint of lamb at the very bottom of the fridge and takes it out the plastic carrier bag. He unlocks the back door. Stepping out into the chilly night, his bare feet make no noise on the little stone pathway down to the end of the garden. The forest that leads down to Barmston Drain is gloomy and silent. A shadow forms in the darkness and Tony holds out the leg of lamb. He's surprised how gently the jaws take it and then, smooth as black silk, and the dog-wolf is off down the garden and over the little fence into the woods.

CHAPTER FIFTEEN

There is one week of the summer holiday left and everyone on the North Hull Estate is ready to get back to normal. The sun is still strong, but there's not too much of summer left. It is mid-morning, late for Tony. On his way to the gym, he sees Lionel coming the other way. The boy is carrying a plastic shopping bag.

"What happened to your face?" asks Lionel, he is wearing his purple arsenal shirt today, which is a lot better than his school uniform.

"I had a fight," explains Tony.

"What happened to the other guy?"

"Nothing really," answers Tony.

Lionel squints up at Tony in the sunlight. Tony wants to change the subject.

"So, your mum lets you go to the shop on your own now?"

"Yes, but only when she needs something and only early in the morning."

"What does she need today?"

"Tampons," says Lionel.

Tony grimaces.

"My mum says she saw the beast, again."

"Where?"

"Behind your house." Lionel cranes his neck upwards. "She says it came to your house. It makes her scared. Susa and me are worried about her. Do you think she's making it up?"

It's not in Tony's nature to lie, he'd rather say nothing at all than that, but he has to say something.

"She sees what's real to her, maybe."

"She came to see you yesterday evening, but you were not there. She brought you foofoo and rice too."

"I was out, I had a fight, like I said."

Lionel examines the bruise on Tony's eye.

"I guess you didn't win."

"No," answers Tony.

Two lads on mountain bikes glide past, with tight padded jackets and their hoods up. They glare down at the world around usually, but at the sight of Tony, with his busted-up face and his white t-shirt showing his arm muscles, they swing out the way. There's no need to shout abuse at this one or prove they are clever, no need to put yourself in real danger.

"My mum says you can come to dinner again," Lionel offers.

"That would be good."

Tony's swollen eye is smooth and a bit purple.

"Tonight, teatime, six o'clock."

"I'll be there."

In the little newsagents, Tony stops in to put some more credit on his electricity card. It has not actually run out yet, but he likes to be prepared. He stands across the counter from Dean, who never leaves the shop. The ginger lad looks red-eyed. He might have started drinking already. He looks in shock and admiration at the bruises on Tony's face.

"Been in the wars?" he asks.

"Something like that."

"Did you win?"

"No, he was better than me," lies Tony. Dean the Gob nods and mentally files this information.

"Have you seen the beast?" he asks Tony.

"What beast?"

"The one that's been running up and down Barmston Drain."

"Sounds like rubbish to me, Dean," says Tony.

"They've seen it up and down Greenwood Avenue, on the Park over by the River Hull behind the industrial estate." Dean taps the stack of newspapers on the counter with his thin finger. "It's been in paper and everything. There was one kid from Newland Ave said he saw it climbing over a fence with a full-sized Alsatian in its gob." He's wide-eyed as he says this. "That's insane," he adds. Tony is stony-faced. Dean carries on. He's enjoying himself. "Maybe it's the same thing that ate the bloke who killed himself. He was your neighbour, wasn't he?"

"Yeah," answers Tony. He looks down at the newspapers on the counter. The headline reads 'Beast seen killing German shepherd' and has a picture of the quieter part of Barmston River with an inset of a local couple who saw it.

"They call them dog men in America, I've seen it all on YouTube," says Dean, "Werewolves, mate. I tell you. You heard it here first." Tony shakes his head. He has passed over his electricity card and a rolled-up ten-pound note.

"A werewolf in Hull?" Tony does not have to pretend how stupid that sounds.

"They reckon there are still wolves up in North Yorkshire, Scarborough way," continues Dean, "things like that would have no problem getting all the way down here. Two women saw it at night on the road out of Wawne, scared them right up it did. They said it chased their car." Dean is brightened by the idea of something horrible lurking in the woods just off the North Hull Estate or maybe even in it. "What do you reckon, mate?" Dean has put Tony's card into the machine and added ten pounds of credit.

"Like I said, sounds like shit to me," Tony repeats.

"Be careful when you're out at night," adds Dean for dramatic effect. "Don't take any shortcuts, will you? Stay out them ten-foots."

Tony takes his card and makes for the door. An old man shuffles past him to the counter and Tony hears Dean start up again to this new customer.

"Have you seen the beast, yet?" he asks in his perky voice. Dean will be spreading these ideas all over

Greenwood Ave. Tony pulls his hood up as he steps out of the newsagent. It makes him feel safe even though it's daytime.

In the gym, it is business as usual. When Tony arrives, the kid's training session has just finished and three eight-year-olds are wrestling outside while others file out into the street. They are red-faced and tired from the session. Inside, Jacko is putting the gloves back into the new mitt cupboard. He looks over his shoulder at Tony as he walks in. Apple is working one of the heavy bags and there is another kid in the weight room. Tony can hear the clang of metal and grunts of effort.

"You got beaten," says Jacko without turning around.

"Yeah," says Tony, "but not in the ring."

"So, what happened?"

"They rigged it. They told me to go down. Wallace got inside my head and messed me up. I lost my concentration."

Jacko turns. Tony notices the wrinkles around his eyes.

"That's not what I heard," he says. "They told me the kid tore you in half. They said you haven't got what it takes, that you haven't got the heart."

"You think that's true?"

"I dunno. That's what boxing does to people."

The air is stale between the two of them. Neither can quite believe the other.

"Wallace knew something about my mum," says Tony. "He says she killed herself… bit her own wrists out. Says it was my dad's fault and mine."

Jacko sighs and looks away when he hears this information. He turns back to the mitt cupboard, closes it and locks it. His movements are deliberate. Jacko goes to the ring at the far end of the gym. His stick clicks on the floor as he walks. He collects an empty water bottle from the floor. Stalling tactics.

"Well…" says Tony. "Is that true?"

The old man turns back to him.

"People say a lot of things, Tony. It doesn't mean they're true."

"It sounded true to me. So, do you know if it's true or not? Do you know how my mum died?"

"It should be your dad telling you this," says Jacko, "not some cocky Scouser, and not me."

"Tell me what?"

"She did die, Tony, and it wasn't nice. She did take her own life. I don't know how, probably Wallace heard that from someone who made it up, or maybe he made it up, but yes, she did kill herself. I know it upset your dad, it would have broken him if it wasn't for you and this place." Jacko steps forward to him, close enough to whisper. "But don't let that man make you feel anything. She was ill in the head, not right, and it was nothing to do with your father or you. He loved that woman, and I know he did because he told me and I saw the way he was with her and what he did for her. I saw how much it hurt him when she was gone, and you, you were just a little baby when it happened. How can it be anything to do with you?" The words are hard for Jacko to get out. "It shouldn't be me telling you this," he repeats.

"Who else is going to tell me?" asks Tony.

"I'm sorry, Tony, sorry you had to find out about it like this."

The boy sighs.

"My dad died less than a month ago, mate and I got punched in the face about a hundred times last night," Tony says. His voice has light humour that papers over the sadness. He needs time to process the information and think it through. "How much worse can things get?" he adds.

Whalebone walks into the gym carrying a brown paper package with both hands. As he walks past them to Wallace's office, he does his false smile to reveal uneven and yellowing teeth.

"Alright there?" he says. "You don't look very clever," referring to the bruises on Tony's face.

Whalebone does not stop. He walks down to the end of the gym and Wallace's office. Tony and Jacko watch him open it and walk through.

"Is Wallace in?" asks Tony.

"Yeah," Jacko replies.

"I better go and see him."

"What for?"

"I need to show him I'm still here, that I'm not gonna disappear. This is my dad's club."

"You know he's controlling you, right?" says Jacko. "I mean he's got me; he's had me from day one. He's not finished with you yet, Tony, not by a long way."

Tony doesn't need Jacko. Tony has everything already.

He follows Whalebone, knocks on the door and peeps through the glass at the two figures inside. He can hear them talking. Wallace asks who it is. Tony responds, and the Scouser yells at him to come in.

Inside, Wallace sits at the desk behind the brown, ripped open box that Whalebone has just brought in. The fat man is beside him, taking little bottles out of the package. They are vaguely like medicine and clink as he sets them on the table. Whalebone removes plastic syringes in vacuum packs and sets them down next to the bottles.

"Come in here, mate." Wallace's voice is at once friendly. "Grab a seat," and he offers the plastic chair at the other side of the desk.

Whalebone does not acknowledge Tony at all. He is separating the bottles into groups of three and putting two needles with each set. Tony sits down and peers through bruised eyes at Wallace. The Scouser has an excited air about him.

"This is the first shipment," Wallace says nodding at the bottles. "Do you know what it is?"

"It's juice," says Tony. Anabolic steroids. Tony has seen

it before in YouTube videos.

"Do you know what it does?"

"Makes thin kids build muscle, shrinks their balls, sends them nuts."

"Good. You don't look very surprised."

"My face is too bruised to show."

"And you thought I was an honest businessman and all that, well, I am. I'm good to my people, my family and the ones that work for me. I'm really good to them. I'm the best to them. You can't run an organisation like I do without being good to people and getting to trust people."

Tony shuffles in his seat. "Why you telling me?"

"Because you're here. You could have stayed away after what happened to you last night, most kids would have."

"I've got nowhere else to go," answers Tony.

"Exactly," says Wallace, "you don't have to be lost any more."

The big Scouser turns to Whalebone.

"Is it all there?" Wallace asks.

"Yeah," Whalebone replies.

"Great. I get it from a bloke I know in Germany and we have a roundabout way of getting it here, sort of. It comes in through the port, just down the road in Hull, King George Dock, all the way down the Humber and Whalebone here goes and collects it. Whalebone used to have to drive all the way over here from Liverpool every Wednesday and collect the stuff. It was a right ball ache."

"A ball ache," repeats Whalebone.

"So, we thought, well, why not set up a kind of network? Why not find somewhere right here in Hull? A place we could use to store, collect and sell our juice, on route to Liverpool, because, on his way back, Whalebone used to stop off at a club we have in Leeds and a place we know in Manchester, like a little line across the country. You join the dots."

Tony watches as Whalebone puts each set of bottles and

syringes into plastic bags.

"Do you make a lot of money?" Tony asks.

"More than you ever could boxing."

"More than fixing matches?"

"Yeah, I just do that for giggles." Wallace is not smiling. "I'm actually glad you're here. You see, a lot of this is yours," and he waves his hand over the bottles of anabolic steroids. "It's for you to get rid of, here, in this club. I mean, a man like me can't be seen to be selling this stuff at his own business, that wouldn't be right, but a tough lad like you, trustworthy - kind of - well, he could sell that stuff and make himself a packet."

Tony sees Whalebone has made up ten or so bags. Wallace leans forwards and picks one up.

"Now, if you're gonna sell this juice on, then you're gonna have to know how to use it. You stick the needle into the top of the bottle, draw out a full dose, right up to the 10-mil mark. Tell the punters to stick it into their arse cheeks or their arms once a day, and they need to keep pumping iron if they want to get any bigger. Once you've shifted that lot, Whalebone will give you some more."

Tony sits in the chair, impassive. His eyes are cold.

"I don't wanna sell drugs," he says.

Wallace smiles.

"They're not drugs like crack, you idiot, they're supplements, aids to help you get bigger and stronger. You can read any science journal, and they'll tell you there's nothing wrong with juice as long as you use it in the right way. There are thousands of people across this country who successfully use this stuff day in and day out, including athletes. Do you think I'd let the kids in my club take something that would seriously damage their health? Besides, they don't take the stuff here, and what someone does in their own home, behind closed doors, is none of my business, is it?" Wallace wipes a bit of spittle from the side of his greying goatee beard. "Don't go calling them drugs."

"I won't do it," says Tony, "it's not right."

"Well, I'm a polite man, Tony, you know, I always like to ask people, but in this case, you see, I'm not asking you to sell this stuff. I'm telling you."

"Or else what?"

"Whalebone."

Tony stands up.

"Look, Tony, I'm a reasonable man here, I know it takes a bit of time to get your head around something like this, and that's okay. If you learn to work with me, then we can do some great business together. I can't stay in this town forever and I'm gonna need someone to run this club for me when things get going, someone I can trust. So, you go on back to your training and think it over, eh? Think about what you might be giving up and the trouble you might be getting yourself into... alright?"

Tony feels the same electricity as he did out in the woods, the same feeling of powerlessness and fear. He feels his mouth dry, his palms wet and his throat itching.

"You don't know anything about me or about the people round here."

"I know everything about you, even things you didn't, and about the people round here," scoffs Wallace. "The people round here are just the same as the people in Leeds or Manchester or Huddersfield or Liverpool. You're a kid, Tony. I'm offering you a way out, a way up. The next time we speak, you better have the right answer for me."

"I'm not afraid of you, Wallace."

It is the first time Tony has said his name.

"You really should be, son."

Tony trains outside Wallace's office in the main gym. It's mid-Saturday afternoon. He feels blank after everything Jacko has told him and the fight the night before. He doesn't want to talk to anyone. He wants to train and think.

The gym is fuller than usual because it's the weekend,

but it makes no difference to Tony. He does all the things he usually would. He works the bags, skips, does sit-ups, shadow boxes, goes into the weight room and presses the bars up, lays on the bench and fly lifts dumbbells. He thinks about his dad and the videos. Lots has changed about the gym, not just the equipment. The people are different too. They're shifty-looking, a bit better dressed with sharper haircuts and bigger muscles. Tony hasn't seen Apple for a week or more, and he hasn't seen anyone from the rugby club.

Two big lads walk into the weight room, they stride into the corner and take turns on the pull-down rope after setting the weight high. They don't notice Tony and he carries on with his sets of twelve. The kids lift heavy to build tissue and look good, the kind of muscle that doesn't move quickly in a fight. He listens to them talk about women and cars, how they hate someone or other and don't like so and so. They're not boxers. Maybe they're on something already; they're not here to learn to fight.

In the main gym, it's busy. Wallace is in the ring with a head guard on. He's covered in sweat and going a few rounds with a squat man built like a bull with almost no neck and a hooked nose. Tony watches the two of them trade blows. The bull man's punches are cumbersome and slow, and he moves more like a tractor than a fighter. Wallace is lighter on his feet, but the jabs he lands are heavy too.

At the water fountain, Apple sits on a stool wiping his face down with a towel.

"Where you been?" asks Tony. Tony meant over the last week, but Apple doesn't answer this question.

"Running," says Apple, "I'm training hard. I heard about the fight in Doncaster. You look like shit."

"Ta. What you training for?"

"Wallace there, he says he can get me a fight." Apple points to the big man still in the ring going toe to toe with the bull.

"Oh yeah?" says Tony.

"Yeah, he says I might have a bit of potential, he says there might be something in it for me, but I've got to train hard."

Tony frowns at Apple,

"You think he's serious?" Tony asks.

"I dunno," says Apple, "but where's the harm in finding out?"

"I found out," says Tony. "Look at my face."

Apple smiles.

"It's training anyway. I enjoy it and it keeps my mum off my back. She'd rather I was in here than on my Xbox or out roaming the streets."

"It's not like it was when Jacko had it though, is it?"

Apple shakes his head. There's an edge to the gym today with aggression and tension that Tony hasn't noticed before. Places where people learn to fight are not often violent. Violent things happen, but they are peaceful in spirit, generally. Wallace is making a good go of it in the ring with the big guy, making his punches sound as loud as possible and the bull fella is snorting as he jabs. Tony notices the blokes working the bags, the lads shadow boxing or skipping, even the kids from the weight room, they are all watching the spectacle in the middle of the gym out of one eye.

"Look at him," says Tony, motioning at Wallace. The fight is a show for the rest of the gym. Like everything else about Wallace, the expensive watch, the car, the suit, it's all a show. He doesn't know a lot about the people round here or people anywhere.

"What a tosser…" Apple whispers back at Tony and they both grin.

CHAPTER SIXTEEN

Tony presses the buzzer on flat number fifteen and then looks at the grey concrete wall stretching upwards. It's six o'clock. He has cleaned himself up and is wearing one of his father's smart shirts. The intercom crackles and Lionel's voice cuts through the static. When he hears it's Tony, he pushes the button to open the door. Tony steps through.

Inside, the tower block is cold and dark again. His trainers make a squeaking sound that rings out around the empty, eerie stairwell and corridors. It all reminds Tony of zombie video games or horror stories, and despite himself, he feels his heart quicken as he heads up to the second floor. He hears a noise from down the stairs and pauses under a single light bulb to have a look behind him. There's nothing there. When Tony turns back to go up the stairs, his heart jumps; standing in front of him in the pale light, is Whalebone, his face is frozen, and his eyes are cold. There are three scratches down one side of his face, which are still red with blood.

"You come to visit one of the girls upstairs?" Whalebone asks.

Tony steps back.

"No," Tony says.

"They're rubbish around here. They're much better back in Liverpool."

Whalebone wipes his cheek and one of the cuts spreads across his face with blood.

"You don't have to be afraid of me, lad. I don't care what you do…" Whalebone corrects himself. "In your free time, I mean. How have you been getting on with that juice? Have you got rid of it yet?"

"No, Wallace has still got it all," answers Tony. He pauses, wondering if he is going to tell Whalebone he won't do it. Then he goes for it. "I'm not going to sell it anyway, mate" Tony adds. He uses the word mate, to not mean mate at all. Whalebone darkens.

"That is the wrong answer," his accent is thick and rasping. "You know what the boss will tell me to do, don't you? He'll have me threaten you first and then I'll have to do something unpleasant. You don't want that to happen, do you?"

Tony stares back in silence. It's a dumb question he's not going to answer. He's sick of the threats and the angry, nasty faces. It bores him. He's got nothing to be scared of. What can they do to him, beat him up? That's happened already. Take his family from him? That's happened already as well. Take away his boxing club? They've done that too. Tony stares Whalebone in the eyes long enough to be rude. It's enough to make a man like Whalebone mad.

The Scouser steps forward, grabs Tony by his shoulder, and the other hand goes down between his legs - the grip is tight behind his neck, and there's a stabbing pain as Whalebone's fingers dig into his muscles. Between his legs, the man's hand has a tight hold of his bits. It happens so quickly and with so little provocation that Tony feels panic as the Scouser brings his face close. He can see Whalebone's pockmarked nose, and the greasy hair and smell his foul breath.

"I'm not a schoolteacher, mate." Whalebone whispers as he squeezes Tony's balls and shoves him back against the wall. "I am allowed to hurt you." Tony struggles against the grip, but it tightens. He grunts. The pain is sharp and withering. Whalebone's face presses nearer.

"You're gonna sell that juice," he adds, "or I'm gonna pull bits off you… do you understand?"

Tony's free right-hand forms into a fist. There is just enough space for him to swing a tight jaw punch if he wanted, but he does not. He falls back, making his body a little limp so that Whalebone can press home his advantage.

"Do you understand me?" whispers Whalebone again.

Tony could lash out and attack, but he senses this is not

the right time. Close up, Tony can get a better sense of the man. He's strong and fast but not fit, used to winning probably and used to people being scared of him. Tony examines his flabby neck and the ears, sees the soft skin behind his ear next to the greasy hair. Hit a man in the right place, and no matter how many years of karate he's learned or how many heads he has smashed in, he will go down. Tony winces as Whalebone put more pressure on his balls. The pain is real but Tony reasons this is a warning, and so, Whalebone won't rip off his bits at all.

"Do you understand?" repeats Whalebone. Tony nods his head vigorously and Whalebone loosens his grip and drops the young man.

"I didn't have to do that," says Whalebone, implying somehow, that the violence was Tony's fault.

Tony falls to one of his knees and then struggles to his feet, staggers back and straightens up. His balls are stinging, and his shoulder is sore. He would like to see more of Whalebone fighting, to understand how he moves and watch the things he does when he feels threatened.

"It doesn't have to be like this, Tony," adds Whalebone, like he is dishing out friendly advice. Tony nods, and in the movement, there is defeat and Whalebone understand he has won. "You'll learn," adds the Scouser as he hitches up his jeans and heads off down the stairwell.

Tony walks up the stairs and rubs his shoulder with his right hand. Fighting Whalebone head-on might not be a good idea, but at least now Tony knows a bit more about the man and how he works, and like Jacko says, when the time comes, he'll be ready.

The corridor is eerie as Tony walks down towards Lionel's flat. The strip light flickers on and off. He raps at the door and straightens his shirt. Despite the trouble only a few moments ago, Tony's stomach gurgles as he thinks of Susa with her brown eyes and her artful hands and fingers.

His mouth is dry.

Lionel opens the door with a big grin on his face and Tony walks through into a different world. The smell from the cooking is rich and warm again, the Congolese music this time is a kind of melodic jazz. In the little kitchen, sat on her stool, attending two big pots, is Mwamba. Her hair is in a tight bun, and she is wearing a long green dress that reaches to her ankles. Mwamba offers Tony a seat with the gesture of a hand and he sits down.

"Where's Susa?" asks Tony.

"She's at work in the supermarket," answers Lionel. "She won't be back till late."

Lionel has opened a big bottle of fizzy pop and is pouring out a glass with both hands. Tony feels at home, sat in the wooden chair with a cushion under him, the smell of Mwamba's stew in his nose and the natural smile of Lionel across from him. He likes the way Mwamba passes him a plate, the smile as she spoons out the stew, the way they have to say grace before they eat. This time, Tony does not keep his eyes open, and though he can't understand Mwamba's words, the Lingala tongue has a softening effect on him, smoothing out his worries like a massage. The stew is sweet and tasty. Lionel insists it is soup, but it is too thick, more like a stew, and has bits of chicken on the bone and chunks of rich vegetables in it. The flavour is different to Tony, but it tastes of home, somehow.

"My mother wants to know what happened to your face," says Lionel.

"Tell her I had a boxing match."

"I did, she wants to know why you didn't win."

"Tell her I lost my concentration."

"She says you must keep your hands up."

Mwamba holds her fists up in front of her face. She wants to help and that is why he comes here, not because she *can* help but because she wants to. Tony wonders what his father would do if he were sitting there too, probably much the same, be polite, smile, see the good in things. His father would like Mwamba and Lionel. Tony looks around the cluttered room once more, at the photographs and the pictures. It's not as clean as his house, but there is more warmth to it. Tony knows how to wash up and cook and clean his clothes, but he doesn't know how to make a home.

After dinner, Tony offers to wash the dishes but Mwamba refuses. She sits on her stool with the radio up and cleans everything in the sink. Tony sits with Lionel at the table and they talk about boxing. They talk about the greats, Mayweather, Tyson, Ali, Frazier, the English boxers Lewis, Prince Naseem, Calzaghe the Welshman, the Olympic winner from Hull, Luke Campbell. Tony describes the epic 'Rumble in the Jungle' fight between Foreman and Ali. Lionel says he wants to play football for Arsenal or maybe Chelsea. Mwamba rejoins them and night is beginning to creep in outside. Tony can see the orange sun spread across the horizon out of the window. He does not want to outstay his welcome.

"I should go," he says.

Mwamba sits down next to him at the table, her eyes serious, crazy even. Lionel sits closer to the table so he can hear, and Tony gets a sense that this is why he has been invited here, again. Mwamba gets closer to him. She takes his hand in one of hers. The palms feel leathery from hard work and she says something in Lingala. Across the table, Lionel translates, his voice too takes on a different accent, almost as if she were talking through him.

"She says she has seen it again, near your house. In the forest behind, on the banks of the river. She says it is sniffing you out, searching for you." It is fearful to hear an old woman talking this way and in her brown eyes, Tony can see conviction. "She asks if you have seen it," and Tony makes sure he looks into her eyes as he answers, he has to try hard to make it genuine.

"No," he answers.

"It will tempt you," continues Lionel as he translates for his mother. "It will tempt you with the promise of power and wealth, and then, when you take the bait, it will take you and control you too, keep you wet with fear."

She squeezes his hand and for the first time, Tony thinks there might be wisdom here in this old woman from a different world thousands of miles away. He wonders whether the threat she is talking about is not the animal she sees behind his house but something else. Perhaps there is another beast.

"Pretend I did see it, what should I do?" he asks.

Mwamba leans closer still as she hears Lionel translate the words, she whispers, low and throated.

"If you go to it once, it will not leave you alone. It has decided it wanted you. There's no way to run. The Bili ape will find you out wherever you go, chase you through every village and over every mountain, through the rivers and jungles. It will hunt."

"So, what then?" Tony asks.

She whispers a few words and Lionel pauses in his translation. Mwamba repeats and her eyes grow angry at her son.

"You have to kill the beast," translates Lionel.

"How?" whispers Tony.

"You will know how."

Mwamba is shaking as she talks. Whatever struggle she has seen is fresh in her memory. There is horror in her eyes, and they are moist with tears. Tony squeezes her hand.

"Do not be afraid for me," he says, "I'm not afraid and I will not be tricked. There is no promise it can hold me with. I do not want you to worry. Please. Promise me you will not worry. Your family, Lionel here and your daughter, they're worried about you. They want you to get help."

Mwamba does not like her son translating this; her voice shakes.

"She says she wishes she did not have to say these things

through me. She worries about what I hear and see, more than a young boy should see… more than anyone should see. The beast is real."

"I know," answers Tony. "I know it's real, but if you want to help me keep safe, then you have to look after yourself. How can you help anyone if you're not well?" It is something his father used to say. "Lionel says you won't see the doctor, he says you don't talk about what happened to you, he says you never have." Lionel's voice has become a struggle translating words he does not want to. "In all this," says Tony, "you and your family have been friends to me, and you have helped me." Mwamba nods her head when she hears the translation. "You will see the doctor as soon as you can get an appointment, you will speak to the translator, you will let them help you."

Mwamba flares her nostrils drops her eyes and huffs in agreement.

Tony walks home in the darkness down Greenwood Ave. He passes the pub with smokers standing in the doorway, past the bright lights of the Chinese takeaway, past the Polish food shop and the newsagent with Dean the Gob standing at the counter inside. He looks at the headlines of the local newspaper in its stand, 'Beast Kills Local Dog', stops to read the byline, 'family pet Alsatian found half-eaten on Endike Lane'. Tony does not read the rest but carries on walking. His face hurts from the punches the night before, especially when he blinks.

Inside his house, he opens up his laptop and checks up and down the list of videos his father left him. He runs his eyes up and down the words. He is not sure what he needs help with. He clicks on *number 21: Sexuality* but then clicks off it. The idea of having his father talk about that kind of thing doesn't feel right. Perhaps he'll watch it another day. Tony opens up *number 22: Talking to girls*, presses pause, goes to the fridge to get a glass of milk, then returns. He sees the image of his father, this time sat on the edge of his bed in his pyjamas. It's good for Tony to see him. When the video starts, Tony can see his father has a twinkle in his eyes and is wearing a smile.

"Don't get confused between pretty girls and ugly girls," says his father, "there is only one type of girl, and they are all completely different and all exactly the same. The absolute number one thing you have to do is make them laugh…"

There's a knock on the back door, and Tony pauses the video. A whisper comes through the glass.

"I know you're in there, Tony, I can see the light is on." It is Emma from next door.

He opens the door and she comes inside. Under the light, Tony sees she has changed since he last saw her. She's had her hair done, and it shines deep red and smooth. She is less tired, stronger somehow. She wears tight black jeans that hug her hips.

"Do you want a drink?" asks Tony.

"What happened to your face?" asks Emma.

"Boxing match."

"What does the other guy look like?"

She's not the first person to ask this.

"Better than me. You alright? How's Sam?"

"Thanks. He's okay. We're both okay. Much better than we should be… considering what's happened. I've got a new job at the shopping centre on Kingswood. I'm working the evening shift. Sam's got back into playing football. We've had a lot of help."

"From the coppers?"

"Yeah, and…like…emotional support too. We're still grieving, but it's taking time. We'll get there in the end." She sounds like she has forgotten what happened, as if she and her son did not kill her husband at all. "I came round to see how you are."

"Fine," answers Tony a little too quick. Emma may now

be an ally, but Tony does not want to confide in her.

"You don't look fine. What have you eaten?"

"I've been round a mate's for tea."

"What did you have?"

"Some sort of stew," he answers.

Emma approves. She glances at the kitchen around her, it's still clean and in order, there are no dishes unwashed, and there is the very faint smell of washing up liquid in her nostrils.

"I've brought you something," she says.

"Oh yeah?"

Emma fishes in the handbag she is carrying in the crook in her elbow and pulls out a thick envelope. She hands it to Tony. He opens it and sees rows of crisp and straight twenty-pound notes.

"It's five hundred," she says, "and there's more coming."

"I don't want this," says Tony.

"It's yours. I've just had his life insurance come through, only the first payment. It's more than me and Sam have ever had before. You deserve to have some of it after what you did for us."

Tony looks down at the notes.

"You haven't told anyone about it, have you?" Emma asks.

"No," answers Tony. He's surprised she asked. "I'd only get myself into trouble if I did."

"You would."

"There is something I might need though," says Tony.

"Yeah?"

"I might need my Auntie Lynn to make some calls."

She sighs.

"It's too dangerous, Tony, after what's happened. If you get found out then you go into care, that won't be so bad, but if I get found out, we're both going to jail, and my Sam will go into care. It's too dangerous. I've got so much more to lose in this than you have, surely you can see that."

"That's why you brought the money, isn't it? It's like your way of saying you don't want anything to do with me. Is that it?"

Tony watches her sigh and hold her hips.

"I think we can't have anything to do with each other."

"We were hardly friends," says Tony.

Her eyes are cold.

"Like I said, there's more money coming when I get paid properly. You can get something you like, go on holiday or something, get a new game console, get some trainers."

The kettle finishes boiling and the water rumbles inside as it switches itself off.

"Tony, I think it's probably best we don't talk to each other now, don't you? Like you said, we were hardly friends."

"Sure," says Tony. "I'll ignore you from now on."

She stops on her way out and blinks at him through her dark, heavy make-up. Emma opens the back door and steps out into the darkness of the garden.

In the empty kitchen, Tony considers the money in the envelope. He feels let down. In the cupboard under the stairs, he finds the loose floorboard using his phone as a flashlight and pulls it up. He dumps the money with the cash he got from Wallace the night before.

It's blood money.

CHAPTER SEVENTEEN

The gym is closed on a Sunday, so Tony runs. He runs right up Greenwood Ave and through into Cottingham village where the houses are big with gardens at the front and back. The streets are quiet on a Sunday morning. He sees a gang of lady runners in pink, a cyclist and dog walkers, it's too early for most people. He runs through the university gardens and up to the windmill high on Skidby Hill. It's been a jog rather than a sprint and another recovery run, something easy. It's taken Tony an hour to run this far, from the edge of the city to the countryside and the hills rolling north to the Wolds. He wonders how far the beast can go.

Tony runs back down through Cottingham and down the main street, past more posh houses again. The sun is out. Sat outside the King William pub on the main road, is a man with a kind face and a pint of black beer in one of his hands. Tony gives him a nod as he sprints past and the man gives a wave. That's what people do round here.

It must be about half eleven when he gets to the roundabout at the top of Greenwood Ave. There is no traffic on the long street, and Tony stops at the newsagents for a drink. At least he can share a few words with Dean who works there. He unrolls the five-pound note he put in the little pocket of his shorts earlier and steps through the door of the shop. Inside, sure enough, Dean is talking to a tall man in bland but scruffy office clothes. Tony looks at the newspapers and then the fizzy drinks in the fridge. He listens to the scruffy man talking; there's a familiar sound in his accent.

"Do you really think something that big could live around here? I mean, in the wild?" asks the office looking man.

"I dunno," says Dean, "all I'm telling you is what I've heard in this shop."

The scruffy man has glasses and the beginnings of a beard on his jowly face. Tony notices he's writing in a little notebook as Dean rambles on.

"Have you ever seen it?"

"Not me," he notices and points at Tony, "but he probably has. His neighbour got eaten by it." Tony half cringes as he sees the shabby man staring at him from across the shop. "I say, mate," says Dean, "your neighbour got eaten, didn't he?"

"I dunno," answers Tony and shrugs his shoulders.

Tony buys a can of fizzy drink and Dean takes his time giving Tony back the change from the five-pound note. The shabby man watches with curiosity.

"I mean, you've probably seen it mate, haven't you?" says Dean. Tony shakes his head.

"It's just talk," says Tony.

As he walks out of the little newsagents and down Greenwood Ave, Tony cracks the can open and takes a swig. He hears footsteps behind him and turns to see the same shabby guy from the shop.

"Mind if I ask you a few questions?" asks the man. "I'm a journalist."

"I'd rather not, mate," says Tony. He doesn't need anyone to pay him any attention.

"I wouldn't say it was you... I don't even have to know your name."

Tony looks up and then down the deserted street and then back to the journalist.

"I could buy you a coffee," says the man.

Tony hasn't spoken to anyone today. He won't have to give his name. What can it hurt?

Tony boils the kettle in his kitchen and the journalist scribbles in his notebook. Tony doesn't see any harm in letting him in. If push came to shove, Tony could flatten him anyway. The journalist says he's called David, says he was from up north originally but moved to London to work on the papers down there and he's come back home to cover a story.

"Do you think your neighbour got eaten?" asks David. He has spent time working on tabloids in the city and knows that sensation sells, so it's a genuine question.

"I dunno," says Tony. He's getting much better at lying. "They say he went off the rails and lost it a bit and drowned in the river. The guy at the boxing club says foxes would have got to him, only takes a few hours, there's loads of them round here."

The journalist scribbles in his pad.

"Have you seen it?" the journalist asks.

"What?"

"They're calling it the Beast of Barmston Drain. It's quite a sensation on the internet, gets a high rank on Google search. Some high-profile people have tweeted and re-tweeted about it, and with so many sightings, well, you must have heard something."

"I don't read the papers," says Tony as he sets the journalist's black coffee down in front of him.

"Haven't people been talking about it round here? It was meant to have killed someone's Alsatian from a few streets away."

Tony hasn't heard anything, just whispers. He distances himself from the subject and imagines he is someone completely different, someone who has never seen the wolf in the forest near here, a normal boy whose Auntie Lynn does live here with him and who is about to start year eleven in a few weeks. The lying comes easy, natural even.

"So, you don't think there's anything in it?"

"Well, maybe," says Tony, "but nothing has happened round here."

"There have been sightings from as far north as Beverley, Cherry Burton, a couple from Dalton on the Wolds say they saw a 'wolf-like creature' ripping into a dead sheep. A woman from Howden says she saw a dog-like creature running after her car on four legs and then suddenly, on two." At this, Tony shakes his head. "Have you heard of the legend of the old stinker?" asks the journalist.

"No," says Tony. He thinks he read about it.

"A wolfman first reported around here more than two hundred years ago. It preyed on dock workers, ate local livestock and had terrible breath, hence the name. This area was probably the last place wolves survived in the UK. There might well be a few left."

"You think so?" asks Tony.

"You're less than a mile away from the open countryside. East Yorkshire has the lowest density population of the whole country - apart from this city, no one really lives here. You can walk north, and there's nothing but fields and forest, so there'd be a million places for it to hide. I've checked it all out on the ordinance survey maps and on satellite images."

"Yes, but why wouldn't we have seen it before? Why would people suddenly start seeing a wolfman now?"

"That's the question I asked," says David. "Maybe they have seen it, and they just don't say anything about it." Tony thinks of the black dog picture hanging on the wall in the front room. The journalist continues: "Psychologists suggest it might be some form of mass hallucination. People invent a monster to be scared of. That's why they like horror films or ghost stories."

"Or maybe it's a load of crap to get people to read newspapers?" says Tony. He sounds like his dad.

The journalist sips his coffee.

"That could also be true," David says. He looks over his glasses and into his Tony's eyes. "There is another thing it could be…"

"What?"

"Well, it's not something I'm sure I could write about, a

little too strange for our readers perhaps. They call them *Ulfheadnar*. It's an old Viking legend. It means those who wear a wolf pelt, literally *wolf header*. They were warriors called berserkers, often battle mad but feared and respected. Legend has it they were shapeshifters as well but, here's the story, if an Ulfheadnar is badly injured in battle and he's not ready to die, perhaps he's got some unfinished business, a place to go or someone to look after, they would wrap him in a fresh wolf pelt, leave him in the woods and then, with any luck he'd turn."

"Turn into what?" asks Tony.

"A wolf."

Tony's face changes. He stares at the journalist with a blank expression and thinks about his father in the hospital bed. Tony sees the two soldiers dressed in full uniform walk past him in the corridor after his father has died. He thinks about him in the coffin and how they lowered it into the ground, how he threw soil onto the top of the wood and how nobody would look him in the eyes when it was done. He feels sick. He feels angry too. The journalist carries on.

"The most famous was named Freydis Eriksen. He came from the tip of Rutland in Denmark: he was mortally wounded in battle in the northern Baltic state of Lithuania in the eleventh century. The other *Ulfheadnar* left him 'to wolf' in the forests so he could travel back to his homelands to protect his wife and family. If you go to Frederikshavn in Denmark today, there's a statue of him in the town square. It's a huge wolf that was said to prowl the forest for hundreds of years."

"What's that got to do with round here?"

"You're all Viking settlers. York was a Viking city, so were all the villages around here. You're probably descended from Vikings or Norsemen yourself. What's your second name?" Tony doesn't answer. "Sorry," says David, "we weren't going to do names, were we? If it ends in *son* or *sen*, then you're one of them."

167

"That's not what it is. It's real," says Tony without thinking.

"So there is something there then?" asks David.

Tony shrugs his shoulders.

"I've been a reporter for quite a long time," David continues, "and it's been my experience that people usually want to tell me everything, unless they've got something to hide. Especially about something like this, something we all pretty much know isn't true. I think you've got something to tell me."

"Why don't you write about the real stories?" asks Tony, "like people who are struggling to get by on benefits?" He thinks of Emma next door, "domestic violence," and then Mwamba, "or refugees?"

"People like reading about werewolves," says David. "If you can give me anything, I can pay, you know. If you're struggling, I can help you get some easy money. I just need something to write about. Maybe you can show me where they found your neighbour, or where you think whatever it is might be. Maybe you've even seen it."

Tony feels the cold ripple through his veins. He has to keep his calm. Like Mwamba told him, sometimes, you invite a beast into your house without knowing it. He swallows. He needs to get this man out.

"I don't know exactly where he died, somewhere on the drain side. It runs right behind the house here," and Tony points out of his back window. The journalist's jowls bounce as he moves his head. He writes a note in his pad.

"Is your mum or dad around? I could ask them some questions. Maybe they'll need the money more than you do."

Tony is pale.

"They're not in," he says.

"I can come back later."

"They won't be home."

"I want to get to the truth. If there's anything out there,

then people should know, don't you think? It could be dangerous."

"I don't know anything, mate," says Tony.

The ease of the lies that he felt before has left him. Now the journalist has sniffed out something, Tony finds it hard to cover up. His ears have gone red. He swallows. His mouth is dry. David finishes his black coffee and sets it on the kitchen table.

"Are you sure your dad's not home?"

"He won't be home again, mate." The mate in this sentence is stressed, so it doesn't mean mate.

Tony is a few words away from telling him where to go.

"Why don't you try the old abattoir on Stockholm Road? They closed it down last month. That's where the bloke next door used to work?" Tony adds.

Tony does not think the beast would travel that far into the town because it would have to cross too many streets and take too many chances. It won't be there. David pulls out his wallet and passes Tony a flimsy business card with his details on it.

"You get in touch with me if you have anything else. I promise I can make it worth your while."

At the open front door, Tony points him down the street to the little bridge that goes over Barmston Drain. David says thanks as he leaves.

Tony closes the frosted glass door and looks down at his feet for a few minutes as he thinks about the information the man has given him. His heart is pounding and his ears are red. His first instinct is to disbelieve the story of the wolf, but it's not enough, he has to know if there's any proof.

In his father's bedroom, he opens up the chest at the bottom of the bed and begins, more quickly than usual, to examine the items. There is nothing different here. Tony goes through the wardrobes that he hasn't emptied yet, the smart shirts on one side, the casual on the other. He searches through the airing cupboard and the little bedside table. He does not know what he is looking for. A wolf pelt? Even if it were real or possible, then Tony's father was not the sort of man to leave any evidence. As Tony rummages through the plastic wallet with all the insurance papers inside, he reasons his father would have told him something like this, perhaps confided in him and explained what was going on, like he did with everything else. But then he remembers his father hasn't told him everything. He forgot to mention Tony's mother's suicide over the years and years he brought his son up. When Tony thinks about this, he feels anger in the bottom of his stomach, and he throws the plastic wallet down, so the paperwork spills out all over the bedroom floor.

Mwamba said this would happen. She said he would be tricked and everything he thought was right would turn out to be a lie.

He knows men don't turn into wolves, no matter how much unfinished business they have got left. In his bedroom, he pulls out his laptop out from under the bed, opens it up and at the search engine, types in Ulfheadnar. He glances down the wiki page and sees the drawings of bare-chested men with wolf headdresses over their faces and spears in their hands. He searches for Frederikshavn and sees the picture of the statue in the town centre. It's cold and bright, a white, marble carving of a powerful wolf with a thick, arctic coat. It's not a bit like the ragged thing he's seen in the forest, a million miles away from it in fact. He closes the laptop and wipes his face.

Tony does not know what to think.

CHAPTER EIGHTEEN

Early Monday morning the landline phone rings in Tony's house. It's an eerie, high pitched sound. Tony listens to it from downstairs as he lies in his bed. He turns over as the answer machine clicks in, on the other end is Ian, the social worker. He sounds upbeat as usual:

"Hi, this is Ian from Hull County Council Social Services department. I wanted to have a chat with Lynn Petersen regarding Tony Petersen and his situation. We've spoken already, but there are a few details I need to iron out, and a couple of signatures I need on some paperwork. I can appreciate you're busy, so I can come out to you anytime on Monday or Tuesday this week." Ian leaves his number and spends too long on the phone for Tony's liking.

Tony looks at himself in the bathroom mirror. The bruises are starting to go down, but the black eye is worse. He's tired. Despite the running and the training, he can't sleep. He sees the faces of his father and Whalebone, Wallace and Jacko, they crowd him and order him, push him and pull him. He sees the wolf too and feels it looking at him from the darkness with its eyes glowing. He feels sick.

At the kitchen table, Tony sits down and opens the laptop and closes it again. There's no one to advise him now. The videos, so crudely made by his father, are out of date already. Perhaps in the evening, when he's feeling sad or threatened, he can take comfort from the old man's words, but here, in the cold light of an August morning, he needs answers. He has to fix things; he has to make everything right before school starts in a week. Then, he can, at least, try to get back to being normal, to get back to routine and homework and cooking and training. Today, more than any other, Tony senses he is on his own, really on his own, like his father explained, and somehow, he doesn't feel helpless. He's got choices. It's time to stop letting people push him around.

He opens the fridge and makes himself a breakfast of scrambled eggs on toast and washes it down with a coffee and a glass of orange. He cuts up carrots and onions, peels potatoes and takes sausages from the fridge, adds them to the slow cooker with some water and beef stock for something to eat when he gets home later. In the freezer, he rakes through the joints of meat his father has left him, the big chunks of steak and hams. They are expensive cuts, monkfish and bream. It's meat to make you strong. Tony finds the biggest piece, a joint of pork, and sets it to defrost in a pan on the kitchen sink. All the time, as Tony works, he feels better. He feels like he is beginning to sort out his own problems rather than letting other people sort them for him.

Upstairs he rummages through a chest of drawers on the landing and pulls out his father's hair clippers. He takes his father's shaving mirror outside to the garden and gives himself a number four buzz cut all over his head, like he should have done before the Mario Lacey fight. The hair blows away in the light, late summer wind. He runs his hands over the stubble where his hair has been. It makes him feel neat. Tony dresses in his tracksuit and a white t-shirt and packs his gym stuff. Once the bag is assembled, he sets it at the bottom of the stairs and picks up the house phone from its cradle. He doesn't have to listen again for Ian's number, he redials the last caller, puts the phone to his ear and waits for Ian to pick up. He keeps his mind clear as it rings. Ian picks up and greets him with his cheery voice.

"Are you free today?" asks Tony, "at about twelve? Only my Auntie Lynn says she'll be here and can sign any of those documents you've got."

Ian sounds surprised on the other end.

"Who's that?" he asks.

"Tony Petersen from the North Hull Estate."

"Well, let me have a look at my diary..." he's too slow for Tony, "Ah yes...I can be there by then," he answers. "Is she there now? I could have a chat to her."

"She's had to nip out."

"Right you are. To be honest, Tony, I've been getting a bit nervous about all this. I've tried to get in touch loads of times and, if she can't even be bothered to get back to me, then it doesn't send a very good message about her looking after you, does it? I mean, she should be setting up this meeting, not you."

"She's a bit airheaded," says Tony. "You've met her, she means well."

"Well, I hope we can get this sorted. Once she signs the guardianship papers, we can hopefully get this thing moving through the courts."

Tony pretends he does not hear this. He has not planned that far ahead, but he is sure he will work it out when he gets there.

"So, noon then?" Tony adds to make sure the details are correct.

"That's great," says Ian on the other end. "I'll be there then." Tony is about to hang up when Ian cuts in:

"You know Tony, I do worry about you. It's not normal for a fifteen-year-old boy to be, well, to be so organised. What I mean is, it's like you're the adult and your Auntie Lynn is the child I'm chasing. Do you see what I mean?"

"Yes," says Tony without thinking what he has said. "Yes, I know what you mean."

Tony raps on the front door of Emma's house and rings her doorbell. He waits for a minute, hoping she is in. He remembers she said she worked evenings at some new shopping centre. Someone thuds down the stairs and Emma, in a thin dressing gown with messed up red hair, opens the door. She squints out into the summer morning. When she sees it's Tony, she beckons him inside as she does up her dressing gown.

"I thought we'd said we wouldn't have anything to do with each other," Emma says as Tony walks through the door.

"I know," says Tony, "but there's something wrong."

Emma's face immediately drains of any colour it might have had this early in the morning.

"What?"

"I need to meet you at mine, as near as you can to twelve. Come over the back fence. Be normal."

Tony makes to leave out the front where he has just stepped in.

"What's happened?" she snaps, grabbing his arm just under the elbow. Her hands are surprisingly strong. "What's going on?"

Tony pulls his arm back but looks her direct in the face. He could ask her for help, but he knows she won't oblige despite the risks he took for her and Sam. He'll have to lie to save himself.

"Someone saw something, that night," says Tony and her grip fades as she staggers back. "It's okay. We can fix it. I need you to be there to give your side of it."

"Is it the police?"

"No. I have to go."

Tony realises she will unravel his story if he stays and explains. He makes for the door handle again.

"I'll say it was you if I have to you know, Tony," her voice is a whisper. "There's probably enough DNA on you or something in that house to send you down for murder."

Emma's face is at once angry and ugly. He's not seen her this way before. Tony hears but pretends not to as he turns the handle of the front door.

"I'll say it was you, and that thing you've seen in the bushes at the end of the drain," she snarls.

"Just before twelve then?" Tony interrupts, ignoring her as he opens and then closes the door.

Jacko has finished sweeping out the gym and is standing with the double doors open at the front. His wrinkled hands are resting on the sweeping brush. The sunlight is on him. Tony never remembers Jacko being anything but old, but not this old.

"Your face is going down then," says Jacko.

Tony has nearly forgotten he is covered in bruises and has the beginnings of a black eye.

"Is Wallace around?" he asks.

"Aye, in the office," says Jacko. He stops the boy with his broom handle, pressing it to his chest.

"They're no good this lot, Tony," he whispers, "no good at all. Things are happening here that shouldn't happen at a boxing club." Jacko's white head comes up to Tony's nose. Tony doesn't remember him being this short either. "Your father wouldn't be happy about any of this, and he wouldn't be happy if you got mixed up in it either."

"I know," says Tony.

"If I'm honest, you'd be better off finding a different place altogether."

Tony stares into the darkness of the gym.

"What about you?"

"What about me? You're not my kid. I'm not going with you. I'm too old to change now, anyway. You've got everything to live for. Wallace, he's a bad one. I've seen some right characters coming and going here, bringing stuff in. I don't want you getting yourself mixed up in any of that tat."

"I thought you said I wasn't your kid."

"Don't get funny Tony. You know what I mean. You've got a future, and it was never going to be at this club anyway, so why not do yourself a favour? Leave now, before they suck you into a world you can't fight your way out of."

"Do you remember when you came to my house that night?" asks Tony. "You came to me and asked if I would be with you when the time was right."

"I remember," scowls Jacko, his teeth are a little yellow and his eyes are dimmed, "but things have changed between then and now, Tony. It's got worse. The only route I can see for you is to leave."

"I know what I'm doing, Jacko."

"You don't know what you're doing. You're fifteen, for Christ's sake, your dad died a few weeks ago. Go home. These blokes are wrong."

Tony takes a deep breath.

"Will you be on my side when the time is right, Jacko?"

The old man's eyes flash.

"I was drunk that night," Jacko replies.

"Well, will you?"

"I can't promise anything, Tony."

"What would my dad say about that?"

"I dunno, he isn't here anymore."

"Exactly. I thought you promised to look after me? Like I'd look after you."

"You're twisting this, Tony. Nobody knew your dad like I did. He wouldn't have been able to stop this anymore than I could. You have to accept it. Move on. Walk away."

Tony shakes his head.

"This is our club, Jacko. I'm not going to leave. Even if you give up, I'm not going to."

"You'll get yourself killed."

"Good," says Tony.

Tony walks into the gym, and his nose fills with the sweat and the grease from the bodies that have trained before him, despite the refurb. The new bags are still, the weight room empty, the ring deserted, but there's an energy here. Tony walks to the far door at the end of the gym and taps on the window. A voice invites him inside. Wallace has his face in a laptop and is wearing a scowl. He glances up.

"What do you want?"

"I came for the stuff."

"What stuff?"

"The juice."

Wallace stands up and goes to the filing cabinet at the side of the room, pulls open one of the metal drawers and looks in. He beckons Tony over, and they both stare down at the rows of bags inside, just as Whalebone had packed them.

"There it is," says Wallace. "Have you got something to carry it in?"

Tony holds up his kit back and then unzips it. Wallace picks up one of the bags from inside the drawer and the bottles clink as he drops it into the kit bag.

"Whalebone told me he had a word with you. You're doing the right thing, Tony. In a world like this, you've got to make your own way, and sometimes you have to do things you don't want to. People trust you round here, like they trusted your dad, this will be good for you."

Tony simply nods as he puts the juice into his kit bag.

"How much do I sell 'em for?"

"It's testosterone propionate, costs £50 for that vial there. They inject it in their arse or the fatty tissues of their arms, *not* into a vein unless they want to die. There should be enough in a bottle for twenty-one shots of 10 mil. That's once a day for three weeks, in the morning with food. After two weeks, if they keep pumping and eating, they'll see a change, and they'll be back for more. Second time round the price goes up to sixty quid, and when you've got all the money, you bring it back to me. If you sell it for more and pocket the difference, I'll break your teeth. That's twelve bags you've got, should make all in all £600 quid. You didn't get it from me if anyone asks. You don't hand it over in the gym. Be discrete. Don't just walk up to someone and ask them if they want to buy some juice. It'll take time to build up a set of customers. So, I'll need you in here training every night. You don't have to weight train, boxing is good enough, better even, then they know you're hard. You got all that?"

"Yeah," says Tony. He's wearing a kind of grimace as he

takes it all in.

"Good," answers Wallace. "I know you haven't got it all. I told it to you too fast. I'm here if you want any advice and make sure you come to me if you have any questions."

Wallace is professional, clipped and to business. He goes back to sit behind his desk, turns towards his laptop and the screen illuminates his eyes. After a few seconds, he glances up at Tony, who is standing with his gym bag in his hands. "Is there anything else?"

"No," says Tony.

"You work for me now, Tony, so, you best be out there selling juice." Tony is vacant. "And, so as you know, business with me can be good or it can be awful, it's your choice." Wallace cannot help himself. Like a bad action film, he regurgitates dialogue. Tony closes the door as he leaves.

In his house, Tony waits for the knock. It is eleven fifty-four. He waits thirty seconds before he opens the door to Ian, the thin, grey-haired social worker.

"Hope you don't mind, I'm a bit early," Ian says.

Tony smiles and invites him in.

"I see your face isn't getting much better," Ian adds.

"Well, faces get worse before they get better, especially black eyes."

Tony leads him through into the front room and goes into the kitchen to boil the kettle. Out the corner of his eye, he sees Emma hop over the garden fence and walk up to his house. Tony opens the back door before she gets there and gets the chance to knock. She looks worried as she steps inside. Tony puts his finger to his lips to quieten her, and his face is serious and dark, as black as it was that night he carried her dead husband down to the banks of the drain side. She's about to say something when she sees Ian, the social worker, pop his head round the kitchen door.

"Hello," Ian says.

In the split second, she has seen him, Emma's whole

face changes, the wrinkles and the frown dissolve, the eyes smooth over and she breaks into a wide smile. As she speaks, she starts to create a cover story, perhaps it comes from experience. The change is instant.

"Hiya," she says, "I'm just a bit cross with Tony for not hanging the washing out already, on a day like this." She takes over and slips into the role of Auntie Lynn. "Tony's boiled the kettle. Shall I make you a cup of something? It was coffee, wasn't it, black coffee last time?"

Ian steps through into the kitchen. He does not get the chance to answer before Emma begins her quick-fire speaking and picks up the kettle. Tony has left out the coffee and some cups, so she doesn't have to rummage through the cupboards. He steps back and lets the actress in Emma shine.

She is a marvel, more nervous than last time, Tony can see, but the performance is flawless. She explains in detail her life in the house with Tony, the routine of her going to work at the big new shopping centre, Tony's cooking and cleaning, and her returning to meals in the evening. She is careful too, not to put too much of a light-hearted spin on it. This might not be believed. So, when Tony is out of the room, he hears her explain how much he misses his dad and his mood swings. It takes less than an hour for her to work her magic on Ian and although she does not sign the guardianship papers he has brought her, she says she is going to think about it as a permanent solution. They all shake hands as Ian stands in the doorway and Emma takes a look at her watch, saying she's got to get away to work. Tony feels it has gone well.

They wait for Ian's car engine to start outside and for him to drive to the end of the street and turn the corner before they dare breathe.

"I think that went okay," says Tony to break the silence.

Emma slaps him hard on the side of the face and it stings his bruised cheek.

"Do you realise how much shit you've put me and my Sam in?" She is angry; her voice is raised but not quite in a shout. "Do you understand what might have happened if he'd have found me out?"

"I helped you out when you needed me," says Tony. "It was me carried that man down to the drain. It was me that took the risk, not you. All you can think about is yourself. I'm trying to buy myself enough time to get back to normal."

"For what, Tony, for what? So you can live your life exactly the same as your father did, in the exact same house, training at the exact same club? He's dead, and that's a terrible thing, it really is, but he's dead and no matter what you do, how you live, what you want, things are going to have to change. Whatever he may have told you, you cannot live like this here, not for a year or for six months. You might be able to cook and clean, look after yourself, box and whatever, but this isn't a family, Tony. You're fifteen, sooner or later you're going to need support, help, someone to listen to you. You can't live your life like a fight."

She is red-faced after saying too much. She goes to the sink, draws herself some water in her coffee cup and takes a sip. "I'm sorry," she adds, "what you did for me and my Sam was beyond what anyone could ever have done for us, and I have thanked you for that already. But this has got to end. Auntie Lynn has got to go back to Doncaster, Tony. You've got to turn yourself in. If your dad had thought this through or if he were here now, then he'd say the same thing."

They stare at each other for a few moments and the clock from above the door clacks as the seconds tick away.

"You can't do it alone, Tony.. Believe me. I've tried."

Emma leaves, and Tony watches her hop over the little fence that separates their gardens.

He wonders, for the first time, if she might be right.

CHAPTER NINETEEN

It is evening. The realisation that the summer holidays are over is dawning on the children and families of the North Hull Estate. Kids have been dragged to get new uniforms and pencil cases, and mums and dads rub their hands together, thinking of a time when they will have the house to themselves, at least in the daytime. There is a sense of sadness for the end of this summer. It has come too soon. Kids who spent all their time roaming the streets on their pushbikes begin to worry they won't get any time to ride. Kids who spent six weeks on their Xboxes wonder how they'll continue their games once they go back to school. Lionel tries on his school uniform, again, in front of the mirror. He has convinced his mother to buy him a pair of black, named trainers that can pass as school shoes. Jacko is gearing up to teach the last of the little kids at the boxing club. He's grown to know them all now, sees potential in most and greatness in a few.

Tony eats the stew that he set to cook this morning and freezes what he can't finish for other days when he will not have time to make anything. He unwraps the pork joint he took out of the fridge in the morning and puts it in a metal roasting tray with all the juices. He pats the flesh. If he were going to cook it, he would rub the skin with salt and olive oil then stick it in the slow cooker for as long as he could. Tony takes a sharp knife and cuts off bits of the flesh.

He puts the tray outside in the darkness of the garden, about half-way down the path. Then, he waits upstairs in his bedroom, staring down at the trees. He wonders if he can see a black shape moving through the shadows. He blinks, and it is gone. He has thought a lot about the journalist's story from the day before, dismissed it, believed it, dismissed it and believed it again. He knows it can't be right. How could it be? His father wasn't a Viking, there's no wolf pelt and to add to this, Tony saw his father in his last moments, he saw him before he died. He picked up the clear plastic bag with his things after the nurse had covered over the body.

Tony hears the tray clatter in the garden, and he knows something has got to his ham joint. He is already dressed with his trainers on, and he creeps down the stairs and through the dark kitchen to the door. His hand goes round the door handle, and he feels a sense of fear at what he's going to see.

There it is in the garden, head down in the baking tray Tony left on the path. It licks and chews on the chunks of pork and the metal tray scrapes on the stone. He can smell the wet dog stink as he approaches, and it senses him, giving a low, almost inaudible growl as a warning. Tony does not stop until he gets close, nearly close enough to touch it

"Look at me," he whispers, but the beast does not stop nuzzling and biting at the tray. "Look at me," he repeats, and the dog-wolf stops, steps backwards with its haunches up; shows its face to him and growls. It bares its teeth; they are a concertina of sharp spikes under yellow eyes. Its ears are back and warn him not to get any closer. Tony puts out his hand, palm down towards the creature. He can feel the bristling energy radiating from it, the anger and the rage, it makes him feel calm somehow.

"Who are you?" he asks, but the beast keeps moving backwards. "What do you want from me?" The beast growls. A police siren sounds from a few streets away, a sad wailing in and out as the noise gets closer. The beast's ears spin as it listens at the whine that cuts through the silence of the night. Now there are two sirens, getting louder and louder, nearer and nearer, till they race down Tony's street and past his house with a screech of tyres on tarmac. There's the slam of doors and the rumble of boots with shouts in the mid-distance. Something is happening close to home. Not in his street maybe, but near. The beast senses this too and creeps backwards, keeping low before it turns and springs over the back fence into the dense undergrowth and onto the banks of the drain.

Tony slips through his house in the darkness and opens his front door. He sees flashing blue lights of the police and emergency vehicles in the street opposite. Behind this, in a burst of orange light, a fire crackles from the top of the block of flats.

It is Mwamba's tower block.

Tony approaches at a light jog. There are three fire engines around the six-storey building and perhaps twenty firefighters dressed in their heavy yellow outfits, busy setting up hoses. There is a lot of shouting, and, like Tony, the great and the good of the North Hull Estate have been roused out of their houses and flats to see what is going on. They stand in their pyjamas or dressing gowns, looking at the spectacle. From near the top of the tower block, bright flames are belching out of the windows and licking up the sides. Tony can feel the heat as he approaches, even at this distance. Another police car with its sirens on squeaks to a halt a few metres from him, the policeman gets out and puts his hand to his forehead in shock. Tony thinks of little Lionel and Mwamba then jogs closer. Another policeman is telling onlookers to stand back, and Tony gives him a wide birth. He circles round the back of the fire engines as firefighters unravel hoses from great wheels on their trucks. He crawls around a parked car and then another until he is much closer to the building than he should be.

Standing alone on the grass and blinking, is Lionel, his smooth face wears a blank expression, and his eyes are passive. He is watching the flames pump heavy smoke into the night sky. Despite the chaos going on behind, Lionel has not been spotted. Tony appears at his side.

"Where's your mum?" Tony asks and Lionel does not turn round. Tony grabs him by the shoulders. "Where's your mum, Lionel? Where's Susa?" he asks again. The little boy is pale. His expression is frozen.

"Susa's at work. Mum - she made me run," he says. "She made me leave her. I didn't know what to do. She can't get down the stairs. She said it was a punishment for all the bad she's done." Lionel's voice is without emotion.

"Go and tell one of the firefighters she's still inside and tell them your flat number."

"I did," says Lionel. "They say firemen are inside already. On the other side of the building first."

Tony curses under his breath and sees the open door to the tower block. Somewhere high above, the fire is raging into the night sky.

"I'll get her," he says. Tony zips up his top and snuggles into the hood as he approaches the door and without a whisper, he slips inside.

He expects the air to be hot and dusty in the tower block, but it is cold and dark like it always is. He sprints up the first set of stairs in a couple of leaps and is on the first floor with the light still flickering in the stairwell. At the second floor, the corridor is dense with a kind of thin soot. It's hot like a sauna and Tony pulls the chords on his hood, so the material covers his face. There's blood on the walls here, a big fresh streak of it and a bloody handprint as well. Tony can see more blood dotted up the stairs. He doesn't need to go far. At Mwamba's door, he tries the handle, but it's locked. He bangs on it.

"Open the door, it's Tony," he yells.

He bangs again, harder, with, his face pressed close to the wood. "Open the door," he screams. He hears a crashing noise from far up inside the building where something has fallen. It gives him urgency. "Open the door," yells as he bangs, then stops; stands back and kicks at the lock with all his weight behind his foot. The handle collapses and one of the hinges clatters to the floor. With another boot, the door falls in. Tony clambers through into the hall and stumbles to the little kitchen. He finds Mwamba in the front room, sat in an armchair clutching her bible to her chest with her eyes closed.

"Come on," screams Tony, but she does not hear him.

Mwamba is mumbling something as she rocks back and forth in her seat. Her face is wet with sweat. When Tony touches her shoulder, her eyes snap open.

"No, No, No," she snarls through her bared teeth.

There is smoke drifting into the flat from outside in the corridor and another sliding sound from somewhere in the building followed by a crash. Something is falling in. Hot smoke billows through the front door of Mwamba's flat and into the kitchen. Mwamba does not respond.

"We have to go, now!" Tony shouts above the noise outside.

"No," she hisses.

She suddenly grips Tony by the wrist and holds him as she speaks Lingala into his face. She is insane.

Tony has had enough.

He shakes free from her grip and stands up, grabs her arm and pulls her upwards. His movement is quick and powerful as he lifts her over his shoulder. His legs shiver under the weight. Mwamba begins to scream. It's high-pitched and frantic, and the sound hurts Tony's ears. He feels sick from the smoke as he staggers through the kitchen. Into the corridor, he stumbles and follows the wall down to the stairs. The screaming is off-putting, and Mwamba is a dead weight, she wriggles and struggles for periods before tiring. Tony gets to the top of the stairs and there is a boom from far above.

He has to get out soon, or he will not be able to breathe. Smoke pours down the stairwell at them, and Tony's thighs strain at the screaming woman on his back. She digs her nails into his flesh and tries to move her arms, but Tony has a tight grip on her. He can't afford to stop. At the first floor, Mwamba's screaming has lessened, and her fingers have stopped clawing at him. The air is easier to breathe the lower he goes. As he gets to the bottom flight of stairs, Tony sees the main door leading outside is closed. He staggers to it; rattles the handle and he finds it will not open. There are more crashes and bangs from far up the building. Lines of dust fall through the cracks of the ceiling above. Tony hammers on the door with his free hand and yells as loud as he can, hearing his own voice muffled by the smoke and the heat. He bangs until he feels his legs get weaker and his chest seizing up. He splits one of his knuckles on the toughened glass as he punches it. On the other side of the door, Tony hears the bleeping of buttons being pressed on the keypad, the mechanism clicks, and the door opens. He stumbles outside, managing to carry the body of Mwamba a few steps to the grass where he drops it with a thud and collapses down next to her. He gasps in air as he looks up at the night sky above him. Lionel's little face appears above him,

"They locked the door after you went in," Lionel tells him in his matter of fact way.

Tony sits up. He is wheezing and covered in dirt, but alive.

"Is my mother dead?" asks Lionel, staring at the body of Mwamba who is laid on her back.

Tony does not say anything. He's trying to work out what is going on. The firefighters are the other side of the building, some twenty metres away, and no one noticed him as he slipped in and out of the building by the back entrance. Beyond the action of the fire engines, he can see a small crowd of people.

"We've got to get away from here," says Tony. "It's still burning."

"What about my mother?" Lionel asks.

Lionel is standing next to Mwamba's body. She mumbles something in Lingala even though her eyes don't open. Lionel smiles wide and bends down to throw his little arms around her body. He presses his cheek close to her face.

"She says you are powerful."

A fireman approaches dressed in yellow trousers, a long orange jacket and a helmet with a visor.

"What are you lot doing here?" he says. "You should be back behind the line and away from the building." As the man gets closer, he sees Tony is covered in ash with cuts on his face. "Have you been in there?" bellows the fireman.

"He went and got my mother out," says Lionel. The fireman puts his radio to his lips to get help.

They don't even keep Tony in the hospital for the night. He's suffered some respiratory distress but nothing major. The cuts on his hands and the scratches on his body from Mwamba's nails have been cleaned and patched up with plasters and a wrap-around bandage. The nurses ask about the black eye and bruises from his fight, and Tony has to explain, many times, that he is a boxer. The fire, it turns out, was all over the other side of the building. It started in a flat on the fifth floor and spread upwards before it gutted the rest of the tower block.

The policeman that talks to Tony tells him what he did was very stupid, and he could have got himself and others killed as a result. He also tells him he is lucky he isn't going to be charged with anything. Tony doesn't say to the officer about the blood he saw along the walls of the corridor. He keeps his head down and keeps asking to go home. Tony tells the officer his dad works as a bus driver in the station in town and he can go there and get a lift straight home. He gives his name and address as Will Black knowing that Will Black's dad is actually a bus driver. The policeman lets him go with a promise he will be talking to his parents just as soon as all this is cleaned up.

Mwamba and little Lionel have been taken up into the inner parts of the hospital itself because of Mwamba's hip injuries; they want to check nothing has come out of place while Tony carried her. There's no need for Tony to see how they are. If he does, he might get himself into more trouble with the police or some other busybody.

He walks out of the double doors at the hospital and puts his hood up. He doesn't have any money and it must be two or three miles to the North Hull Estate. It's half-past ten on a Sunday evening, but Tony does not feel afraid or disheartened. He zips up his grey hoodie, now filthy from the fire, and begins a slow jog over the railway bridge behind the hospital. There's a slight, fine rain beginning and a cool breeze. His legs feel stiff and worn and his chest is tight, but somehow, Tony feels good. This time, he feels like he has won. He sees himself breaking down the door and pulling Mwamba onto his shoulders. It felt good. He knows, as he runs past the posh pubs of Princes Avenue, that his father would be proud of what he did, because he is proud of what he did.

He runs along the back streets and out onto the far end of Beverley Road which is quiet but for a few taxis and the last of the night buses. With each thudding step, he feels better, like some piece in him has fallen into place, like he is of value, like the world is better because he is in it.

Tony does not feel tired as he gets to Greenwood Ave and turns into 6th Avenue, even though he's sweating and shivering in equal measure. Across the road from his house, there are ambulances and fire engines. The blaze is out, at least, but the mess will take months to clean up.

Inside, Tony warms celery soup his father froze many months before. He eats it with brown bread, and because he feels hungry, he opens a tin of mackerel. A boxer's meal, to keep him strong. He looks out of the upstairs window at the still, patchy forest around the drain and for some reason, he does not feel the creature is watching him from out there.

Not tonight.

CHAPTER TWENTY

Tony wakes to the sun streaming in through the thin open curtain of his bedroom window. He wants to wake up early and that's why he didn't close them the night before. In the bathroom mirror, he sees his beaten-up face, the bruises and the black eye from the Mario Lacey fight and the cuts from the night before where Mwamba's nails dug into his lower back. He rubs some of his father's antiseptic cream on the wounds and feels the sting as the medicine works into them.

He's ready.

It's now, or not at all.

Next week, everyone will be back at school and the world will have moved on. It has to be today.

He eats a good breakfast, puts the radio on, opens the back door so the summer air can come in, drinks coffee and thinks about the times he sat there with his father. For an hour, he sits and reads through his medical book and rereads the chapter on finding muscles and trigger points, massage techniques and tendons. Though he has read the chapter many, many times before, he pours over it. The familiarity of the words and the diagrams he has looked at for so long, make him feel safe. Tony traces a finger along the back and neck of the picture. He loses himself in the pages.

At ten, after he has cleaned the kitchen, he leaves the house and walks up the street in the sunlight. Tony marvels at the block of flats burned down the night before. There are still people gawping at it and a television news crew stationed nearby. A couple of old men stand together and shake their heads as they point to the charred building. The six-storey tall block stands as it did the day before, but with gutted blackened windows and fire stains creeping up the sides. It's like something out of a disaster movie.

At the newsagent, Tony sees Dean who is usually inside, standing in front of the shop, staring at the burned block some distance off. He calls Tony over.

"Hey," he says. "Did you see it burn down last night?"

"Yeah," answers Tony.

"Someone started it, they reckon. On the fifth floor. You know some girls were living up there, don't you? Well, a punter was pissed off with them, poured petrol all over the flat and set it alight."

Dean is enjoying himself as he tells the story. He has told it to many people up and down the estate and worked it into something better than it was when he first heard it. Tony doesn't say anything. He doesn't have to. Dean talks at him rather than to him. "That's eighteen flats gone, eighteen families with nowhere to live."

"Did they get everyone out?" asks Tony.

"In the end... there was this bloke who went back in there to get someone out, some African woman. He carried her down the stairs." Tony swallows and looks behind him. "Nutter," says Dean shaking his head.

"Who was he?" asks Tony, though he knows.

"Dunno, it's probably made up. One bloke told me the fire brigade are looking for him to give him an award, and this copper told me they want to arrest him for criminal damage. You know what people are like round here, they'll spread all sorts."

"Like all that Beast of Barmston Drain stuff," adds Tony. To this, Dean frowns.

"That's straight-up though, mate. They found another dog mauled to death on Beresford Park and a ton of the swans and ducks that live up there have been killed too. Didn't you see it in the news?"

"No," says Tony.

"They reckon there really is something. There's too much evidence for there not to be. I've heard the council has called in pest control to try and find it. They'll have enough on their plate with this fire happening though. Who'd have thought it, North Hull Estate, the centre of the world? Who'd have thought anything would ever happen here?"

An old man shuffles into the shop, and Dean nips back in after him to resume his post, leaving Tony staring at the tower block. Up the road is the gym.

He swallows. Today's the day.

It's too late for Jacko and the kids. They will already have finished their training session, and Jacko himself will probably be at home reading the racing post. The door is open, but there is no one in. The bags creak uneasy against their fittings on the roof, the ring looms silent at the far end, and the door to the weights room is ajar. Whalebone sits at the back of the gym on one of the fold-out chairs, flicking through the screen on his phone with a fat thumb. He knows someone has walked into the gym, but he does not move. Tony walks over to stand in front of him.

"Where's Wallace?" Tony asks.

"Dunno," answers Whalebone. He is watching some sort of video on his phone and making a grin, which is forced.

"Know when he'll be back?"

"No."

"Someone burned that block of flats down last night," says Tony. At this, Whalebone looks up, his flabby, cold face suddenly angry.

"She deserved it, did that woman in there," he snaps. "Horrible bitch… you know if she got burned?"

"They got everyone out, all eighteen families."

Whalebone's expression goes back to a scowl and then back to his phone.

"You set that fire, didn't you Whalebone?" The big man with the cap and long greasy hair is impassive.

"Say that again, and I'll rip your head off," he whispers without looking up.

Tony steps back. His heart is beating shallow. His legs

are bent and ready; his heart rate slow. He checks behind and around him to make sure no one is there again and feels his mouth dry up.

"I told you, the boss is not here, so, what do you want?" asks Whalebone.

It doesn't feel right, not now. There are too many things that could go wrong. The open door to the street outside and the fact that anyone could see, but, there's no use in wasting an opportunity. Maybe he can learn something.

"Who taught you to fight?" Tony asks.

"What's it got to do with you?"

Tony examines Whalebone's flabby chest and the size of his neck and looks for where the muscles might fit together down his neckline and onto his powerful shoulders. Whalebone cocks his head.

"What is it you want?"

"The boss."

"You got that he's the boss into your head now, have you? Good. Well, he's not here, I already told you that."

"It's about the juice."

"I don't know anything about any juice."

Tony realises he should not be talking about it so publicly, but he wants to see more of Whalebone.

"I promise you, mate," Whalebone continues. "If I have to stand up to deal with you, I will pull bits off your body. Do you get me?"

Tony steps back.

"See you later then, Whalebone," he says.

He makes sure his voice sounds cocky and arrogant and that he has pronounced the fat man's name with as much disrespect as possible. Whalebone stares at him with his nasty, black eyes. Tony steps backwards, turns and walks out of the gym.

Whalebone will have to wait.

In the kitchen, Tony has put the laptop on the table and

is watching a video made by his father. He's watched the sentimental ones again. They make him feel weak. He has watched the ones on plumbing and electrics, the ones about online banking and haircuts. The only one he has not seen is *Number 50* called simply, *Delete everything*. He's clicked on it before, but the file does not open at all, as if whatever was there had been deleted. He tries it again, and nothing happens, except an error sign flashes up on the computer.

This is it then. This is all he has left of his father, 49 videos of between 3 and 5 minutes long. He rubs his forehead. There's a bleep from the front room, an alarm sound like the one his father used on his phone to wake them both up in the morning. Tony follows his ears to the phone he has left plugged in on the sideboard. It is buzzing and playing a little tune. He picks it up and presses the off button. There is a memo, not a message.

'Hi Tony, this is your dad. Please watch this. I love you.'

He feels weak and sits on the couch. It's like his father is still there somewhere and has just sent him the message. Grief suddenly becomes real again. His father must have planned this, to set an alarm with a message on it, he must have planned this from the hospital. There is a link in the message, it's a video link. He clicks the button and rotates the screen so that it is horizontal. His father's weak and thin face fills the screen, his eyes are soft, but the skin around his cheekbones is stretched tight. He's in bed wearing the black bandana he used to wrap round his head to stop him looking bald. His voice is strained, and he smiles into the camera.

"Hi Tony, it's me," his father begins, "that's the kind of stupid thing I would say to you." He smiles. "This is video number fifty in the list. This is 'delete', and it's my final one of the set. For a long time, I wondered whether leaving you a video log about all the things I wanted to tell you would be the right thing to do. I talked to the doctors here they thought it was a positive thing, something you could keep and look back on in years to come. I always had it in my mind to make them and then hide them away for you until you were older, but the logistics would have been too much to organise. I'm going to set the alarm for you on this phone and hope you keep it plugged in for long enough. I'm going to set the date for 25 days from now. I think I'll be gone by then. You might also have had the chance to watch all the videos by now. So, here's what I want to say in the last one. I want you to delete them, the videos I've made, all of them."

"You see - I can give you all the advice in the world, tell you how to talk to girls, fight, wash your clothes, cook; but in the end, the one who has to make all the final decisions is you. You know that, of course you do, but that's why you should delete the videos. No kid ever needs to have their dad's advice recorded for evermore. It's not natural. How are you going to be able to forget and ignore it? If you've heard it once, then that's enough. I'll be gone. My advice won't always be right for you, if you stick to it, you'll lose, just the same as if you never listened to it all. I've seen the way you've handled all this so far, Tony, I've seen what you've had to put up with and - I can't imagine it's going to get any better. You need to trust yourself more than anyone else. Now I'm gone, no one is ever going to believe in you again, except yourself."

The man puts his thin fingers over his eyes; the words are hard for him and just holding the smartphone camera is exhausting. "I love you, Tony. Love yourself, trust yourself and when you are ready, delete the videos." The camera switches position as Tony's father drops it onto the bed. There's a noise of someone entering the hospital room, and then he hears his father again, this time muffled because the microphone on the camera is covered by sheets. "Hiya Tony," says his father. "Turn me phone off will you, kid? It's on the bed here." The screen clicks and goes black. Tony does not remember that day. He does not remember switching off his father's phone.

He sits with his head in his hands in the front room.

He thinks about what he's heard. He knows all of it is true, that he's on his own and he has to make his own decisions, but he doesn't need to be reminded. It's like being told that you are going to die - we all are, but to hear it so many times is draining. Tony feels like he needs to talk, to be heard by someone. He thinks, fleetingly of Ian the social worker, a man who he could confide in, but he would not want him to get too close for fear he would find out he is a minor living alone. He thinks of Emma next door, but he's burned his bridges there. He thinks of Jacko and then shakes his head. It's time. He's had enough of wallowing and feeling sorry for himself.

Tony drinks a cup of very sweet coffee and warms up some soup. He doesn't feel hungry, but he eats a tin of sardines and drinks the oil, cracks four eggs into a jug, adds some milk and drinks that too. He will need the energy. He washes his face and looks at his bruises in the mirror. He imagines for a moment that it is not him who is staring back at him in the reflection but some other poor kid. What does he think of the eyes? What can he see in him? He sees someone who is angry, not red-faced or put out, but angry deep inside, burning angry, white-hot in the centre, but controlled. If Tony does not get rid of this heat, he thinks, it will eat him up. He has to take care of it now, today, rid himself of it if he can, or at least, start on a path that will lead him there.

He picks up his kit bag from where he left it in the morning, opens it and sees the little bottles of juice and the needles. To this, he adds the money from the floorboard under the stairs, the money Whalebone and Emma gave him and zips it up.

In the kitchen, he searches through the tub of pens his father kept in an old plant pot and takes the silver one; he thinks it might be the strongest. He attaches it to his t-shirt by the lid. At the front door, he turns off the light and looks back inside. He's gripped by a sudden desire to go upstairs and touch his father's Lonsdale belt, it might give him luck, but he thinks better of it. Luck isn't going to help him today; it hasn't done so far. He locks the door and pulls up his hood as he walks down towards the gym and the row of little shops. He has everything he needs.

Tony can hear the noise from the gym as he walks up the street. It's Thursday. On a summer evening like this, the windows are open to let the sweat out After the heavy workouts of Monday to Wednesday, Thursday is for sparring and learning techniques. Tony slips in and no one seems to notice him, but that does not mean they do not see him.

Jacko is working with some young lads and wearing pads. They are doing combinations and he spots Tony setting his gym bag down on one the benches. Whalebone stands at the open door of the office, leaning on the frame. He spots Tony too. On the outside corner of the ring, dressed in a grey vest and blue tracksuit bottoms, is Wallace. He has a towel around his neck and is shouting instructions to two blokes in the ring in front of him. He does not notice Tony warming up in front of one of the bags.

At this time of night, most lads have finished their workouts and are watching the sparring. Tony has watched the sparring lots and lots of times. If you get to fight, it's a good place to test something out and have the other lads tell you what you're doing wrong. If you watch, you see what to do and what not to do. Tony walks to the back of the gym and sees Whalebone coming round the corner of the gym towards him. He feels his pulse quicken as he catches the Scouser's eyes.

"I want a word with you in the weight room," says Whalebone, real matter of fact. "I can't hear myself think with all this noise going on." He takes Tony by the arm and spins him round, so the lad is walking in front; they move through into the silence and the stink of the weight room.

Whalebone closes the door.

Tony's ready for this.

He knows what Whalebone will do and readies himself for it. The fat Scouser lurches forward much faster than Tony expects, grabs him by the neck and, like before. His other hand goes straight for his balls. Whalebone pushes Tony up against the weight room wall and brings his face close.

"Just a friendly chat, like…" he whispers in a snarl. "I wondered how you were getting on with the juice. How much you'd sold and that?"

Tony feels the vice grip around his throat and crotch. He wriggles backwards and feels the fingers tighten as the blood rushes to his head and the pain and discomfort spirals from his balls. He can see the happy, confident twinkle in Whalebone's eyes and wonders how many boys he has done this to, or worse.

He isn't going to do this to Tony again.

With his free right-hand Tony reaches up to the neckline of his t-shirt and grabs the silver pen he put there earlier. He swings it back in his fist and hammers it into the exposed muscle on Whalebone's left shoulder. He feels it slide into the sinews and jangle the nerves. Tony's has been looking in his medical book for the right place to put it.

Whalebone grunts and his grip loosens as Tony twists free. He does not hit Whalebone but pushes him, so the Scouser stumbles and crashes backwards into a row of dumbbells. Whalebone doesn't lose his footing somehow and grimaces back at Tony a few feet away from him.

"You shouldn't have done that," Whalebone threatens.

Tony's stomach drops in fear. It did not play out like this in his mind. He had hoped to put the pen through his neck and kill him where he stood, or at least injure him. Now, he's only pissed Whalebone off. The man darts forward again, like he did in front of Wallace a week or so ago. He snaps out his hand in a punch, but Tony has already moved out the way, and Whalebone's strike crunches into the soft plaster of the wall behind him. Tony seizes his chance. His hand has come to rest on one of the 4kg hand weights on a rack, he grabs it and swings it up into the side of Whalebone's head. It connects with his skull in a dull clunk and Whalebone's flat cap falls off his head as he pitches forward into the bench like a sack of potatoes. Tony steps to the side and pulls the whole of the weight-lifting rack down over Whalebone's body. There is a crash as the bar hits his back, and one of the heavy weights clips his head. He groans, face down and then slumps flat to the ground. A trickle of red blood paints a thin line from his face.

"Karate that," whispers Tony.

He takes the key that is in the lock, opens the door, steps out into the busy gym, closes it and then locks it again. Behind him, the club is watching two lads going at each other and listening to the shouts from Wallace over the thumps and slaps of their heavy gloves. They have not noticed a thing, crashes and groans always come from the weight room. Tony's plan has gone a little better than he had hoped. Whalebone is Wallace's eyes.

Tony walks to his kit bag, takes out his black gum shield and looks down at the envelope of money inside next to the bottles of juice and the needles. His heart is beating heavy in his chest. He's done Whalebone, so he could walk away from this now, walk away and never come back to the gym again. His hands are shaking as he picks up the kit bag and he turns to the men fighting in the ring where Wallace is shouting orders and advice. They do not notice him at all.

At the far end of the gym, Tony sees Jacko. He stands alone and small against the new white wall. He is putting gloves away and watching the sparring out the corner of his eye. He notices Tony and nods at the lad. Perhaps he knows what's happened to Whalebone. He is on the young man's side, somehow.

Here it is.

Tony checks his surroundings, so he knows what is where. He looks around the gym at the bright white walls and the clean, full-length mirror on the wall. He sees the twenty or so boxers gathered around the ring. Some of them have been at the club for years and knew his father even, others are newer and are meatheads, weightlifters or kids who want to be big to look good or nasty. He hears the squeak of trainers on canvas and the heavy steps and the grunts as the boxers hit or get hit. Wallace calls out to one of them, simple, arsehole instructions 'get your hands up, step back, move, stop messing about'. Tony walks through the little crowd to the front so he can see. He's nervous, more nervous than at any of the fights, more than at his dad's funeral. He wants to pee, needs a drink, wants to sit down, wants to do anything but what he is about to do; but Tony knows if he does not make a stand right now, then he'll never be able to come back into this gym again.

The two amateur boxers fall back to either side of the ring, tired and sweating Wallace whispers something into the ear of one of them in earnest, his cold blue eyes sparkle as he talks. Though he can't believe he is doing it, Tony calls out, loud, so everyone in the gym can hear him. He tries to sound tough and solid, but it comes out a bit limp.

"I want a word with you, Wallace," he shouts. He's like a little kid shouting up to a giant.

Though the men of the club hear him, no one stops what they are doing, not least Wallace, who carries on whispering to the amateur fighter. Tony repeats it. His heart is beating in his chest, and he clambers up into the ring, through the ropes and says it again. "I want a word with you, Wallace, I said."

Wallace glances at him and hears, but again does not attempt to stop what he is doing. The other men of the gym start to disperse. They've heard Tony, but since he's so keen on making whatever he wants to say public, they don't want to get involved. Tony walks up to Wallace, still talking in the corner, and stares at him while holding his kit bag in one hand. Wallace finally turns his way and speaks; his voice is gentle.

"I'll be in my office in a minute, Tony, if you want a word. It's not the way to deal with things, is it, shouting your mouth off around the gym?"

Tony steps back and clambers out of the ring as Wallace finishes off talking to the fighter. Wallace takes his time now he knows Tony is watching him. Other eyes are on them as well. Wallace climbs down from the side and shoots Tony a friendly look. It's for the other lads, so they know Wallace is not a monster. He beckons with his head to his office at the far corner of the gym and wipes his head with the towel round his neck, casual, and then stops to take a drink from his water bottle.

Tony knows the minute he gets into Wallace's office; he's done for. The only game he has is out here, on the gym floor, not in the ring but on the floorboards. Tony rushes forward and shoves Wallace hard in his back with his hands, sending the big man stumbling forwards and then onto his knees in the middle of the gym floor.

Faces turn. It's like a schoolboy fight and should not be happening in a boxing gym. A gentle hand comes to rest on Tony's chest as he steps forward.

"Easy mate," says a blonde kid in a vest with muscles too big to be a fighter. "What's all this about?"

From the floor, Wallace gets from his knees, and his face is red. It's undignified.

"What is wrong with you?" Wallace snaps.

Tony lifts his kit bag, unzips it and empties the contents. The bottles clink as they hit the floorboards, but do not break and the needles crackle in their plastic packages. The envelope full of money splits open and twenty-pound notes flutter to the floor.

"This is what I want to talk about, Wallace, the juice you wanted me to sell. I haven't sold any of it, and I'm not going to. You can keep your money too. It's all here, and more. You can keep it and piss off back to Liverpool."

All eyes are on the scene. The blonde kid steps closer to Tony with a worried look on his face. Wallace cocks his head. He allows a minute for the whole gym to see how he is going to respond.

"I have no idea what you are on about, mate," he comments. His answer is earnest. "I don't know anything about any juice or money, and I don't like you suggesting I'm involved with anything like that." Wallace is flustered, "Where's Whalebone?" he calls.

The faces around them wear expressions of concern, what's all this about juice? Fighting in the gym? Real fights don't happen here, just the ones in the ring.

"Why don't you tell everyone what you told me?" yells Tony. "That when the drugs come off the boat here in Hull, you ship them on across the country, through Leeds, Manchester and back to Liverpool. You're a criminal. All the blokes know it, they maybe don't know how much, but they know you're dodgy."

Wallace steps forward. He is becoming angry.

"You better watch your mouth, Tony, spreading lies like that can get you hurt" he warns.

"Well, go on then? Let's have it now, me and you."

Wallace shakes his head, and his face has a mocking scowl.

"Where's Whalebone?" he calls.

"Just me and you, Wallace, no one else. Are you scared of a fifteen-year-old lad?"

"I'm a businessman, son, I don't get into street fights."

Tony steps forward and shoves Wallace in the chest. The bigger man moves backwards but not by much. They are hopelessly outmatched, Tony is small and wiry, Wallace, big, bulky, experienced and more muscular. The shove has pushed it too far for Wallace, and he changes.

"Lock the door," he says to anyone around him as he

removes the towel from around his neck and takes off his tracksuit top. "Lock the door. No one gets in or out until this is done. I'm gonna teach you a lesson, Tony. It's not gonna be nice, you'll get hurt, but I can't have people saying stuff like that about me, whoever they are. I'm not gonna do this because I enjoy it. It's just business. There's no gloves and no rules. I'm saying this to everyone here, and no one pull me off him when I get started, do you hear? No one stop me. This is gonna be an example to all of yous."

Tony slips in his black gum shield and rocks his head left to right to loosen his neck muscles.

Here it is.

"You're not going to fight him, are you?" asks the blonde man who put his hand on Tony earlier. His voice is incredulous.

"You want to go at me first, do you?" asks Wallace.

The blonde man shakes his head and steps back. A loose circle forms around Tony and Wallace. The air is still and thick with tension as they face each other. This should not be happening in a boxing club.

Tony puts up his fists. Now the fight is here, he feels calmer, he knows what to do here.

It begins.

Wallace moves quickly for a man of his size and weight. He does not punch but slaps at Tony's head, the weight and power are enough to send the lad reeling to one side. Wallace hits him with his other hand. He claps Tony around, like a rag doll, before grabbing him by the shoulders and throwing him across the gym into the full-length mirror. The back of Tony's head hits the glass and spiral cracks spider web outwards from the impact. Wallace moves on his advantage and Tony has enough time to bury his head in his arms before the Scouser begins to punch his body. He throws heavy, unnecessarily hard blows at the young lad's ribs. Tony tucks his head into his elbow, and his body rattles as the punches hammer down. He tries to move, but it's all he can do to keep on his feet with his back pressed up against the shattered mirror. He can smell the sweat coming from Wallace and hear his grunts as he delivers punch after punch.

It's pathetic to watch.

After a minute of full power, Wallace steps back, breathing heavily with his face wet.

"I warned you," he says. "I warned you."

Tony's head spins and his eyes blink. His forehead is cut and blood is running down his face. He feels sick and his legs feel too weak to stand on. This is not the same as any boxing match he's ever had. Wallace is faster, crueller and more experienced. There is no bell.

"Never pick a fight you can't win, Tony. Do you hear me?" Wallace spits.

Wallace has dropped his guard and is speaking to Tony down his nose through bared teeth. He's still out of breath. Tony hears the Scouser speaking and he can understand the words, but his brain is too shaky to make sense of them. His stomach turns and his throat burns.

"Have you had enough, mate?" mocks Wallace.

Tony sees his chance. In his arrogance, Wallace has left himself open. The boy springs forward, fakes a left and bends his whole body into a right hook. The world slows down and his senses heighten. In front of him, frozen in time, stands Wallace. Tony can suddenly see the gym around him, the two strip lights above, the worried expressions on the men watching and Jacko's frown of concern from the far wall. The world races forward. The fake Tony sold Wallace has paid off and the big man, now shocked by the boy's movements, has his head in the wrong position. He realises too late, and Tony's right fist connects with his jaw. Tony feels the bristles of Wallace's unshaven beard under his knuckles and feels the bone crack under the pressure. It's the sweet spot, the point on a chin that, if you hit it right, will send someone to the ground. Wallace's legs buckle under him as his head snaps backwards from the punch. Tony stands as the big man crashes back onto the floor with a low groan.

Tony could leap on Wallace and smash his head into the floor, but he stands away and feels the blood running down his face. He wipes it away from his eyes. He's shaking.

"Get up," he says through his gum shield.

Wallace turns over and gets to his feet. His eyes are dull and glazed over.

"Lucky little bastard," he whispers.

Tony fits his gumshield back into place, and Wallace rushes him. The man is too angry to fight well. He runs and Tony waits until the last second to slip to the side and bring his fist up, directly into Wallace's nose. He feels the soft bone breaking. Wallace staggers forward a few steps and then collapses forward into the floorboards.

"You're out of shape," states Tony. There is no emotion or anger in his voice. "Get up."

Wallace gets to his knees and then to his feet.

"Do you know who I am?" Wallace asks. His face is bleeding too, "Do you know what is going to happen to you - with all the people I know?" Tony spits out his gum shield.

"Two punches," says Tony. "I've only hit you twice. I'm fifteen years old. Everyone here saw it. I'm gonna hit you again as well."

At this, Wallace lurches forward and grabs at Tony's shoulders, leaving his stomach and solar plexus wide open. Tony steps to the side and swings into him, his boney knuckle finding the soft spot under Wallace's ribs and above his belly right in the solar plexus, exactly where the man had failed to hit him. The Scouser staggers backward, winded and Tony follows up with a flurry of punches to his stomach and chest. He works on him, feels one of the ribs pop as he delivers his whole weight and hip into each blow. Wallace staggers and then slumps to the floor on his arse, groans again, and clutches his stomach.

"That's enough, Tony," says one of the blokes watching. "He's had enough."

"I didn't hear you saying that when he was on me?" says Tony. "He hasn't had enough. Get up," he calls to Wallace.

The man struggles. He has cut the back of his shoulders and palms of his hands on the broken glass from the mirror.

"I'm gonna kill you tonight," he whispers as he gets to his feet.

Tony darts forward and hits him again in the face so that his head cracks back against the mirror once more. Wallace slides down to a sitting position. His eyes glaze over.

"Boxing career?" he scoffs. "I'll tell you what Wallace, you are full of shit. You're not a boxer. You're a liar. I bet you paid for every win you ever got. You're a bully. It just takes someone to stand up to you. This is our club, and you just got put on your arse. I thought you were meant to be the hardest man in Liverpool?"

At the far end of the gym, old man Jacko smiles.

There's a banging sound coming from the weight room. The door is rattling. There's another bang, and another and then, the thin wood around the lock of the weight room brakes and the handle falls outwards. Whalebone pushes it open and staggers out into the gym. He's pale and is not wearing his cap. He staggers over to the little crowd and sees Wallace slumped against the wall. Tony backs off and his heart quickens. Whalebone does not register anything as he runs for the office at the end and goes inside. They hear the filing cabinet slide open.

Tony hesitates. He's unsure.

Whalebone returns. In his hand is a black sawn-off shotgun and he holds it at Tony as he walks forward. Apart from being pale, Whalebone's face is as serious as it always is. When he gets close enough, he shoulders the gun and aims at Tony's head. There is no hesitation or emotion in him, like he's done this a hundred times before. Tony steps backwards. He has no idea whether to run or dodge or attack. It's all too quick.

"Run, Tony," Jacko shouts as he limps with pace across the gym floor towards Whalebone. His stick clacks on the wood as he moves. "Run, Tony," he shouts again. It's the sound the boy needs. Whalebone readies his gun and his finger wraps around the trigger. Jacko falls on the fat man with a right hook and they crash backwards.

There's a gunshot.

Tony takes to his heels and another gunshot booms out across the gym as Whalebones fires. The men scatter. The boy ducks behind the ring, runs into Wallace's office, jumps onto the table and climbs up, through the little window and slips down behind the gym into the night air. In a few seconds, he is running down the road, his heart pounding and blood running down his face.

He wonders if Jacko is dead.

He wonders if he'll be next.

It does not take Wallace too long to get back on his feet. He worked as a bouncer in the eighties and knows how to take a beating, though it's been a while. He is angry, roars at Whalebone for being so stupid and promises retribution. The lads at the gym have disappeared. Jacko was dragged away by one of them. There's blood on the gym floor.

The police will have been called. Wallace thinks quickly. He'll have to work hard to build a reputation again, and Whalebone will have to disappear back to Liverpool. Wallace mops his bloody face with his gym towel. There's one job he has to do before anything else, one thing he and Whalebone have to see to. They have to kill that kid, Tony. Wallace knows where he lives.

The two of them do not speak as they prepare themselves in the office. Whalebone loads the shotgun with shells while Wallace makes a phone call to someone he knows who can get rid of stuff. In a few minutes, they are closing the front door of the gym, locking it and then walking down Greenwood Ave towards Tony's house. Whalebone carries the gun covered in a coat.

"I hate the people round here," says Wallace. It's his real voice without any of the show.

Whalebone does not say anything at all.

At Tony's house in 6th Avenue, Wallace turns the front door handle. It's unlocked. He steps inside. The hall light is on and there's a bloody handprint on the wall. Whalebone follows behind him; takes the coat off the shotgun he's carrying and walks through into the kitchen.

The light is on here too and the backdoor is wide open into the night outside. Whalebone searches the little downstairs toilet while Wallace checks upstairs. The lad has gone. They both walk out into the garden and Whalebone focuses his eyes as they grow accustomed to the darkness.

"He's in the woods," says Wallace.

Whalebone nods and they both climb over the little fence into the blackness of the trees. Wallace's feet sink into the soft earth and they feel their way through the tree trunks in the moonlight with outstretched arms.

"He can't have got far," says Wallace. "The state he's in." His voice is lost in the still night around them.

They struggle down the bank and alongside the smooth water's edge where the trees open out. Whalebone scans the other side.

"He could be anywhere," whispers Whalebone. "We have to make this quick. The coppers will be all over the gym by now."

"He's here," says Wallace, "somewhere."

Tony melts out of the darkness behind them. He has picked up a spade from the end of his garden and he swings it flat at the back of Whalebone's head. It connects with a dull thud and the fat man pitches forward into the mud. This is Tony's place. He pulls the spade back to swing again, but Wallace turns, grabs the handle and pushes forwards, so he and the boy are face to face. They wrestle with the spade, but Wallace is much heavier and stronger than Tony. He shoves the lad backwards, so he falls onto the mud with Wallace on top of him looking down into his eyes. With Wallace's full weight on his chest, Tony cannot move. He struggles bucks and writhes beneath the heavy man. Wallace puts his hands around Tony's throat and leans into him, bringing his face close.

"You picked the wrong fight, mate," whispers Wallace as he squeezes.

Tony feels his face getting red and his chest heaving, the heavy hands around his neck constrict the air in his windpipe. His eyes roll back and the world swims.

A low growling comes from the trees. Wallace turns his head to see a shadow moving out of the darkness towards him through the trees. His grip around the boy's neck loosens as it looms nearer. He feels fear and the beast can sense it. The warning growl is louder as it shows its rows of jagged teeth, so Wallace removes his hands from Tony. His face is a grimace in the moonlight, his heart is pumping in his chest and he swears lightly under his breath.

Wallace is not nearly angry enough for this.

The beast flashes out of the darkness at him, and Wallace disappears under the weight of the animal. He brings his arms up but too late. It goes for his neck, the heavy jaws ripping a deep gash in his throat. It has a tight grip, and Wallace flails around on the floor, making a muffled screaming sound as blood coughs out of the wound and his mouth. The beast rags him.

It does not take too long.

When the thrashing stops, the beast does not release its grip but settles next to the body. It snuffles at the neck it has ripped open.

As Tony gets to his feet, he can see that Wallace's eyes are still open. Perhaps he's still alive. He won't be for long. The beast growls at Tony.

"He's all yours." The boy staggers backwards in the darkness. He picks up the sawn-off shotgun that Whalebone has left and carries it up the hill, then climbs over the little fence and goes in through his back door. He turns off the light and sits down at the kitchen table in the darkness. He feels the dried blood on his face.

Tony does not sleep.

He waits until the dawn breaks over the river behind his house and the light is pale blue. He considers the heavy, black shotgun on the kitchen table.

Things were not meant to go like this.

His father was not meant to die. He was not meant to lie to social services. Little Sam was not meant to murder his dad, and the beast was never meant to be here at all. It was never meant to save him. Tony cannot see his future. He cannot imagine how his life will be. Will he start school again on Monday morning in the new uniform his father got him before he died? Will he get to go back to that boxing gym? Tony holds his head in his hands.

There is a noise from the front room. It's the alarm sounding from his father's phone. Tony stands at the doorway and watches the light flash on and off. He picks it up. It's a reminder from his father from the day previous. The alarm that he did not delete is repeating. It's the same message. 'Hi Tony, this is your dad. Please watch this. I love you.'

Tony goes back to the kitchen and picks up the sawn-off shotgun. What chance does he have, here, alone? It's only been a few weeks and he's fallen apart. What's the point? The last video from his father runs through his mind, the advice - that he doesn't need any advice and that his life is his own. He thinks about the journalist too, and the story of the wolfmen.

Tony knows what he has to do.

He opens the back door to the still half-dark morning,

and walks down his garden path, climbs over the little fence and goes into the woods. It is a different place to a few hours ago, with the light glimmering through the leaves and the cold wind in his hair. Tony goes down to the water and walks along the bank. He sees Wallace's body on its back. The head is at an odd angle, and there is a large, dark red gouge in his throat. His stomach has been torn open and there's gore on the mud around him. Tony does not want to see it. Whalebone's body has disappeared.

Tony moves on down the bank to the thick bushes where there is a mass of brambles and dark foliage, where something could hide. His arms are trembling, and they make the gun rattle in his hands. His heart is racing. Tony squats down and moves deep into the undergrowth. He hears the low growl from the beast he has seen for the last three weeks since his father died. It is hidden and perfectly still at the back of the bushes. How something so big can be so secret is a sense of marvel. He can see its eyes looking at him, full, in the semi-darkness of the thorns and leaves. Tony brings the gun to his shoulder in a slow movement and aligns the barrel as close to the animal's face as he can get it. He takes a deep breath to stop himself shaking, closes his eyes and sees his father in his hospital bed. Silent tears run down his dirty face.

"I know who you are," he whispers to the beast. "I worked it out. You can't be here, not like this."

Tony can see what will happen when they find Wallace's body. They'll find this beast they'll find it and kill it. The dead body and the fight with Wallace will lead them to Tony. Questions will be asked that he cannot answer. He will be discovered. He has to control the situation, like a fight, steer it in the direction where it will work out best.

"It's better I do this," whispers Tony to the beast. "Better me than someone else."

Tony needs to start again.

Like his father said, he needs to start at the beginning

and make his own way. He needs to delete the files of memories that will only drag him into what was and what should have been but is not.

He pulls the trigger and feels the recoil on his shoulder, listens, as it rings out along the still water of the river. The beast slumps to the floor. It wouldn't have felt a thing.

In his kitchen, Tony picks up the house phone and presses the redial button. It rings, and Ian the social worker's answerphone, delivers the message that his hours of work start at nine. Tony leaves him a recording:

"It's Tony from the North Hull Estate," he says. His voice is shaky. "My Auntie Lynn has gone back to Doncaster, for good. I've had some trouble with the man from the boxing club too. I've had a fight; something's happened to him in the woods behind my house. I think he's dead. I need some help. Please could you ring me back on this number?"

Tony lays the phone down. He feels like he has failed because he could not do this on his own, because he was not strong enough and because he needs help. Tony hangs his head and weeps into his hands, the tears, finally, hot and wet, relief and sadness spilling through his fingers onto his kitchen floor.

The woman from the wildlife sanctuary shakes her head at the dead wolf on the floor of the forest. It's one of the biggest she's seen, even though it's thin. She pokes at its chest, looks at the markings on its back and examines the hole in the side of its head where most of the buckshot entered.

"It's not one of ours," she says.

"But it could be?" asks the policewoman.

"No," she says, "it's not one of ours. This one is black and grey. It's far too big to be one of ours."

"Are you sure?" asks the officer.

"I've been working with wolves for over twenty years. None of them have escaped, and this couldn't be one of them. Is that clear enough?"

"So, where could it have come from?"

"That's your problem."

"Could have escaped from somewhere else, a private collector, maybe?"

"Maybe, but there's nothing on this animal to indicate it's been captive, the claws don't look like they've been cut, the teeth are in poor shape, there are scars on the face from fights. If I were to make a guess, I'd say it was wild."

The police officer writes something down in her little book.

"Thanks for your time," she adds.

Lionel stands small in front of the enormous punch bag. He attacks it with short combinations, two left jabs and then a right cross. The bag hardly moves. Jacko shakes his head as he watches the lad.

"Do that for the next hour," he says, "and I might show you something new next week."

You have to earn Jacko's respect. He's worse for discipline than he's ever been now he's got his club back and he's survived a gunshot. Lionel's face twists in pain as he carries on hitting the heavy bag with his thin arms, Tony approaches and stands behind to watch.

"Keep at it mate," says Tony. "The technique will come the more times you hit the bag." Lionel turns.

"Can't we go home?" he whispers. It's odd to hear Lionel say *we* and *home* in the same sentence.

"You've got another ten minutes. I promised your mum I'd make you train properly." Jacko walks over to his little office at the back of the gym and comes out carrying a wide cardboard tube. He summons Tony over.

"Get the step ladders," he orders. "You're gonna hang this with me, I hung the last one with your dad."

Tony sets the ladder up behind the ring. Jacko undoes the cardboard tube and unrolls a long poster. It takes Tony a couple of minutes to pin it up. Then, the two of them step back to look at the black and white poster of Muhammed Ali. It's different from the last one. This time, young Muhammed holds his fist in front of him, the perspective makes it look huge, on the white background are the words 'Impossible is nothing'.

"How's school?" ask Jacko.

"Yeah... alright."

"You come to me if you need anything. You should have come to me before."

"I know."

"I'm serious," says Jacko. "I don't need any of this hard man stuff, the people and kids round here need this club. They need people like you to look up to. I can't do it alone. I know you don't want to; I know you want to hide away, but you've got too much talent, Tony." Jacko has his eyes fixed on the poster. "I need you back in the ring. I need you to train. I need you to believe in yourself and I need you to fight. Local-level to start with, but we'll get bigger, we'll take it all the way, right to the top, right to the Lonsdale Belt like your dad and beyond. Are you with me?" Tony stares at the poster too. He looks at the smooth skin of Ali, at his tight muscles and the glint in his eye. Tony nods.

"I'm with you," he whispers.

"That Congolese woman feed you ok?" asks Jacko.

"Her name's Mwamba. Her cooking's good. I've been there for three weeks."

"You're going to need to eat right. I'll talk to her. Five nights a week training. No excuses." The two men turn to face each other. "When do you want to start?" Asks Jacko. Tony looks at his shoes and then back to the poster. Impossible is nothing. He feels a tingle down his spine.

"How about right now?" He asks.

Printed in Great Britain
by Amazon